"Are you not at all even curious as to how my essence ended up inside a terran body?"

Zeratul's head turned toward them at that, his eyes glowing. Jake tensed. He knew, of course, the basics—that Zamara had been evading Ulrezaj's assassins, that she had left a note in her own blood and clues as to how someone might find her. But the details she had not shared with him. He was not sure he wanted them.

"I . . . am curious," Zeratul admitted. The protoss had always struck Jake as catlike—not in how they looked in any way, but their grace, their power, and their overwhelming curiosity about first the world and then the universe around them. "I did not know that humans were capable of containing the essence of a preserver."

"He is not," Zamara said bluntly. "The duty is killing him."

Zeratul's eyes narrowed slightly, and as he regarded Jake, the archaeologist knew that this time, Zeratul was not seeing Zamara. He was looking at Jake.

"Did you undertake this duty freely, human?"

Jake shook his head uncomfortably.

"No."

STARCRAFT™

THE DARK TEMPLAR SAGA

BOOK THREE OF THREE

TWILIGHT

CHRISTIE GOLDEN

POCKET STAR BOOKS
New York   London   Toronto   Sydney

A Pocket Star Book published by
POCKET BOOKS, a division of Simon & Schuster, Inc.
1230 Avenue of the Americas, New York, NY 10020

This book is a work of fiction. Names, characters, places, and incidents either are products of the author's imagination or are used fictitiously. Any resemblance to actual events or locales or persons, living or dead, is entirely coincidental.

First Pocket Star Books paperback edition July 2009

POCKET STAR BOOKS and colophon are registered trademarks of Simon & Schuster, Inc.

For information about special discounts for bulk purchases, please contact Simon & Schuster Special Sales at 1-866-506-1949 or business@simonandschuster.com.

The Simon & Schuster Speakers Bureau can bring authors to your live event. For more information or to book an event, contact the Simon & Schuster Speakers Bureau at 1-866-248-3049 or visit our website at www.simonspeakers.com.

Cover art by Glenn Rane

Manufactured in the United States of America

10 9 8 7 6 5 4 3 2 1

ISBN 978-0-7434-7129-9
ISBN 978-1-4391-6357-3 (ebook)

This book is dedicated
to all those who fall down
and keep getting up.

PROLOGUE

IT WAS TIME TO WELCOME THE TWILIGHT.

The young acolyte was so deep in his studies that the singing of the crystals startled him. Simple things they were, gentle chimes that did nothing more or less profound than call the scholars of the Alys'aril, the "Sanctuary of Wisdom," to gather together at the end of the long, scorching day. He jumped, grasping the precious khaydarin crystal tightly in his four-fingered hand rather than dropping it; such had been the rigors of training from a young age here in the Alys'aril. The crystals were everything. They must always, always be handled with care, training overriding instinct so that no careless hand would risk dropping such a precious item.

He forced himself to relax, carefully returned the crystal to its slot and stepped back to survey his handiwork with pride. Today, he had successfully negotiated the transfer of information held by no fewer than seven ancient, time-worn, and damaged crystals into gleaming, freshly-quarried, and charged receptacles.

His mentor, Krythkal, came up behind him, ducking and tilting his head in a smile. "Well done," he said. "Seven. An impressive number. But you must always take care that you do not rush the task. It is better to accurately salvage the contents of a single crystal than to imperfectly translate a hundred."

The young alysaar fought back annoyance. He had been here for forty years; he was no novice. Nonetheless, he inclined his head. "You speak truly. And yet, there is so much that remains to be done."

He spread his hand to indicate the Chalice of Memories. An enormous bowl carved from soft stone by those among the dark templar who had once been of the Khalai caste, it towered stories high in front of both master and apprentice and was filled to brimming with khaydarin crystals. A levitating platform would bear the scholars to the top, where they would place no more than five crystals at a time into special padded satchels strapped securely to their bodies. Some crystals stored but a single memory. Others had hundreds. Some were still largely clear, needing only slight refinement. Others required the sharpest, most highly disciplined minds the alysaar, the "Keepers of Wisdom," could bring to the task to understand the memories and successfully transfer them to purer crystals. No one dared even make an educated guess regarding how many crystals were cradled in the Chalice. It would take the lifetimes of many—and the lifetimes of the protoss were long—to chronicle all it contained. And there were always new memories coming.

"It is a duty whose joy lies in the doing, not in the finishing," Krythkal chuckled. "For it will never be finished, not as long as a single dark templar lives. But come. The sun sinks to its rest, and so must we. Weary minds can miss a detail, and that is most certainly not what we want."

The little moon was arid and almost unbearably hot, and because of this the scholars who manned the Alys'aril ventured forth from its dark, cool stone halls at only dawn and dusk to take nourishment. Three centuries ago, when the first dark templar had come here in a xel'naga vessel, banished from their home-world of Aiur, they had thought it destiny that they found this place so quickly. Not only was there a warp gate, a relic from the xel'naga, that marked this place as one that had been visited by the Great Teachers, but there was a rare combination of energies that had modified—some said "purified"—the khaydarin crystals that were to be found here.

The Alys'aril had been constructed atop one such clustering of energy. There were two others, one deep below the surface where khaydarin crystals manifested in riotous profusion, and one that had been detected but never explored, below the floor of the moon's single large ocean.

Ehlna, "Haven," they had named the moon, and spent many long years constructing a settlement and, of course, establishing the Alys'aril. It was well into the second century of habitation before other voices clamored to expand beyond this place, to seek more information and more hospitable worlds. But Ehlna was not forgotten, even as the dark templar continued to wander and learn and explore the cosmos. The warp gate that linked this, the first place to know the tread of dark templar feet, and other worlds visited by the exiled protoss still occasionally hummed and brightened to life, as pilgrims came through to add their memories and discoveries to the whole. They were made welcome, and an alysaar sat with them as their memories were channeled into a crystal.

The youth nodded, erected a glowing force field of mental energy to protect his unfinished task, and accompanied his mentor outside.

Ehlna was a lovely place at twilight. The dust that would settle into skin and clothing during the day also scattered out the sun's blue and green lights, and the sunsets were spectacular. The one hundred and thirteen protoss who had pledged their lives to remaining on Ehlna to tend the Alys'aril stood and lifted their faces to skies that went from yellow to orange to purple, and then slowly to gray. Clad only in a short robe that exposed most of his skin to the life-giving rays, the youth absorbed the nutrients from the setting sun. He felt himself growing stronger as one by one the stars came out, looking like small crystalline spheres to his eyes, although he knew they were suns or worlds all to themselves.

He wondered what was out there, on those other worlds. He was glad of his choice to stay, for he hungered for knowledge, for lore, more than he hungered for adventure. But he was growing weary of simply transferring memories from one khaydarin crystal to another. The protoss who had exiled them had preservers. The dark templar, who embraced the power and strength of the individual and abhorred subsuming one's will to the collective surrender of the Khala, did not. Thus, they had to find an alternative way to preserve memories; a technological way. When he was younger and did not question so much, he trusted that the decision to thus artificially create preservers was a wise one. Now he was not so sure. It seemed to him . . . wasteful. Certainly some memories—such as learning how to create a weapon or ship, or developing a new skill, or the recollections of a great battle or discovery—were extremely useful to future generations. But an old protoss's remembrance of a humorous story? Or beholding a sunset such as this one? Those memories might be important to the individual, but surely not to those who had no personal stake in them. The Keepers of Wisdom exclaimed over such things, regarding them almost reverently, and the youth was hard put to conceal his growing annoyance with such petty memories.

The Wall of Knowledge, now . . . *that* was what he yearned to explore. One of the reasons he had chosen to stay behind and devote his life to being a Keeper of Wisdom was because he wanted to help his people. Anger burned in him when he recalled the stories of how the dark templar had been so badly treated at the hands of their supposed "brethren," for a crime no more horrible than not wishing to share their most intimate selves with all other protoss. He wanted the dark templar to surpass their banishers—grow stronger, wiser, better than the protoss who remained, wrapped in smug self-satisfaction, on Aiur. Surely there was knowledge in these crystals to help the dark templar achieve that goal. But ritual and habit had evolved so that the Wall of Knowledge remained largely untouched. The reasoning was that while all knowledge was considered important, not all knowledge was considered wholesome. Some knowledge was deemed too dangerous to come to light, even among the general population of the alysaar. He would have to labor at the Chalice for many, many more decades before he would even be considered for such a coveted duty. And *that* knowledge chafed at him.

The idea had occurred to him before. The Wall might be forbidden to him, but it was never guarded. Certainly not at night, when all the scholars slept. He'd planned it all out: how he would stay awake at night, and see just what the Wall of Knowledge held, what secrets it kept to itself and the select few deemed worthy of plumbing that information. But something had always held him back. Respect for tradition, perhaps. Or a desire to eventually prove himself trustworthy.

Or perhaps simply fear.

It was at that moment, even as the song of the crystals faded and the night sky went utterly black, and the Keepers of Wisdom turned to their beds for deep, refreshing rest, that the fear abruptly vanished. No more waiting. No more hesitating. He had been here forty years. Would he wait forty more, too afraid to take the opportunity that was right in front of him?

No.

Quickly the youth buried his thoughts. It was unlikely anyone would read them; most of the time, it was only surface thoughts that were heard, unless one was engrossed in a private conversation. And now everyone's attention was focused on sleep. He pretended tiredness as he accompanied his fellow alysaar back to their sleeping quarters. Beds consisted of blankets placed on the stone floor. There was not much luxury here; the scholars lived a simple, focused life. Tonight, with his new resolve burning in the back of his brain, the youth saw it all with new eyes. The alysaar were custodians of the most significant knowledge the dark templar possessed. And yet they were content to simply drowse on the floor, feed from the twilight skies, and transfer knowledge from one crystal to another rather than actually *learn* it.

What glories were locked up inside those glittering crystals? What information, insights, wonders, power? What means to help the dark templar protect themselves from and even surpass the protoss who had banished them? He was so agitated he could barely lie still long enough to feign sleep while waiting for the others to drift off to slumber. After a time, he gently touched their minds with his own, and when he was certain they were all deep in their dreams, the youth rose. His feet barely whispering over the cool stone floor, he quietly made his way to the Wall of Knowledge.

He gazed at it raptly, hungrily. Where to begin? So much wisdom here . . . how could one choose just one crystal? The task was both daunting and yet inspiring. He settled his mind, extended a hand that trembled only slightly, and let his fingers close at random upon a crystal.

And gazing down at the glittering shard cupped in his palm, the youth had his first fluttering, glimmering glimpse of true power.

CHAPTER 1

WE MUST GO, ROSEMARY.

Rosemary Dahl's head whipped up at Zamara's voice speaking in her brain. She didn't think she'd ever get truly comfortable with such a method of communication, but after the last several minutes, when she and the protoss inside Jake's mind had worked together to repair the damaged warp gate, she was getting used to it. She fired one last time at the zerg, swarming far too close for comfort, even though their target was elsewhere, and let her gaze linger for just a second on the glowing darkness that was lumbering toward them.

They'd come here because of Zamara, the . . . spirit, Rosemary guessed was the best word, of a dead protoss preserver who housed every memory every protoss had ever had. And among those memories was something so important that Zamara had been determined to find a way to continue on after death—to share those memories with one Jacob Jefferson Ramsey, archaeologist, who was now possibly going to die because of those memories. Zamara had brought them here to locate a fragment of an extremely pure and powerful crystal, thinking to save Jake's life with it.

All well and good, but they hadn't counted on a lot of things. They hadn't counted on finding two separate and determined protoss factions practically at war with one another. They hadn't counted on Valerian Mengsk, son of Emperor Arcturus Mengsk and Rosemary's employer-turned-hunter, tracking them here. They hadn't counted on confronting Rosemary's former lover Ethan Stewart, seemingly raised from the dead and horrifically modified by someone he referred to as the "queen," leading a pack of zerg. And for *sure* they hadn't counted on discovering that one of the protoss factions—the Forged—was being controlled by a monstrosity called a dark archon.

An entity comprised of seven of the deadliest assassins in the history of the dark templar, his name was Ulrezaj. Dark archons were an abomination to the Aiur protoss, and Rosemary had her own deeply personal grudge against the thing out there. The misguided followers of the monstrous being had dredged up the very worst parts of her, the parts she had thought she'd shed long ago. They had captured her and smeared some kind of drug they called "Sundrop" on her skin, and she'd toppled immediately back into the dark pit of addiction. Her eyes narrowed even now as she recalled what the drug had done to her.

She tore her mind from the memory and focused on the pleasant image in front of her. Attacked on

three sides, he was stumbling now, the oh-so-mighty
Ulrezaj, and her heart leaped to see it. More than anything she could recall wanting—well, wanting with a
clear head at any rate—she wanted to see Ulrezaj die,
fall beneath the chittering living carpet of zerg, the
powerful onslaught of Valerian Mengsk's Dominion
vessels, and the stubborn attack of what few protoss
remained on Aiur.

*I sympathize with your desire, but the gate will soon
close.*

Gotcha, Zamara.

Rosemary whirled and headed for the gate at top
speed. Right before she plunged into its swirling, misty
center, she called over her shoulder, "Jake, come on!"

Beside her ran the last few protoss to escape Aiur.
Those who stayed behind would die. She knew it, and
they knew it, and they were content with their choice.
As for the gate, Rosemary wasn't sure what to expect.
The ground seemed solid beneath her running feet the
entire way, but darkness descended almost instantly.
Rosemary clutched her rifle and slowed, unsure if she
was through yet or not. The consistency of the earth
seemed to change, become less firm, more like sand
than hard-packed earth. It was still dark, but there
was some source of light, dispersed and faint, like
starlight. She could just start to make out the shapes
of the protoss around her and—

HALT!

The order that slammed into her brain was so
intense that Rosemary gasped and stumbled, falling

into one of the protoss who had also come to a stop beside her. He caught her quickly and steadied her.

Information flooded her brain, a cacophony of mental shouting and explanations, and she bit back a gasp of pain. The protoss next to her squeezed her arm reassuringly. Good God, was this how it was all the time? Until this moment Rosemary hadn't fully appreciated how much Zamara had shielded her—

"—from Aiur. There is one other who is still coming—"

—images of battle, of death, of Ulrezaj, of dead protoss lying in the chambers beneath the protoss homeland—

"—zerg and a dark archon—"

"—Sundrop, a despicable drug—"

"Zerg?"

Rosemary winced at the horror emanating from the protoss who surrounded the little band of refugees; she knew now that they were surrounded here, wherever "here" on Shakuras was.

"What were you thinking? Zerg? You'll lead them here! Redirect, redirect and then shut it down!"

Rosemary shoved her way through the press of protoss surrounding her; they were too tall and she couldn't see these new protoss who were—

Clarity struck her like an armored fist as she suddenly made sense of the jumble of words and images with which her poor human, non-psionic brain was being bombarded. They were going to close the gate.

Which would leave Jake stranded on Aiur.

"No!" she shrieked. Rosemary lunged for the nearest protoss, seizing his arm. His head whipped around and he stared at her, and she got a hint of just how alien she must appear to these beings. Unlike the refugees who had just raced through the warp gate, these protoss were fit, healthy, and armed to the teeth—well, they would have been if they'd had any teeth. The templar she'd dared lay hands on freed himself easily and backhanded her, training his weapon on her as she fell hard on soft sand. The wind knocked out of her, she gasped inelegantly like a fish, staring up at a purple sky that was not quite day and not quite night, still instinctively and foolishly trying to form words when intellectually she knew that thoughts would do as well or better.

Bless them, the other protoss rallied. The one who'd caught her before—Vartanil, she thought his name was—now gently helped her to her feet, while the others shot streams of information to the guards of the warp gate.

"You must open the gates, if only briefly!" Vartanil was saying. "There is a terran male named Jacob Jefferson Ramsey still on Aiur. He houses within him one of the last preservers."

The guard who'd struck Rosemary gazed coldly at Vartanil. "The hardships you have endured over the last four years must have damaged your mind, Vartanil."

Rosemary wondered as breath finally came back to her how the guard had known Vartanil's name. Oh yeah—that instant thought stuff. And even as that realization hit, she found that she knew the guards' names as well. This bully, his skin dark gray and his face angular and dotted here and there with sharp, small hornlike protrusions, was Razturul. The other was Turavis.

"He's right," Rosemary said, "and it's a hell of a long story. Zamara will tell you, but first you need to open this damned *gate*!"

She was astonished at how upset she was at the thought of Jake being stranded in Aiur. Or being taken by Valerian or Ethan or reduced to a little cloud of atoms by Ulrezaj. He didn't deserve to wind up that way, not after all he'd been through. And whatever little mysteries Zamara had locked in her dead-but-yet-still-living consciousness were obviously very important to the protoss.

Razturul's eyes, glowing in the dim light of a twilight evening, narrowed as he regarded her. "It is true that you all tell the same story," he acknowledged, obviously reluctantly.

"Yes, Razturul, but none of them can enter the Khala, so we cannot verify their claims in a place where there can be no deception," said Turavis. His face was smoother than the bully's, and his nerve cords, neatly pulled back and tied, hung down to his waist.

Razturul pointed at Vartanil. "This one claims that the protoss you have brought with you, terran, have been subjected to a drug called Sundrop." His eyes widened slightly as, unbidden, Rosemary recollected

the abject shame and self-loathing she'd endured while in the throes of that wretched drug. "Ah, you, too, claim to have been addicted."

"No claim about it," Rosemary muttered. She fought back her anger and fear. "Please," she said, a word she did not often use. "My friend and the preserver he houses are in terrible danger. Just open the gate for a second."

"It is too late," Turavis said, compassion lacing his words. "But if it is any consolation, your friend has been redirected to another gate."

Rosemary looked at him, uncomprehending.

"The warp gates are xel'naga technology, and they can be found on many worlds," Turavis continued. "Any warp gate can open onto any other active gate. When we saw that there was a risk of invasion— by zerg, or the Dominion, or this dark archon— we redirected anyone who was already within the boundaries of the gate to another one. Jacob will have walked through the gate thinking to arrive on Shakuras, as you have, but instead will find himself in another place entirely."

Rosemary gaped at him. "Oh, great. Can you tell which one?"

Razturul shook his head. "No. While it is not entirely random, there are still many possibilities. The redirection is designed so that if it is an enemy, they will not be sent anywhere that they could do harm to our people, but if it is one of our own, they will be able to survive."

"Well, yeah, but in case you haven't noticed, bud, I'm not a protoss. What about toxic atmospheres? What about predators? What about food? We humans can't live on sunlight like you guys can."

"You said he is with a preserver," Razturul said, casting a slightly disapproving glance at Vartanil. "If this is true, then she will be able to program the gate to take them somewhere else, if where they are is inhospitable. Do not worry about him, Rosemary Dahl. I would think you should be more worried about yourself."

"What—hey look, Pointy-face," Rosemary snarled, drawing herself up to her full diminutive height. "Right about now my buddy is figuring out that he's somewhere that's *not* Shakuras, where he needs to be to get the preserver out of his head and save his damn *life*, and that he *is* someplace else all by himself with no clue about how to reach anybody who can help him. I think it highly appropriate that I worry about him, and oh, by the way, are you threatening me?"

Rosemary found herself surrounded by templar, both kinds, all with those weird energy blades pointed at her.

"It was not a threat; it was a warning," Razturul said smoothly. "Come with us, Rosemary Dahl. We have no wish to hurt you, but you must be confined and interrogated."

Her eyes widened slightly at the last word. She knew what that was code for where the Dominion was concerned, and she'd rather die right now, speared on a glowing blade of mental energy made physical, than be subjected to the impersonal and deliberate brain dismemberment that—

—images of a room, spartan but not devoid of comforts, and answering questions filled her mind.

"Oh," she said, relaxing slightly. "That's a bit better."

She got a hint of something that might have been "barbaric."

"My friends," she said, gesturing to the protoss who had accompanied her. "What will happen to them?"

Turavis turned to regard the protoss who had escaped the carnage that was now the surface of Aiur. "They are brothers, to be welcomed home," he said. "We will help them recover from the grip of this . . . Sundrop . . . and question them as well. Once they have shared their information, we would joyfully have them rejoin protoss society."

She couldn't help it. The thought, *and what's going to happen to me?* was formed and was read.

"That remains to be seen," said Turavis. "It will depend on what the executor decides."

As Rosemary and the little group of refugees trudged through soft blue sand to a gleaming vessel that awaited them, Rosemary thought darkly that "executor" sounded a bit too much like "executioner" for her liking.

CHAPTER 2

JAKE RAN TOWARD THE MISTY SWIRL THAT was the center of the warp gate and, overriding his instincts, didn't slow as he raced through. It was suddenly very dark, and then suddenly very bright, and very *cold*, and the ground beneath him was very slick, and his feet shot out from under him.

He tried to roll and would have succeeded, had the surface upon which he attempted said roll not been ice. As it was he hit the ice hard, slid wildly along its length, and found himself in a pile of snow.

I thought Shakuras was a sort of desert, he thought irritatedly to Zamara as he stumbled to his feet, floundering in the snow that reached his thighs rather than attempting to rise on the ice.

It is, came the maddeningly unruffled reply. *We are not on Shakuras.*

Jake shivered as the wind knifed him. When he ran through the gate, he'd been sweating heavily from the clammy heat of the Aiur climate, exertion and, yes, nerves, and now he was feeling his soaked clothing actually begin to freeze to his skin. He folded his arms tightly around himself. *Where the hell are we then, what went wrong, and what do we do now?*

Jake squinted against the brightness of sunlight reflecting off of snow, turning to look in every direction. The only thing he could see in the arctic landscape was snow, more snow, and for a little variety what looked like icebergs over there. The gate was the only evidence that an advanced intelligence had ever been to this place.

I do not know where we are, and it does not matter. As for what happened, I have, as you humans would call it, a "hunch."

She asked him to surrender his body to her will for a moment, and he obliged, marveling quietly as she moved his legs securely across the slippery surface and lifted his arms to touch the softly glowing surface of the gate. The cold receded, just a bit, as Jake again marveled at the technology of the xel'naga. The combination of nature and science, of mental power and things he, a simple human, could not understand . . . it was wondrous.

He felt her disappointment and worry seized him. *What is it? What's wrong?*

It is as I suspected, Zamara replied. *The way to Shakuras is blocked. We have been—I think the term you would understand is "locked out."*

Locked out? Why the hell would they lock us out?

It is a wise precaution, though inconvenient for us. The last time protoss fled to Shakuras from Aiur, zerg followed them. Shakuras suffered terribly. It was only through a great deal of effort that it and the protoss as a race survived at all, and the planet bears the scars of that battle to this day. I believe that once the protoss guarding the gate realized that Rosemary and her companions had come from Aiur, they ordered the Shakuras gate closed and redirected us here. A hint of humor. *Wherever "here" may be. The warp gates are xel'naga technology, not protoss. I have no memory of this place at all. I believe I am the first protoss to have seen it.*

Jake was a scholar, and fascinated by mysteries and discoveries. At any other time, he'd have been as intrigued as Zamara was to explore a new place. But he was freezing, he was scared, and a sudden shooting of pain in his temple reminded him that he was dying.

But . . . you just said you think Rosemary and the other protoss got through. Do you think they will convince the guards to open the gate?

She, too, was concerned, he knew, but at his words mirth flowed through him, warm and light.

If you were a protoss, how would you react to Rosemary?

Oh my God, he thought. *You're right. She'll probably punch the first one who gets in her way.*

I do not think so. She may wish to, but she has learned much. She has been tempered.

Unbidden, the term the misled and misused followers of Ulrezaj had chosen to describe themselves came to Jake's mind: *Forged.*

In a way, yes. That is apt. However, I believe the protoss will eventually agree to admit us to Shakuras.

Eventually? I can't stay here for that long. Not even for another few minutes, not without shelter or food.

I know. Let me think.

He did, taking his body back from her and moving as quickly as he dared on the slippery surface to stay warm. Cut-off pants, a sleeveless vest, and a light shirt, perfectly appropriate garments in Aiur's stifling humidity and unforgiving sun, served him not at all here.

I have reached a decision. Your hands again, please.

He watched as again she lifted his hands to the gate and began to do—whatever it was that programming the gate entailed.

So what are we going to do?

We go back through the gate.

He laughed, a short harsh bark of a sound. He was starting to lose feeling in his limbs and face. *We can't reach Shakuras; where do we go? How do we find these dark templar you need to reach?*

If we are prevented from reaching Shakuras, the home of the dark templar, for the moment, then we will seek aid from a certain dark templar who is probably not *on Shakuras.*

Who is that?

Prelate Zeratul.

Jake's mind was suddenly awash in images and memories, none of which he could grasp in their entire complexity at this point but all of which served to give him a good idea of the nature of this dark templar. Age and wisdom were the predominant characteristics that graced this being. Although Jake knew that the Aiur protoss and the dark templar were the same species, there were subtle physical differences.

The protoss he had befriended had skin that came in a variety of blue and gray. Zeratul's skin seemed almost purple, very dark where it encircled deep-set eyes, but lightening to pale lavender along the various ridges that also made him stand out from other protoss. Alzadar and Ladranix had almost smooth skin, with no bumps or ridges to mar the curves of their features. Zeratul's chin was long, thin, and ivory-colored.

There were other differences, too, differences of perception and sensation that Zamara imparted to him. The Aiur protoss had been fond of gold hues, as of the sun, but the dark templar in his mind's eye seemed almost swathed in shadow. One of Zeratul's arms was encased in a bracer that looked familiar to Jake; he'd seen similar bracers in action when Ladranix had sliced off the crystal Jake now carried in one of the many pockets of his vest. This piece of armor channeled psionic power and enabled the templar to wield the beautiful, graceful, and deadly psi blades. Zeratul's bracer was darker, and Jake wasn't sure if it was his imagination that made him see shadows swirling around the armor. The rest of his garb was also dark— soft, heavy robes of a rust color trimmed with brown fur. Jake knew that in keeping with dark templar tradition, his nerve cords had been ritually severed. All that was left of them was a short cluster, tied back in a ponytail. Dark templar could never enter the Khala because of this self-mutilation, even if they wished to. It was a defiant and permanent action.

Jake thought back to young Raszagal, of her pride

and astonishing intellect. He thought of the other dark templar, herded like animals onto a ship of alien construction, a vessel no one was certain would even work properly. Exiled because the Conclave was afraid of them.

I didn't realize you had the memories of someone who had known a dark templar! I mean, known one after they were banished. I'm looking forward to learning about them firsthand—well, as firsthand as preserver memories can be. They seem very wronged.

They were. The true tragedy is that the Conclave honestly believed that killing them—a stance Adun forced them to later mitigate to banishing—was the best thing to do for the protoss as a race. But the dark templar were not idle. They learned many, many things as they explored the Void in their centuries of exile. If we are fortunate, you will get to meet Zeratul as well.

You know where to find him? Exciting as the idea of meeting this powerful dark templar was, Jake was more immediately interested in getting out of the frigid environment. As if in answer to his thought, the gate began to glow and hum, active once again. Within its boundaries, a mist formed, and began to whirl in a clockwise direction.

Zamara hesitated. . . . *Not exactly.*

Great. They were going to start warp gate–hopping around the galaxy in search of a dark templar who might or might not be able to help save Jake's life, while over on Shakuras, Rosemary Dahl was an accidental terran ambassador to the protoss.

Zeratul spoke once about how he found the peace to locate the center from which all true strength comes. All protoss meditate. We also utilize the khaydarin crystals to focus our thoughts. But there are times when we need not just the calm of the mental senses, but those of the physical ones. Sensory pleasures, too, have a place in soothing the spirit.

Jake thought of the smell and taste of the sammuro fruit, and Zamara agreed.

The mental conversation took only a fraction of a second. As soon as the gate was fully active, Jake hurried through. Again darkness descended, and then again the world was bright. But this was no arctic wasteland, no sweltering rain forest. He looked around, blinking, stunned at what he beheld.

The color of the sky was pink. Not a rusty red indicative of high iron content in a dusty atmosphere, but positively pink, like a rose. The grass beneath him, for it was recognizable as such, was thick and soft and a soothing purple-blue color. The air was entirely breathable, and as Jake inhaled deeply a profusion of scents, everything from fruity to piney to a rich deep earth smell, filled his nostrils. The sun, a rose-yellow, was warm and the breeze that carried the scents, gentle. For a moment, Jake wondered how he could exist on a planet that had a clear, noontime, rose-colored sky. The little he knew about oxygen-nitrogen atmospheres and something called Rayleigh scattering told his brain that he should be having difficulty surviving here.

It is an unusual phenomenon. Shall I explain it in detail?

Jake closed his eyes, welcoming the warmth on his skin. He shrugged off his wet jacket and shirt.

No. I'll just accept it.

It was then that his eye fell upon a vessel. It resembled the small scout ships Jake had seen on Aiur, but it was slightly different. It was more—"squat" was the only word he could think of, solid, rather than elongated and graceful. Its creator had eschewed the gold that seemed to be the preferred hue of protoss vessels in favor of a black that seemed almost completely nonreflective, as if it absorbed the rosy sunlight that struck it. Here and there were dull bronze highlights.

Jake felt hope surge from Zamara, and at the same moment couldn't stifle a yelp of pain. His body stiffened and then began to tremble, and for a brief second he lost consciousness. He came to on his hands and knees, panting, and cautiously sat upright.

Zamara . . . what . . .

For a wild moment he thought—he hoped—that whatever had just happened to him had somehow been caused by the alien vessel. Or there was something in the atmosphere that was harmful after all. But he knew better.

The tumors are growing worse. You are beginning to feel the effects of the pressure they are putting on your brain, Zamara informed him, the blunt statement strangely more comforting than any misguided false sympathy would have been. Jake knew he could trust Zamara to tell him the unvarnished truth.

Well, at least I get to keel over in a beautiful place, he said. He'd always appreciated gallows humor.

I will do everything in my power—use all of my knowledge—to keep you alive and safe, Jacob.

. . . I know. The seizure had passed and while the headache remained, it had subsided to the point where Jake no longer had the urge to rip off his own head. Shakily he got to his feet.

The vessel is of dark templar design, Zamara said. *I do not know if it belongs to Zeratul, but seeing it here is a promising sign. Let us see what we can learn.*

Jake took deep, steadying gulps of the deliciously scented air and approached the vessel. He felt Zamara's excitement as he extended a hand and ran it along the ship's curving sides. It looked like it had been sitting here for a while. Pollen, dust, and leaves all dulled its surface and now coated Jake's hand.

I know more about the dark templar than most protoss— both their origins and their current status. But I am accustomed to knowing almost everything, and this—ah, this is new. I look forward to learning.

Jake smiled, softly. There was a dreadful direness about their situation, and the fact that the brain tumors—plural, mind you, no longer just "a brain tumor"—were worsening pointed up the fact that time was running out. Running out for him, for Zamara, who also would cease to exist if his body died, running out for whatever information she held that was so damn valuable. Maybe running out for the universe, if the secret was that important.

But still, with the smooth, cool curve of the dark templar vessel beneath his fingers, a sense of leashed power emanating from it, and the almost childlike awe of a protoss who knew more than Jake could even begin to comprehend weaving in with his own wonder, Jake Ramsey felt himself a lucky man indeed.

The vessel responded to Zamara's touch—apparently dark templar and Aiur protoss were not that different when it came to an innate understanding of how their technology worked—and a ramp slowly extended. His heart racing, Jake climbed aboard. Looking around he found that everything was both somehow familiar and completely strange. He sensed that Zamara shared the feeling.

He heard a soft hum and whirled just in time to see the door sliding shut. It was dark inside, darker than it should be considering there was at least one viewscreen in the forward part of the ship, and Jake suddenly felt nervous.

Uh . . . Zamara, do you know how to operate this thing at all? Or maybe at least open the door?

I am sure I will be able to comprehend it. Zeratul shared much with Tassadar about the source of dark templar energies. I may not be able to control it as he does, but perhaps I can . . . intuit . . .

Jake relinquished control of his body and let her ease it into a chair. The controls of the ship were barely visible, buttons and indentations on an otherwise flat surface. Zamara passed Jake's hand, fingers spread, over the controls, and they hummed to glowing green life.

Ah! Excellent. Let us see how long it has been since the vessel was operated.

Symbols appeared, flashing faster than Jake could register them. But apparently Zamara had no such trouble.

It has been several months since anyone has operated the ship.

That doesn't sound promising.

It is neither promising nor dispiriting; it is simply a fact. There is no way to determine the identity of the ship's owner. Now to find coordinates.

Zamara waved Jake's hand again, in an undulating pattern, over part of the controls, and a screen lit up. Alien symbols raced over it. *The dark templar have certainly suffered, and many are still resentful. However, they still revere Aiur, and have never sought to deny their protoss heritage. They did not create a new written language . . . which is fortunate for us. There are several flight paths entered into the knowledge banks of this vessel. Let us see where they take us.*

What—you're stealing this ship? Jake had a sudden rather comical mental image of a protoss off catching some cosmic rays and seeing his ship lift off without him.

I have programmed the vessel to scan for any protoss life-forms. There are none within several hundred kilometers, and as I told you, the vessel has not been operated for many months. I suspect that this ship, located in such close proxim-

ity to the warp gate, is waiting for its pilot to return from his or her travels beyond the gate.

Well, that makes sense, but what if he comes back and his ship's not here?

Why then, it will be necessary for him to make contact with us, and that is precisely what we wish to happen, is it not?

And before Jake quite knew what was happening, the dark templar ship had powered up, lifted off, and was moving swiftly and silently among pink clouds.

CHAPTER 3

ETHAN STEWART HAD ONCE BEEN MERELY human. A fine specimen of his species, to be sure, with a body powerful and toned and a mind disciplined and sharp, but only human nonetheless. He was more now. Augmented, enhanced, improved. He was the consort to Kerrigan, Queen of Blades, mistress of the zerg, whom he adored and would serve to the last drop of . . . whatever passed for blood now surging through his veins.

Rosemary Dahl had once been his lover, and he had once honestly cared for her. But now he lived to serve his queen, and Ethan, part human and part zerg, could think of no worse fate than disappointing Kerrigan.

So when his quarry, a simple archaeologist, who admittedly happened to have a protoss preserver in his brain, ran through the swirling blue mist of the warp gate on Aiur, Ethan let out a roar of combined outrage and agony. He had only been a few paces behind Ramsey—but it might as well have been light-years. The man had escaped.

She knew; she saw through his eyes when she

chose to, and she saw what he saw, and her fury chilled him.

"The first task I set you to, and you fail me! Apparently capturing a single human male was too difficult for you, even when I give you control of my vast army!"

"My queen . . . we could not possibly have expected the Dominion or the dark archon—"

"One's mettle is tested by how well one reacts to the unexpected. I am disappointed in you, Ethan. Perhaps my creation was not as perfect as I had thought."

"Trust me, my queen, you have wrought excellent work."

"Then prove me wrong. You have let Ramsey and the girl escape. Find them, bring Ramsey to me, and I shall be mollified."

He stared at the battle that still raged, even though the prize he, the Dominion, and the dark archon were apparently all after had slipped through their collective fingers. Rosemary, Jake, and the protoss in his brain had gone through an active warp gate—they could be anywhere another warp gate opened.

Maybe anywhere in the universe.

How the hell was he to find them?

Ethan regarded the zerg under his command as they slashed, chewed, and clawed at what remained of the protoss, were shot to pulpy bits by the Dominion vessels, and launched themselves at the swirling, huge, crimson mass that was the dark archon.

He did not know how to operate the gates; that

was protoss knowledge, and nearly all the protoss were dead. Some he himself had killed, quickly dispatching them in frustration when they gleefully revealed their ignorance of the warp gate technology. Apparently such was not just protoss knowledge, but *rare* protoss knowledge. Furious, Ethan gathered himself and stared out over the blood-saturated ground. A few protoss still stood, making a noble but ultimately futile last stand against the thing out there. Even if the dark archon fell, even if the Dominion departed, both Ethan and the doomed protoss knew he would turn his zerg upon them.

He looked around, waving the extra pair of scythe-like limbs with which Kerrigan had gifted him, itching to slice and maim and kill. There. There was one, downed but not dead.

Not yet.

Ethan sent the order, and a pair of hydralisks immediately ceased their attack and hastened to the injured protoss. Before it fully understood what was happening, they had lifted it and borne it to their commander.

The wounded protoss raised his head with a great effort and peered up at Ethan. His armor had been rent in several places and he was slippery with blood. He would not last long without treatment.

"Do you know how to operate the warp gate?" Ethan demanded.

The protoss nodded weakly. "Yes. But I will not aid you."

Elation and irritation both filled him. "You do not understand the gravity of your situation, protoss."

The alien closed its eyes and tilted its head. "It is you who do not understand. I am redeemed. I would never compromise my redemption for you. I am Alzadar, and I will die a templar, as I once was."

Ethan muttered, "I do not have time for this . . ." and at once one of the hydralisks impaled its hook-like blade into Alzadar's thigh. The protoss arched in silent agony, reminding Ethan of an insect impaled on a pin.

"You will find no one among my people who will help you recover Jacob Ramsey. We face death gladly."

"Death yes, but torture?"

The protoss's eyes, which had dimmed, suddenly brightened. "Even that. I pity you. You do not understand what it is to love something greater than yourself." He shuddered. "My life . . . for . . . Aiur."

Perhaps Alzadar would have broken eventually, had he not been so severely injured. Perhaps he could have been "convinced" to cooperate. But the protoss was badly injured, and before Ethan quite realized it, Alzadar was dead. Ethan cursed.

In the end, Ethan thought with more than a touch of worry, Alzadar's prediction about the nature of the protoss was more than likely correct. How, then, was Ethan to track Jake? Panic fluttered inside him for an instant, but he resolutely pushed it down. He would simply have to find another way, that was all.

He summoned the mutalisk and climbed atop it again, surveying the battle that raged below from an aerial vantage point. Perhaps a fresh perspective would give him insight.

What was happening should not have been possible.

Ulrezaj raged even as he realized that he was likely about to die. How could such a thing happen? He was Ulrezaj! It had been his mind that had seen possibilities where others saw only atrocities. It had been his daring that had taken him to a place where no one, no thing, had ever had the courage to venture. It had been fear that had caused the dark templar, long ago, to forbid the creation of such power. He understood why they feared it; such power, whirling out of control, could do more harm than good.

But Ulrezaj was completely, entirely in control.

Until this moment.

Stubborn protoss, Dominion vessels, and zerg. Anyone, anything else would have perished under the onslaught. Ulrezaj would have vanquished them and reduced Zamara and the frail terran in which she'd secreted herself to handfuls of shredded flesh, had it not been for the psionic storms that the few remaining protoss had inexplicably been able to summon.

He felt his strength ebbing. He swayed as the attacks continued, and knew with both confusion and fury that he would soon fall. They would be upon him then, and he would not recover. All his knowledge, all his power, all the glory that was going to be his, was *supposed* to have been his—lost.

It was, he would have thought mere moments ago, impossible.

And then, like the eye of the hurricane passing over, there was a pause. The fighting ceased for the most part, and even as hope that he might indeed survive gave him fresh energy, Ulrezaj realized that his prey had fled.

Zamara, clever, despised Zamara, had eluded his grasp a second time.

He did not waste precious time and energy fighting to move forward to discover if the gate was still open. He knew it would not be. Zamara was not a fool, she would not leave such an easy trail for him to follow.

There was nothing to do but retreat and try again. Ulrezaj gathered himself and sent his instructions to those Forged who still stood with him.

The treachery of the Shel'na Kryhas and the attacks of these new foes weakens me. Protect me while I return to the chambers, where I may rest and grow powerful once again.

Xava'tor, we hear, and we obey.

Immediately the ships that had been pressing the attack closed in around Ulrezaj's swirling essence as the enormous dark archon changed direction and moved swiftly toward safety.

"It's hurt," breathed Devon Starke, former ghost and now devoted employee of Valerian Mengsk. "The protoss mental attacks were able to hurt it."

It had been difficult, protecting himself against the power of the dark archon's mind—minds? It was hard to tell which—but Starke had managed to do it. He could not read the thoughts of the dark archon per se, not the way he could those of terrans, but he could get bits and pieces. Enough so that he understood that the protoss had utilized a psionic attack that had managed to harm this seemingly unstoppable juggernaut of darkness that was moving implacably toward—

And it was then he realized that Jake and Rosemary had indeed made their escape. Starke rubbed his head, which was aching terribly. The combination of battling protoss, zerg, and this monstrous thing that had appeared out of nowhere had been too much of a distraction. Starke had come for one thing, one man, and that man was gone.

"Contact Mr. V," he ordered.

"Sir," the pilot said, his voice strained, "I can't raise anyone. Not even the other ships."

"What?"

"Whatever the protoss did somehow short-circuited our communications system. We're damned lucky we're still flying."

Damn it. Starke was used to following orders. He needed to know where to go, what to do—regroup with the others, or attempt to figure out the warp gate, or—

—or follow the dark archon, who was now retreating almost more swiftly than it had advanced.

Starke closed his eyes, willing his body to accept the pain, trading the agony for information.

It was indeed hurt. Wounded, even. Exhausted. It needed to rest. Recover. In . . . *below*. Then it would attack again. It would find the preserver and destroy her. There was no place she could hide from—

"Ulrezaj," Devon whispered. He had a name now. Maybe that would help. In the meantime, he knew what he had to do. There was no following Jake Ramsey through the warp gate. But it was clear that this being, this Ulrezaj, wanted Ramsey as badly as Valerian did.

"The dark archon is going to ground," he told the pilot. "Let him think he's shaken us, but don't lose him. When he makes his move, which he will, we will follow him at a distance."

The pilot looked uneasy, but nodded. "Of course, sir."

"In the meantime, I will take a hawk and rendezvous with Mr. V's vessel and apprise him of what has happened." Starke rose and then gripped the arm of the chair as his vision swirled. Such close contact with Ulrezaj, plus uncomfortably close proximity to the—storms, he supposed he would call them, of the protoss had tired him more than he thought.

He sat back down hard in the chair and forced a laugh. "I'll do that in . . . just a few moments."

Fear skittered along Valerian's mind. He liked Devon Starke. He did not want to think that the man had perished. Beside him, his personal assistant,

Charles Whittier, muttering under his breath and looking even more distraught than usual, frantically moved his hands over the controls, trying to raise the ghost. Or indeed anyone, as all the screens were still ominously dark.

"Sir, I-I'm afraid that whatever it was the protoss did may have shorted out communication."

Valerian nodded his blond head, brushing absently at a stray lock that fell into his eyes. "Keep trying, Whittier." He clapped a hand on his assistant's shoulder in what he hoped was a heartening manner. Instead Whittier jumped about a foot.

Valerian folded his arms across his chest, thinking. It was quite possible he'd just lost all his vessels. He'd put every resource available into this, and if they were gone, he'd have to start from the beginning. He thought about the last thing he'd heard from Starke. *It's all we can do to stop this dark archon from killing them. The protoss are doing something—I'm not sure what—but it's giving the thing pause.*

The moments ticked by. There was no response.

Valerian had sent every ship save his own down to Aiur to capture Jake. None of them had reported in. The best case scenario was that their communications systems were damaged; the worst, that whatever it was the protoss were doing had wiped out his entire fleet.

"This is Captain Macey for Mr. V, are you available, sir?"

Captain Dennis Macey had a smooth, confident

voice that sounded like nothing in the universe would take him by surprise. Even now, he sounded so calm one could almost imagine he was bored.

Valerian leaned down and pressed a button. "This is Mr. V., Captain—have you had any contact with your vessels on the surface?"

"Negative, sir, not for several minutes. I'm attempting to raise them, but with no luck."

Valerian was left with only one option.

"Captain, I'll be on the bridge in a moment." He ended the conversation and turned to Whittier. "I'm going down there, Whittier. Prepare my hawk."

"Sir! You can't possibly—what would your father—"

Valerian turned. Gray eyes narrowing, he fixed a gaze on Whittier that silenced the man in mid-sentence. "I came here to find Ramsey. If Ramsey is dead, I need to know. If everyone I set to that task is dead, I need to know. They are my responsibility. Keep monitoring, Whittier."

"Y-yes, sir."

Captain Macey, a tall, taciturn man with skin the color of coffee and eyes that never revealed what he was thinking, turned without surprise as his employer entered and nodded acknowledgment of the Heir Apparent's presence.

Valerian gazed out the huge windows and regarded Aiur turning slowly in space. From this distance, nothing could be seen of the fighting on the surface.

"Starke said that the protoss were doing something—utilizing some kind of psionic attack," Valerian told the captain.

"I don't know that much about the protoss, sir, but I know they know how to ruin a planet. It's entirely possible our ships are—"

". . . to *Illustrious,* come in *Illustrious.*"

The voice sounded exhausted, but it was clearly recognizable as belonging to Devon Starke. Valerian felt a grin spreading across his face.

"Devon! Are you all right?"

"Not quite sure how to answer that, sir, but I am alive. And I have quite a lot of news."

CHAPTER 4

ROSEMARY THOUGHT BACK TO THE LAST TIME she'd been in a cell. It had not been all that long ago, though it felt like she'd lived a lifetime since then. It had been right when Valerian had double-crossed her. She'd been about to turn Jake Ramsey over to the tender loving care of the marines aboard the *Gray Tiger* and collect her payment. Instead, the marines had arrested her too.

She'd been put in a tiny little makeshift cell that she had paced too many times to count. Rosemary recalled kicking the prefab walls in anger—that had not been her smartest moment. She owed her eventual freedom to the very man she'd planned to betray. A smile curved her lips as she recalled the door swinging open and Jake entering. She'd jumped him before she realized who he was, and they'd both hit the floor hard. Jake had not had Zamara in his head very long at that point, and he'd been exhausted by the ordeal. Though he had been the one to unlock her door, it was Rosemary who got them to safety when Jake passed out.

Rosemary realized that not only was she worried about Jake's safety and, yes, that of the protoss in his brain, but . . . she missed the guy.

She surveyed her current living quarters with a wry grin. No tiny prefab-walled cell for her this time. If this was any indication, the protoss did things on a much classier scale than humans did. The room was spacious, with a large, soft mattress on the floor, tables and chairs (a bit too large for a human frame, let alone her petite one, but tables and chairs nonetheless), and a spacious window that nearly took up half the wall. It opened onto a purple-blue landscape of swirling sands and buildings, the latter only distinguishable in the apparent eternal twilight by faint lights. She had had only three real complaints, some of which were more easily taken care of than others. One was the lighting; it was apparently controlled by telepathy, and Rosemary was sorely lacking in that quarter. She had had to knock on the door and ask her guard to turn the lights on and off. The second was food and water. Rosemary remembered Jake saying that the protoss got all their nutrients from the sun, moon, and stars. She needed something more substantial. Which led to her third complaint—a rather pressing need for a chamber pot.

The food had seemed to pose the biggest problem. She'd not seen much of Shakuras—the brief glimpse of an outside area when she and the other protoss had run through the gate was pretty much it. Rosemary had been ushered onto the ship and not been allowed to look outside during the brief flight to—wherever it was.

She frowned a little. Make that *four* complaints—no one had told her very much since they'd brought her here and put her in this very nice, comfortable, spacious room that was, in the end, still just a prison cell.

Her stomach rumbled. They'd brought the chamber pot, but still hadn't brought her anything to eat. She had no way of telling time, but knew she had been here several hours already. They had gotten her water; she reached for a bowl containing the precious liquid and took a sip.

She heard the sound of the door opening and turned, expecting to see her protoss guard. Instead a stranger entered, a female who was clearly of high rank and well aware of it. She stood proudly, a commanding presence. The newcomer wore armor that Rosemary recognized marked her as a templar. Rosemary thought it was largely symbolic at first, as her gaze swept over this imposing figure. Good protection at the vulnerable backward bend of the knee and upper arms, and the sweep of gleaming metal that lifted like slender wings at the shoulder should effectively block blows to the throat. But the waist and thigh showed smooth gray flesh. Then again, if this was the head of the templar, which Rosemary suspected an "executor" was, this female probably would halt any attacker dead in his tracks before he got close enough to get in a blow.

Rosemary had seen bits and pieces of armor on the Aiur protoss, but she now realized how dreadfully battle-worn that armor had been. What the protoss before her now wore was gleaming and bright, catching even the dim blue-purple light that came in from the window and the light from the glowing, gemlike spheres set into the armor itself. The dangling appendages that Rosemary knew were nerve cords and that definitely marked her as a traditional protoss and not one of the dark templar fell almost like long ropes of hair, with golden metal pieces adorning their ends. Beneath the armor, she wore a slender drape of fabric that looked very luxurious and soft, a night-black, velvety swath that protected her gray skin from the gleaming, gold metal.

In her four-fingered hands, which still looked so very weird to Rosemary, she carried a shallow golden bowl that had some vaguely spherical things and a couple of long, grassy things in it.

Rosemary did not attempt to hide her scrutiny, and she realized that the newcomer was in all likelihood sizing her up as well. At the moment, exhausted, hungry, and physically filthy as she was, Rosemary knew who'd win that competition. She decided she'd add the lack of a bath to her list of complaints.

"Who are you?" Rosemary asked.

The protoss placed the bowl down with almost ceremonial precision on the table, turned, and inclined her head. It wasn't quite a bow, but it was a gesture of respect.

"I am Executor Selendis," she said. "I have come to query you as to the nature of your purpose on our world." She indicated the bowl. "It has taken us no little effort, but we have located fruits and tubers that I believe you will be able to consume."

Rosemary eyed the contents of the bowl and hoped Selendis was right. She was starving. But even more than food, she hungered for information.

"I'm Rosemary Dahl, and you know exactly why I am here. I get that you all live much longer than we do, and that protocol and ceremony and stuff mean a lot to you, but there's not a lot of time for things like that right now."

Executor Selendis regarded the terran with luminous, unblinking eyes. "There is always time to do something the right way, Rosemary Dahl."

"It depends on whose definition of 'right way' you use."

Selendis half closed her eyes, tilted her head, and hunched her armored shoulders slightly in the gesture that indicated humor. "I suppose that it does. Do you wish to feed before we speak?"

Feed. Like she was a pet, or an animal to be fattened for slaughter or something. Selendis narrowed her eyes; she'd read Rosemary's thoughts, of course. Man, this was getting old.

"I'll skip the chow for now. Like I said, we don't have a lot of time. What do you know so far?"

"What the protoss who accompanied you have told me. I cannot verify their statements in the Khala as of yet. They are still ridding themselves of the influence of the drug with which the dark archon polluted them." A great deal of distaste was in the words. Rosemary wasn't sure if the detestation was directed at the drug or at the thought of the dark archon. Or maybe even at her.

Rosemary glanced away. "The Sundrop, it's . . . bad stuff, yeah."

Selendis nodded, slowly. Rosemary sensed the executor was still making up her mind about everything.

"Let me get right to the point. I understand why your guards redirected my friend Jake. It was a smart thing to do. But unfortunately Jake has a preserver in his head with some really important information—information she was willing to kill a whole lot of people to protect. And because she's inside my friend's brain, he's dying. She wants to put what she knows into a dark templar crystal, so the information isn't lost. Jake wants her out of his head, so he can survive. And I want—"

The rush of words was suddenly dammed as Rosemary slammed hard against the fact that she actually *didn't* know what she wanted. A few years or months ago, she'd have named it in terms of creature comforts, personal challenges, and a whole lot of credits. Even recently, she was planning on using the archaeologist as her pass to safety and fortune. But now—

The protoss before her waited patiently, with that freaky stillness that was so unsettling. Time to them was utterly different than it was to terrans. Their life-times lasted centuries; humans, generally less than one. They could afford to be patient.

Rosemary opened her mouth, closed it, opened it again. "I . . . I guess I want Jake to be okay."

"That is all?"

"Well, I want to be okay too. I just—" Rosemary grinned self-deprecatingly. "I guess I just don't know what that looks like anymore."

"I see."

Rosemary wasn't at all sure that this gray-skinned, imposing female did. "Look—find Jake and bring him back so Zamara can get out of his head. How hard can it be?"

"What you do not understand, terran, is that what you ask is a serious matter indeed. I must be certain that it is not just the right thing for your colleague, but the right thing for my people."

"It's a damned *preserver*!" Rosemary cried in utter exasperation. "Isn't helping her survive the right thing for your people?"

"You yourself have confessed that you were sub-jected to a mind-altering drug," Selendis continued, completely unperturbed by Rosemary's outburst. "So were the others. Until the drug has cleared their sys-tems and we can meet their minds and hearts in the Khala, I must wait and listen and learn."

Suddenly the import of the words struck Rosemary. "You mean—wait a minute. Are you saying that all the protoss who came through with me were the

Tal'darim—the Forged? That there are none of Those Who Endure among them?"

"No. There are not. Only those whose minds were affected by the Sundrop."

Rosemary sank down in one of the oversized chairs, stunned by the news. She thought of the moment when she was certain she was going to die at the hands—well, pincers, claws, whatever they had— of the zerg and the wave of protoss had descended to save them. She thought of their ready forgiveness of her almost-betrayal. She passed a shaking hand through her hair, telling herself it was exhaustion and lack of food that made this news so upsetting.

"Your concern does you credit. Do not belittle it so."

Rosemary shot Selendis an angry glare. "Don't read my mind. Wait for me to talk, damn it."

"I have not yet determined if you are truly friend or foe, Rosemary Dahl. I will do as I see fit to ascertain the truth. The others may have granted your request to not read your mind, but I have made no such promise."

Rosemary found her hands clenching into fists and forced herself to relax. "Listen to me, Selendis. You are wasting precious time. Jake and Zamara are in danger, and they're out there alone. They could die while you wait for the others to detox to verify *the same damn story we're all telling*!"

The glowing eyes flashed, and Rosemary realized she'd finally gotten to Selendis. "There is no reason I should trust you, and every reason I should doubt you. We protoss have encountered only a few humans. And the single human female we have dealt with does not make us at all inclined to be welcoming."

There was nothing Rosemary could do, and she sagged slightly, still in the chair. "Fine. But I'll tell you this. If Jake dies because you are all sitting around on your hands waiting for verification in the Khala, I personally will make sure you regret it."

Selendis had recovered herself and seemed as immovable as ever. "If it turns out you are telling the truth, and if Jacob Ramsey and the preserver he bears die because of my choice to delay, then I will regret it more than your human brain can possibly grasp. But I am the executor of the templar, and such decisions are mine to make and their outcomes my responsibility to bear. Is there anything else you require?"

Jake . . . aw, damn it.

"Nothing you'd be willing or able to give me," Rosemary said, momentarily defeated.

Selendis hesitated. "If the nourishment we have provided is inadequate, please inform your guard and we will make another attempt at providing you sustenance. In the meantime, I will send for hot water and fresh clothing for you. I hope to have your account of events verified shortly."

Rosemary supposed she should say thank you, but she was too angry and frustrated and heartsick. Instead she stayed put in the chair, arms folded, while Selendis left. Then, sighing, she grabbed a piece of what she thought was fruit and bit into it. It was mushy and bland, and she thought with regret of the sammuro fruit she and Jake had eaten on Aiur. Of the protoss who had risked their lives to gather it for them, and to hunt the prey whose flesh had provided necessary protein for the two terrans.

According to Selendis, none of the Shel'na Kryhas had made it. They were all lying dead on Aiur.

Didn't look like they were Those Who Endure after all.

CHAPTER 5

VARTANIL HAD BEEN VERY YOUNG WHEN HIS LIFE had been so violently disrupted. Less than a century old, he had lived the peaceful, orderly life that all protoss on Aiur knew. His family was of the Furinax bloodline, and their specialty had been crafting objects of beauty. Others built the physical infrastructure of the cities and vessels and weapons; others crafted the armor as well as the bracers that channeled the templar's psionic energy, manifesting it in powerful psi blades. But Vartanil had been a carver of the light-and-dark wood of the spotted shuwark tree, shaping the soft wood beneath clever hands, bringing forth the images of beasts both native and alien for the delight of the senses. Even as it dried, the wood smelled good—clean and healing. Vartanil polished it until it was smooth as a river stone to the touch, and he knew that the images he created delighted the eye.

That had all been destroyed when the zerg came to Aiur.

His family had gotten separated and had scattered, as many familial units had done in those horrifying days. Vartanil never knew what became of them, and could only hope that they were among the lucky ones who had made it off planet. With what he had come to regard as blind luck, Vartanil managed to elude the zerg, only to nearly be slain by a ravenous omhara. He had been saved by a small group of protoss, mostly khalai like himself, although there were a few templar, led by Alzadar, and a judicator, Felanis. His skin becoming mottled with his overwhelming emotions, Vartanil had sworn himself to the service of this group. As time passed, Felanis and Alzadar found other protoss, and their numbers swelled.

Vartanil still helped with his carving talent, but this time, he carved arrows, bows, spears, throwing sticks. Weapons to stave off the wandering zerg and more natural, but no less dangerous, native animals. Alzadar taught him how to use the weapons he created. Vartanil knew he would never be a true warrior, not like Alzadar was, but he took pride in being able to help protect his new family.

When conflict arose between the two factions, Vartanil left with Felanis's group—"the Forged," as they eventually called themselves. He had no animosity toward Ladranix or the other protoss, but he had vowed to follow Alzadar, who had been so kind to him.

And when later Alzadar revealed the true horror of the "Benefactor" the gulled Forged had been following—a dark archon, perhaps the most powerful and dangerous the protoss had ever known, and who, far from protecting them, had been preying upon them—he had passionately rallied behind Alzadar to forsake the false benefactor and cleave again to his fellows.

When it became clear that Alzadar was choosing to stay behind and die defending the terrans, buying the precious time they and the preserver Jacob carried needed, Vartanil almost panicked. Who would lead them? Who—how—

"There is no protoss wiser than a preserver," Alzadar had said. "Follow Jacob. Protect him and the precious being he bears." Vartanil promised to do so.

Vartanil had been stunned beyond measure when he stumbled through the warp gate to arrive in Shakuras, only to discover that his new leader, the one he had promised the likely-now-dead Alzadar he would protect and aid, had been diverted to somewhere else entirely. And when Rosemary had come under verbal attack—Rosemary, a mere terran, non-telepathic, who had still managed to turn her back on the exquisite pleasure offered by the Sundrop—he had rallied to her defense immediately. She was the one closest to Jacob Jefferson Ramsey; he would help her.

Vartanil and the others were separated from Rosemary shortly after their arrival. A small vessel had been summoned, to bear them to who knew where. He watched two templar, each over half a meter taller than the petite human female, flank her on either side as they marched her away. And then the first pangs of withdrawal hit, and Vartanil quite forgot about Rosemary, about Jacob, about Alzadar, or Aiur or Shakuras, indeed anything that was not the intense, all-consuming craving that racked his body.

How long it took for the vile drug to clear his system, he did not know. Later, he would be told it took three full days. He was unconscious for most of it, waking now and then to find himself surrounded by other protoss sending him caring, concerned thoughts, bearing him to a place where starlight could fall upon him, giving him a lifeline while his body shuddered and hunched and his limbs flailed, sending him back into blessed unconsciousness for another brief respite.

He blinked awake, clear-headed and feeling wrung out. He was in a room with several others of the Forged. Some slept on, others moved about quietly. Many stood at the large window, their faces turned up toward the life-giving rays of the cosmos, regaining their strength after the ordeal.

On the sleeping pallet next to him, a figure stirred. Vartanil recognized him as Korlendir, and extended tentative thoughts to his friend.

"Korlendir, are you well?" He could have probed to find out for himself, but refrained, knowing that Korlendir, too, must have suffered greatly in breaking free of the Sundrop.

"Drained. Exhausted. Empty."

Vartanil nodded. He felt the same way. "But that will pass, and we will be free of Ulrezaj's deception. The Sundrop has left our bodies, and now we can again meet in the Khala."

". . . yes. This is true."

Vartanil looked about. "I see only former Tal'darim here. Where are those who aided us?"

"Gone, no doubt, to sit in the Khala and purge themselves of the taint of having touched our minds."

The thought was laced with so much bitterness that Vartanil recoiled. "I am certain that is not the case."

Korlendir turned to look at him. "Truly? I am not. What I said to those whose minds touched mine was harsh and angry and terrified. I would have felt sullied were it my mind that had been exposed to such filthy thoughts."

"Perhaps. But the Khala teaches us compassion above all else. Those who sat with us gave us a link to what it is to be protoss. . . . They did so out of caring."

Korlendir had no answer to that. At that moment, the door opened. Several protoss entered, bearing clean robes. One of them Vartanil recognized as Rishagar, who had sat with him a long time. The protoss, smaller than most and almost painfully slender, drifted toward him, warm affection rolling off her.

"You wake, friend Vartanil. And your mind is as clear as the waters of the Shushari pools. I am so very pleased."

She placed the clothing on the bed, and he rose and bowed to her. Rishagar extended her hands, palms up, and Vartanil imitated her. Energy formed and glowed softly in the space between their nearly-touching hands.

He met her in the Khala, and the beauty and wonder of the union caught him by surprise. It had been so long, and he had grown used to his isolation, though he had never learned to not miss the connection, the ache for it.

Sore trials you have had, my brother, and it was more than words, more than thoughts, he *felt* this mental communication. *But you have survived. You have come home.*

Vartanil could not hide the slight reluctance he felt at the words, and Rishagar's puzzlement floated around him. Scorning words, he held in his mind's eye and his heart encountering Jacob Jefferson Ramsey, and Zamara, and Rosemary Dahl. He showed her the desiccated corpses of what had once been worshipful Xava'kai, the whirling dark raging monster that had descended upon the fleeing preserver and her host. She had sat with him and comforted him mentally as his body rid itself of Sundrop, but now she *felt* the craving, the terror of the inexplicable separation from the Khala, the joy at the reunion at this deep level.

Gently they drew apart, warmth filling both of them. "So it is true, what the terran female has said."

"It is true. Zamara must be found and saved—as must Jacob Ramsey. He is a friend to the protoss. We have had so many casualties; it would grieve me if he were to be another one."

Rishagar nodded. "Executor Selendis will want to speak with you. And with you, Korlendir," she added, drawing the other protoss into the conversation. "Once she has met with you all, you are free to leave."

"And go where?" Korlendir was angry. "This is not our home. Our home lies in smoking ruins, crawling with zerg. And we sit here doing nothing about it."

"Executor Selendis, too, is passionate about our homeworld," Rishagar nodded, her calm a contrast to Korlendir's agitation. "Once she is informed, she and the hierarch will decide what the best course of action must be. But truly, this is your home now, Korlendir, as much as it is mine. The dark templar have done their best to make us welcome."

It was only because he had so recently been with Rishagar in the Khala that Vartanil picked up on the slight hesitation. Directing his thoughts privately to her, he asked, "Is there trouble here on Shakuras then?"

"Only what was to be expected—ancient enmities cannot be solved in a day, or a year, or even four years. But most of us are working hard to recover our former kinship."

Vartanil understood. Such divisions ran deep. He had seen one of the dark templar at the gate, Razturul was his name. Unlike most protoss from Aiur, for years Vartanil had known only a touching of minds, not souls. He had been denied the Khala because of the Sundrop; in a way, while fanning hatred of the dark templar among the Forged, Ulrezaj had actually been forcing those under his control to become like their exiled brethren.

"It is all . . . very complicated," he said finally. Rishagar half closed her eyes and warm humor washed over him. He shared it with her. But beside them, still angry and more than a touch confused, Korlendir sat in silence.

Hard on Rishagar's heels had come the executor. Korlendir had come to know that a female now occupied the place of power where Tassadar had once stood, but it was still unusual. Raszagal, the late matriarch of the dark templar, had led her people for many centuries. He had learned that among the dark templar, females in positions of power were not at all uncommon. But he was unused to such things. There had been none among the Conclave, and few among the templar. To see this powerful female in her beautiful, shining armor, to feel her gaze upon him, was unsettling.

It was with reluctance that he followed her lead and stepped into the Khala again. Worn out from both the physical and mental toll the detoxification had taken on him, reentering the Khala in the company of such a strong spirit as Selendis was more jarring than comforting, more intense than soothing. Nonetheless, her pleasure that he had escaped was genuine, as was her concern about the terrans.

The human female did not lie, then. There is a preserver's spirit trapped inside the human male. And she, too, was in the grip of the Sundrop.

She drew from him everything. Korlendir did not fight Selendis, but he could not hide his agitation from her. She was brief, and before she withdrew, she thanked him and sent calm to him. It helped somewhat.

Had union in the Khala always been like this? Korlendir was a templar. He had, along with every other protoss he had ever known, loathed and slightly feared the rebellious dark templar. Such he had been taught. But now it made him feel too vulnerable, this intimate joining, with no feeling, no thought, hidden from this stranger.

Selendis was clearly troubled by what she had learned. Nonetheless when she had finished, she bowed to him, and moved toward Vartanil. Korlendir was free to go now. There was a place here, in the capital city of Talematros, where records were kept. Korlendir, like all the others, had been encouraged to go there and locate his family. If he could not—if his family had perished on Aiur—he would be welcomed by Selendis and the other templar. No protoss was without a place, a position, a role to play.

Except Korlendir.

He found that he did not particularly care if his blood family had survived. The Forged had become his family, with the Xava'tor as its head. The Sundrop had calmed and comforted. Perhaps it had indeed driven them out of the Khala, but after what Korlendir had just experienced, he was not certain that was a bad thing. They had been close under the care of the Xava'tor. Even though the Benefactor had been revealed to be of dark templar origins—a dark archon, no less—Korlendir wondered, keeping the thought shielded, if perhaps Ulrezaj had been wronged.

Korlendir glanced over at Vartanil. He and Selendis sat palm to palm, and the young khalai was deeply at peace and happy. For a moment, Korlendir envied him.

He sat for a while longer, then rose and left the building.

He did not head toward the record chambers, nor the templar tower. He let his feet take him where they would. They took him through the city, bathed in the near-constant twilight and pocked with the strange architectural designs he was beginning to understand were typical of the dark templar. Korlendir glared up at them once, then lowered his head. He walked almost all day, until the buildings began to thin and the purple, hazy sky above him opened up. Finally, he lifted his head, and his eyes widened at what he beheld. He knew what it was, even though he had never seen it before.

It rose majestically in the distance, towering over the blasted landscape that encircled it. Four triangles that met at the top, it seemed at first to Korlendir to be comprised of multicolored lights. He realized as he drew closer, breaking into a loping run even though he had been walking for hours, that it was a solid crystalline structure.

The xel'naga temple. The reason that the dark templar had chosen to settle here instead of anywhere else they had discovered on their long journey. They had taken its presence as a sign, and now, as Korlendir hastened toward the temple that seemed a shining beacon of hope, he took it as a sign as well.

For the last few years, he had dwelt in such a place. Deep beneath the surface of Aiur was a labyrinthine world of swirling, beautiful, luminous harmony, and the Forged had made it their home. Not all of it, for the Benefactor forbade them to explore certain areas, but much of it. The xel'naga had made those chambers beneath Aiur, and they had made this heart-stoppingly beautiful temple that reached toward the swirling blue clouds.

He slowed as he approached, wondering how he would be received, and stood hesitating on the stairs that climbed upward. A sound reached him; a sort of humming, singing sound, more melody than random noise. For a moment, he closed his eyes, the better to simply listen to the song. Then, still listening to the haunting sound, Korlendir opened his eyes and craned his neck, gazing raptly at the sheer beauty of the structure. A thought brushed his, gentle, soft.

"Welcome, brother, to the temple of the xel'naga."

Korlendir turned to regard what must be one of the acolytes of the temple. The figure, light gray in color, bowed deeply. He was dressed in white robes that draped his body with artful effortlessness. In the light of this sacred place, the garb seemed to have a soft radiance of its own. Peace flowed from the acolyte.

Korlendir, templar born and bred, gave the acolyte a stiff and formal salute. He felt large and awkward amid this place of seemingly fragile beauty, next to this delicately made tender of the temple, whose name he knew was Taarim. The chambers beneath Aiur were kin to the one he stood in now, but subtly different.

Reading his surface thoughts, Taarim brightened. "Ah! You are one of our lost brethren from our ancient and longed-for homeland, returned to us. Welcome, welcome indeed. What brings you to the temple?"

"I—do not know," Korlendir answered truthfully. "I did not feel like I belonged anywhere else."

He did not meet Taarim in the Khala, not quite, but he freely opened his thoughts and experiences to the younger protoss. Taarim did likewise, and Korlendir learned that those of the Shelak bloodline were now the main guardians of this temple, even though they were not dark templar. They had a long history of understanding and protecting xel'naga artifacts, so it was no difficult decision to turn the care of this precious place over to them.

"Yes . . . I and the other Shelak descendants were born to care for this place," Taarim said, spreading his arms wide and seeming to embrace the temple. "But others are sometimes called to come here, others who are not of Shelak lineage. Judicator or Khalai or . . ." and Taarim half closed his eyes and tilted his head, ". . . Templar caste, it matters not here. Even some of the dark templar have stayed, working together with us. The songs of the crystal are merely pleasant sounds to some. To others, they sing to their very souls."

Emotion flooded Korlendir. He staggered and Taarim caught his arm with steady yet gentle support. "You have endured much," the Shelak said. "Come, my brother, for if I am certain of anything, I am certain you belong here."

Taarim steered Korlendir inside. Almost overwhelmed with a sense of belonging he had not felt since Alzadar had disrupted the calm and tranquility known by the Forged, Korlendir let himself be led into a cool alcove. He sank gratefully to the floor, which was covered with soft pillows. The illumination was provided by glowing crystals, which hovered gracefully as though borne by unseen hands. All around him still, the crystals sang.

Other acolytes were there, and more drifted in, piqued by curiosity. Korlendir saw that Taarim had spoken truly, for while most of those he saw were clearly of the Shelak bloodline, others were from different castes. Indeed, he even saw the sharp, spiked features of a dark templar.

Taarim began to speak. He told of the day four years ago when, frightened almost beyond reason, thousands of terrified protoss fled from their homeworld to this twilight world of Shakuras. He told of Tassadar's sacrifice, the attack of the zerg upon Shakuras, the need to harness both traditional and dark templar energies to activate the great crystals, the Khalis and the Uraj, in order to save a second protoss world from the zerg. Korlendir listened raptly.

He had been raised to believe that it was the templar who protected the protoss. And in times before, it was. But now he realized that it was the Shelak who had always kept alive what it truly meant to be protoss. The Khalai caste built the infrastructure, harnessed science and technology, and created beautiful things simply because beauty was as necessary as air and light. The Judicator caste defined the laws and kept to the true path, and the Templar caste protected the physical bodies of the protoss.

Beyond and deeper than all this was the true essence—the knowledge of the xel'naga, the Wanderers from Afar, the Great Teachers. They and their wisdom were there before the protoss found even the Khala, and they and their wisdom were here now, at this vital juncture in time, at a crossroads for protoss history.

"Let me be part of this," Korlendir all but begged, his skin mottling with deep emotion.

"You already are, brother, by coming here today," Taarim assured him. "Do you turn from your path of templar, then? Do you seek to be a guardian of the ancient things, a protector of old wisdom, and a harbinger of a glorious future for our people?"

"With all that I am, I do."

They met in the Khala then, and Taarim could see the sincerity in Korlendir's heart. Taarim turned to another white-robed protoss and nodded. The other bowed and hastened away.

"There is no turning back when you start this path. For this is a path of deep secrets and lore and knowledge. There is more to us than this simple temple, my brother. Far, far more. If you betray us, retribution will be merciless and swift."

"I understand."

And then joy leaped in Korlendir as he detected a familiar, sweet, cloying scent.

He had come home indeed.

CHAPTER 6

IF IT HADN'T BEEN FOR THE FACT THAT HE WAS dying and that Zamara had a universe-shattering secret she needed to share, Jake thought he might never have been happier.

The place was gorgeous. He could understand why Zeratul—or indeed any sane member of a sentient species—would see this place as a refuge. Too, there were all kinds of remnants of alien races, which Jake spotted longingly as the small vessel flew with startling speed and silence over the planet's surface.

Maybe one day I'll get back here, he said to Zamara as the enticing pile of clearly non-naturally-occurring rubble below him retreated into the distance.

I hope you do, Jacob. But we must find the most likely spot to encounter the prelate. We wish to be found, not hide amongst ruins.

Jake sighed. *I used to love doing that. Hide amongst ruins.*

But now you are at the forefront of a battle that will change everything.

If I live long enough to tell anybody.

We will. The firmness of Zamara's reply was heartening.

So, what exactly are we looking for?

The place where Zeratul either is . . . or to which he will return. I will know it when I see it.

Jake's mind went back to worrying about the warp gate. Zamara seemed to think it would eventually open for them.

Yes, Jacob, as I said before, I think at some point we will be permitted on Shakuras. However, I would imagine that all gates that open onto Shakuras are closed at this time. Unless Rosemary and the others can convince the protoss that the information I bear is more important than a possible invasion of Shakuras, I doubt they will open the gates any time soon.

Oh great.

Do not lose hope, Jacob.

He tried not to. He really did. But the headaches were growing more frequent and more severe, and he knew that despite her calm demeanor and words of reassurance, Zamara, too, was worried that time would run out on them.

I should have been faster, Jake sighed. *I lingered too long. I gave them enough time to shut the gate before I tried to go through.*

True, said Zamara mercilessly, and Jake winced slightly. *But it is difficult to blame you for your desire to see the destruction of Ulrezaj. I admit, I, too, would have taken pleasure in knowing for certain that he was no longer a threat. Regardless, what is done is done, and regret serves us nothing.*

He nodded, still gazing at the landscape unfolding beneath him. If it hadn't been tinged with that peculiar yet soothing rose-gold wash, it would look like the holovids of old Earth he'd seen. Meadows, oceans, trees, mountains . . . glorious.

Tell me about Zeratul.

I will show you. But it will take . . . context.

Trusting her completely, Jake let her take charge of piloting the vessel—she was anyway, really, he was more or less just along for the ride—and opened to the wave of memories.

Clad in the glorious, graceful ceremonial armor that was his right to wear as a high templar and the leader of the vast protoss fleet, Tassadar stood on the bridge of the Gantrithor, *staring out at what remained of the human colony they called "Chau Sara."*

"It is done," he said, sorrow tingeing his mental voice.

Jake tilted her head and regarded—

"Holy crap, Zamara, I'm you! I mean, it's you!" Jake had always had an instant understanding of whose identity he was sharing in these moments. He *was* that protoss, as well as himself, but it felt odd to be both Jake Ramsey and Zamara, whom he had come to know so well.

"Indeed you are, and indeed it is. These memories are but a few years old, and they are my own. I thought I had made that clear."

"No, but it's a nice surprise."

• • •

—the executor. "It was you who first found the probes, Executor. It is thanks to you that the zerg have not spread farther."

"Perhaps, Zamara. But it is also thanks to me that every terran on this world is now dead."

Jake waved a dismissive hand. "Unfortunate, but necessary. The zerg must be stopped. Extreme measures were demanded, the responsibilities of the Dae'Uhl notwithstanding."

"I'd . . . forgotten how callous you were when we first met," Jake muttered.

"I have not. But I am glad that my sentiments changed. Just as Tassadar's did. We are not omniscient, infallible gods, Jacob. We know much—and preservers remember all that our race knows—but we still have much, much to learn."

Tassadar touched one of the communication crystals and informed the Conclave that the mission had been accomplished.

"Well done, Executor," said Aldaris, his imposing visage filling the holographic viewscreen. "It sounds like the first step was a complete success."

"First step?" Tassadar asked.

"Of course. This is not the only planet in the system. We cannot afford to assume that the zerg would confine their efforts to a single world. You must investigate all possible sources of infestation and root them out. Then and only then may we consider our job accomplished."

Jake kept her thoughts to herself. "Our job" indeed. It was Tassadar and the hundred-plus ships he commanded that had come to confront what could have been an attack. Aldaris and the others had taken an extreme position from the outset, and yet they were not the ones who had to do the deed. Still, that was how it had always been, since shortly after the Khala had been established.

Ever the obedient arm of the Conclave, Tassadar inclined his head. "As you wish. I will investigate the sister world to this one. And if it, too, is infested beyond hope, I shall destroy it."

Aldaris hunched his shoulders in displeasure. "If it is infested at all, Executor, or is even likely to be infested, you shall obliterate it. We cannot afford to take any risks. Those are your orders."

Before the conversation could continue, Aldaris had terminated it. Tassadar did not move for a moment.

Jake regarded the world before her, or rather, what was left of it. Incongruously beautiful smears of light pocked the planet, and Jake knew that the spikes of orange marked where the protoss purging of the infested world had gone deep into its heart, so deep that the planet's magma had boiled to the surface. Some of these orange spikes marked where the terrans had had settlements. Some of them were far away from the terran population, but not the zerg. Eighty percent of the atmosphere was now gone.

"... I had friends there," Jake said sickly.

"They would have become zerg. The infestation was irreversible."

"Yeah ... but still ... to see this ... wow."

• • •

Tassadar gave the order to move to the sister planet of the one he had just destroyed. He kept his thoughts to himself, and Jake did not pry. Tassadar had been in the forefront arguing against the action he had just been ordered to take; it was to be expected that he would harbor regrets.

"Executor, we are detecting terran vessels."

"I am not surprised, after what we have just done. Display."

The crystal hummed and an image appeared before them. "Vessel is identified as Norad II, Colonel Edmund Duke in command. It is a Behemoth-class ship. . . ."

Jake paid little attention as the statistics of the terran vessel were described. The protoss had long kept a watchful eye on the terrans; the Dae'Uhl, the "Great Stewardship," demanded it. The protoss had watched this young race grow and expand, marveling at how they managed to thrive despite almost constantly attacking one another. It was the Dae'Uhl that Tassadar had cited when he had been ordered to utterly destroy Chau Sara. The protoss knew a great deal about terrans, their weaponry and ships, and what they were capable of. And while the Norad II was a powerful ship by terran standards, it was but a single vessel, and posed no real threat at all. It was a buzzing insect, easily swatted away.

Except Tassadar gave no order to do so.

"Executor?" queried the pilot. "Shall I destroy the terran ship?"

Jake watched both her friend and the vessel. It was mov-

ing quickly to intercept. No doubt it would begin attacking them as soon as it was within range.

"There are no other ships. It comes to its doom," Tassadar said. Jake felt Tassadar's respect and sorrow wash over her. "They are . . . courageous, these humans."

"Sir? They are almost within range."

Tassadar's next words stunned everyone. "Deploy the subwarp field and give the order to retreat."

Jake stared at her friend. "You are supposed to destroy Mar Sara, Tassadar. This ship is nothing to us."

"No, it is not," Tassadar said, "and you know well it is not fear that makes me choose this course of action."

Jake nodded, slowly, as every ship in the powerful protoss fleet disappeared to human eyes, and sat back. And waited. And watched.

Jake opened his eyes and realized he was trembling. It was always profound, of course, when Zamara shared the memories she tended with him. And he knew he'd been privileged to see the actual unfolding of historic events that had shaped the protoss more than he could possibly grasp. But this—this was a moment out of his own history, not that of an alien's. He'd been witness to the great cataclysmic event of his generation—hell, perhaps that of all humanity, ever. First contact with an alien race—two alien races, if you counted the zerg on Chau Sara, and he supposed he should count that.

Zamara's detachment chilled him, even though he knew she had revised her opinion of terrans a great deal since she'd been hitchhiking inside one for so long. But he would have expected nothing less from the Zamara he had first met. Tassadar's actions, however, did surprise him. He knew what it cost a templar emotionally to defy the Conclave.

Some of this I know, of course, he told Zamara. *But it's all been filtered through Dominion propaganda. It's fascinating to see it from the other side.*

Zamara chuckled, and gently commandeered his body to land the ship. *There is more . . . so much more that you must see. I hope you can learn it from Zeratul himself. I do think we are in the right place.*

Why are we setting down here? Not that Jake minded. The site Zamara had selected was a beautiful meadow high in the mountains, and Jake spied what appeared to be a makeshift shelter. The idyllic setting included a waterfall to complete a holo-card–perfect image, if one discounted that luscious pink sky. Hell, even that was starting to seem more perfect to Jake's eyes than blue sky now.

I analyzed all the coordinates. Several sites were visited more than once. This one seems to be the most frequently inhabited by the original pilot of this vessel. It is a logical deduction that this is therefore the most likely site to encounter Zeratul, if it is indeed he who owns the ship.

And here I thought you picked it because it was scenic.

That is merely a pleasant coincidence.

Using Jake's body, Zamara landed the ship gently. They disembarked and Jake closed his eyes and breathed the clean, soft air.

I'm beginning to see why Zeratul likes this place so much, he said. *I had no idea human and protoss ideals of beauty were so similar.*

I think this planet was selected not for aesthetic reasons but for practical ones. Zeratul was looking for a place to restore himself. Negative ions in the atmosphere, which produce a sensation of calm and well-being in both humans and in protoss, are increased by higher altitudes and proximity to moving water, especially waterfalls. And it has been established that rose hues are soothing and relaxing because of the vibration of the wavelength.

Jake shrugged. He just thought it was pretty.

We do admire beauty and harmony as well, Jacob. We just desire it to be . . . useful as well as pleasant.

Dragging his eyes from the waterfall, he looked at the lean-to. It was rough, but functional, and appeared sturdy enough to protect its occupant from whatever weather might manifest. It seemed to be constructed of organic material—branches, vines, moss to seal out rain. Whoever built it didn't care about privacy, but then again, this place seemed to be uninhabited.

His stomach rumbled. He was willing to bet the water was safe to drink, but he'd check to make sure. Rosemary had the Pig—more properly termed the Handheld Personal Information-Gathering and Navigation Unit, "HPIGNU," conveniently shortened to the porcine abbreviation—so he'd have to rely on Zamara and whatever technology he could find here. Approaching the shelter, he found an oval metal box of some sort. He fiddled with it until it opened to his touch. Inside were all kinds of equipment.

Dark templar technology, Zamara said, her excitement plain.

Anything you recognize?

No, but I should again be able to intuit.

The sound of the rushing water was soothing, yes, but Jake realized he was parched. He'd found that barring something toxic in the soil or in something that swam in it, water was water, and generally just fine. Of course he'd always had the equipment to analyze it before. He took one of the alien pieces of equipment in each hand and went to stand beside the water, feeling the spray patter softly on his skin, and swallowed dryly.

Hurry up with that intuiting, Zamara, or else I'll die of thirst before you figure it out.

But he didn't. He lay down on the soft grass, purple-hued but comfortable, and peered up through a filter of leaves at clouds scudding past a pink sky. All the exhaustion he had staved off over the last several days seemed to descend on him at once.

Rest, Jacob. Rest and dream.

There could be no better guardian, and so, trusting her completely, Jake filled his lungs with the cleanest air he'd ever breathed, basked in the warm sunlight from an alien star, and obeyed.

"We have waited long enough," Kerrigan stated.

"My queen, Ulrezaj has only been underground

two days. He was obviously gravely injured by our attack. I am certain that once he is well enough to travel, he will lead us directly to Ramsey."

"Who could be so far away by this point that we might never locate him again." Kerrigan's voice was icily angry. "Ramsey might be on Shakuras, he might be somewhere else entirely. He could be dead by now for all we know."

Ethan had no reply; her words were the truth. He inclined his head in acknowledgment, even though she could not see the gesture.

"I obey your will, O my queen. What is it you would have me do?"

In his mind, he felt her smile, and his heart filled with longing. If only he could stand before her, see that expression of gleeful, hungry delight with his own eyes. Oh, how he adored her.

"Ulrezaj has fled to the chambers beneath the surface. I'm not sure what is down there, but it looked as though his only protection was that handful of protoss he had corrupted and enslaved. Most of them are gone—they either deserted him and fled with Ramsey or else they were killed in the battle. He's weak now, and we could kill him easily."

"But that is not your wish, is it?"

"No. But he does not know that. We will descend into the tunnels, a flood of zerg that he will not be able to stand against." Her amusement grew. "We'll light a fire under his glowing dark ass. Flush the quarry. And follow."

"It shall be done."

Ethan was Kerrigan's general, and the zerg obeyed him as they would their queen, utterly and without question or pause. He had permitted them to forage, killing what they could to sustain themselves, or feasting on the carrion that was once living protoss, human, and even zerg. They came like dogs to heel, awaiting his command.

Mounted atop a mutalisk, Ethan led his monstrous troops steadily toward the entrance to the underground chambers where Ulrezaj, wounded and no doubt disheartened, had fled. He smiled slightly, his gaze lingering on them as they scuttled forward, shiny carapaces catching the sunlight, covering kilometers of earth with their undulating bodies while the air was thick with those who could fly.

The army reached the entrance and began to flow inside. Ethan was reminded of pouring water into vermin holes, to either drown the things in their burrows or flush them out. It was an amusing thought.

From her seclusion on Char, Kerrigan watched through the eyes of first one of her creatures, then another. The beauty of what she beheld in the labyrinth did not escape her, but the zergling whose brain she was temporarily hijacking cared nothing for it. This was obviously xel'naga technology, this blend of artifice and nature that yawned deep into the bowels of Aiur. It was not the first time she had seen this; she had been here before. Not in this particular section, to be sure, as the place was staggeringly vast, but beneath the surface of this world, and there was at least a little familiarity mixed in with her admiration.

The zergling hurried along with its fellows, pressed tightly together, filling the stairwell, then exploding into a cavern. Kerrigan noted jeweled control systems and panels and desiccated bodies, with slight interest. It looked as though they had been drained— sucked utterly dry of fluids and life force both. Did Ulrezaj feed on his little sycophants? That might explain how he continued to exist, rather than dissolving after a brief time as was customary with ordinary dark archons. And if he did drain the protoss, and he was as badly wounded as she had hoped, then he might have gotten rid of any resistance her zerg might encounter for her.

Five oval doorways opened onto five different corridors and the zerg stopped in their tracks, awaiting orders. Kerrigan's first thought was to tell them to simply follow the protoss scent, but if Ulrezaj was clever, he could have dispersed his followers in anticipation of just such an assault. Kerrigan shrugged and her wings flexed, the sharp bits of bones clawing momentarily at the air.

"Split into five groups. Investigate all passageways. Kill all protoss you encounter."

They obeyed immediately, gracefully forming five branching streams of the flooding river, moving implacably forward. Kerrigan flitted from mind to mind, seeing everything simultaneously and filtering it all as it was necessary. She sat, clawed hands grasping the arms of the towering thronelike chair, chitinous and organic and honeycombed, which she had had wrought for herself. Her glowing eyes stared into a gloomy, sullen red darkness and saw something else light-years away.

In two of the corridors, protoss rushed forward, some with the remnants of templar armor on their bodies, some clad in tattered robes. Another time, Kerrigan would have been amused at how swiftly they fell, but now their deaths held little pleasure for her, only irritation. Where was the dark archon?

In two other corridors, her creatures surged on unopposed. The technology they passed was startling. In some places there were glowing inscriptions on the walls. Her creatures rushed past too quickly for her to even attempt to read the language. So much here to plunder, to learn, to absorb that would enhance the zerg. Another time, Kerrigan promised herself, she would explore it at leisure, for she was certain that all kinds of useful tidbits of information were hidden here. But for now, there was one single goal.

She knew she was close when she came upon desiccated husks littering the floors. No neatly organized bodies on slabs here, no. Although they looked almost mummified, as if centuries of aridity had taken their toll, the carelessness with which they had been tossed aside told her that they had died recently, their essences drained to serve their master. Her clawed hands tightened in excitement and she smiled.

"This way," she said, rerouting her mindless minions to follow the trail.

They came upon him then in a vast cavern glittering with crystals, and she told her army to halt. They did so with an abruptness that caused several of them to barrel into one another, unable to halt their forward momentum so quickly. Kerrigan hungrily drank her fill, waiting, watching, ready to react to the dark archon's next move.

Here in a place where the only illumination was the eerie, otherworldly glow of the khaydarin crystals, Ulrezaj's presence was more like an absence of light, an absence of . . . being . . . than an actual physical thing as he had been on the planet's surface. All light seemed to be absorbed by him, save for a shimmering green glow that provided the unnatural thing's outline. It pulsed, as if he was breathing, although Kerrigan was willing to bet that it did nothing so mundane.

For a long time, Ulrezaj did not move. Kerrigan's servants stood still as well, although waving antennae and the occasional snap of mandibles betrayed that the zerg were closer to living things than the entity they confronted.

"Do something," Ethan muttered, fidgeting aboard the mutalisk.

"Do something," growled Kerrigan, light-years away, staring straight at Ulrezaj.

He did.

It was almost like a nuclear blast of darkness. Absence of light poured off the dark archon, and every zerg within its radius collapsed without a sound. It took Kerrigan by surprise as the zergling whose eyes she used died so abruptly the Queen of Blades almost didn't realize what had happened. She recovered quickly, selecting another one, and then that one died too, and the next one.

It was happening so fast she couldn't even monitor it. She brushed the mind of her general, whispering, "Tell them to withdraw. It is all up to you now, my consort. He is coming."

Except he wasn't.

To Kerrigan's astonishment and outrage, the dark archon simply winked out of existence. He was gone, leaving only carcasses to mark that he had ever been there.

"No!" she shrieked, leaping up from her throne. She'd been a fool. Ulrezaj was powerful and intelligent, an entity that was unprecedented in the history of the universe as far as she could tell. She could not have anticipated that he would teleport . . . but she *should* have anticipated that he might have unusual abilities. Faster almost than the speed of thought, her awareness flitted from zerg to zerg, searching each of the four other branching paths. Ulrezaj was nowhere to be seen.

"Ethan! He has escaped me! Find him! *Find him now!*"

Find him now!

Ethan bit back horror at the words and instructed

his zerg to scatter. What the hell had Ulrezaj done? Kerrigan shared with him what she had witnessed through the eyes of the now-dead zerg. It looked as though somehow the dark archon had managed to teleport himself to safety.

Both anger and admiration filled him. The kind of power that it took to do that—he'd never heard of anything that could. Ships, yes, even the warp gate used such technology—but a single being?

And then he uttered a short, harsh laugh. "My queen, he may have eluded us for the moment, but such a feat takes more energy than I think even Ulrezaj possesses at this moment. I don't think he's left Aiur. . . . He may not even have left the chambers. It was a trick to unsettle and deceive us, but we will be victorious in the end."

Her admiration and pleasure was like wine to him. "Yes—yes, I suspect you are right. Zerg will pour through every crevice, every chamber, every nook and cranny, and cover every exit we can find. He cannot possibly escape. Still—we will not make the novice's mistake of underestimating him again."

"Indeed, we will not." Somehow, Ethan knew, he was to anticipate what could not possibly be anticipated. And somehow, he would do so.

Flushed with relief and eagerness to hand over the prize to his queen, Ethan stared intently down as the mutalisk hovered. Many of the zerg were rushing back out as swiftly as they had rushed in just a few moments earlier, hastening to spread out and monitor all possible exits from Ulrezaj's hiding place. Others were scurrying deeper into the bowels of this labyrinth. They would find Ulrezaj.

It was one of the scattering zerglings whose eyes enabled Kerrigan to witness what happened not three minutes after Ulrezaj had disappeared. The very earth in front of the zergling was suddenly pierced with a precise line of white light emanating from beneath the surface. Quickly the line spread, forming a rectangle, and then the chunk of earth suddenly flew upward.

The xel'naga vessel, for such Kerrigan instantly realized it had to be, rose from the gaping hole in the earth. Like the chambers below, this craft was a melding of the natural and the technical, all swirls and curves and grace. The zerg swarmed toward it, hurling themselves at it. Kerrigan hoped it was convincing enough—she had to make it look as though she was trying to stop the dark archon's flight.

A heartbeat later the thing crackled with energy. Zerg dropped like stones, both those that were scrabbling to climb atop the thing and many others who were simply circling it in the air. The xel'naga ship continued to rise, striving toward freedom.

From what Kerrigan knew about protoss vessels, the pilots were an integral part of any technology's operating systems. She wondered if it was the same here—if Ulrezaj was expending some of his own psionic energy to control the vessel. She hoped so; he wouldn't be able to give them the slip quite so easily then. She'd just have to wait and find out.

The blast of energy made the very air ripple. Ethan clung tightly to the mutalisk who bore him, directing it to flee with a brutal tenor to his mental commands, hoping that it and he were safely out of range. The mutalisk hurtled away so quickly Ethan nearly lost his grip. He held on and turned his head back to see what had happened.

It was almost balletic. Glowing and radiant, the xel'naga ship ascended to the skies of Aiur like an angel from Hell, all pursuit caught in its deadly radius falling instantly to the earth. He'd been lucky—this time.

Ethan barely had time to summon a behemoth and, along with the other zerg of which he was in charge, enter a hollow area deep inside the creature's dense hide before the xel'naga vessel containing a dark archon disappeared entirely.

"Follow," he told the behemoth, and it obeyed.

CHAPTER 7

THEY WERE HEADING HOME, A SILENT AND SOMBER
fleet. Everyone knew that this was what would occur when
Tassadar had held back, had disobeyed orders out of what
the Conclave believed to be a thoroughly misguided sense of
compassion. Executor Tassadar, the best and brightest warrior
the protoss had, was being summoned home. The Conclave's
order had been almost churlish and petty—Jake realized that
they wanted not just to discipline Tassadar, but to humiliate
him. They were offended that he had disobeyed, and, rightly,
worried about the consequences that disobedience would have.
After all, the zerg were not simple omhara.

But they had not stood beside him when he made that
choice, had not felt the mental anguish and worry that the
internal struggle had cost Tassadar. Jake had. And she was
reminded of another high templar who had disobeyed the
orders of the Conclave when he felt them unnecessarily cruel
and wrong. Adun was a hero to the protoss people, because
history—crafted by the Conclave of that era and those who
had come after them—had willed it so. They were not about
to tarnish Adun's memory with something as pesky as truth,
especially not when that truth would compromise them.

Adun had been too good, too pure for this world, and after banishing the evil dark templar had somehow mystically departed mortal life. That was his legacy. He had sacrificed himself in a way no one yet understood in order to weed out the dark templar taint—to keep the protoss safe.

"But that's not what happened. I—you—God, this is confusing. Vetraas knew the truth! Adun died, for lack of a better word, trying to help save the dark templar!"

"Indeed. Preservers know all sides of an issue, for we have all memories. It is why preservers were utterly forbidden to become members of the Conclave."

Jake tried to grasp this. "You mean—you're not allowed to tell the truth?"

"What preservers know, the Conclave knew. Preservers are keepers of the past, Jacob. We are not crafters of policy. We have our orders, and we remain utterly neutral. It is not our place to judge, to praise, or condemn. It is not our place to act, but simply to observe. At least . . . it has always been so until now."

"You would have let Tassadar be executed then?"

He felt her discomfort. "It is difficult to explain. But yes, then . . . perhaps I would have. I am glad I was not faced with that choice."

"Will you recant?" Jake asked Tassadar privately, her thoughts only for her friend.

"No." Tassadar did not even have to think twice. "I regret having to defy those I have sworn to obey. But I would make

the same decision again." He turned his lambent eyes on her. "*That knowledge lets me face my fate with peace. I know that—*"

The cry hit them all with its force. The most sensitive among them winced in pain. Desperate, frightened, longing, calling out for aid, crying out a specific name . . . "*Tassadar!*"

Images flooded Jake. A burned-out world, covered with soft gray ash, pain unimaginable—and zerg, so many of them—here, here was where the enemy was hiding—

"*Char,*" Tassadar said. "*I know the world. The cry for aid comes from there.*"

And just that quickly, Jake knew what they were going to do. Tassadar touched the crystal that communicated his thoughts to his fleet.

"*You all followed me without question when I chose to disobey the orders of the Conclave. You must trust my orders again now, when I tell you to continue your journey to Aiur. The* Gantrithor *will not be accompanying you. I have received a telepathic distress call that I know I must investigate. I also believe that there is a chance to eradicate our true enemy, the zerg, once and for all—here, on this planet. Repeat, all vessels, return to Aiur. Your loyalty . . . is moving beyond measure.* En taro Adun.*"

Lifting his hand from the crystal, he broadcast his thoughts throughout his flagship. "*Those who do not wish to follow me to investigate this distress call are also free to return home. You will receive nothing but the highest praise from me, and I will do my utmost to see that the Conclave vents its anger upon me and me alone.*"

Jake strained for the replies, and was touched, but not surprised, when not a single protoss aboard the Gantrithor chose to disembark. They were templar, all of them, and they followed their leader. Almost overcome, Tassadar momentarily lowered his head into his hand, blocking his emotions.

"No commander has ever had such a crew," he said, the words heartfelt. He turned to Jake. "Zamara—you, however, should return."

Jake shook her head. "I will stay with you."

"I would be easier in my mind if I knew you were safe in the Sanctum."

Jake tilted her head and half closed her eyes in a smile. "Executor . . . Tassadar . . . for so long, I have been a holder, a keeper of memories. I wish to make some of my own, and I believe in you—what you are doing. It is my choice to go with you. I am not the only preserver, Executor. If I fall, others will continue on. We are the one constant."

"True. But I would not see you come to harm, and I cannot guarantee your safety. Zamara . . . you are one of the great treasures of our people. I have caused sufficient alienation without endangering a preserver. And I do not know what fate awaits us on Char."

"You know that whoever called to you was in deep pain, and is a powerful telepath. There is a puzzle here—you have sensed it, as have I. You know that this is, if not the seat of the zerg, certainly a place where many of them can be found. And there are no guarantees in this life regardless. At this juncture, nothing is stable anymore. I have made my decision."

He gazed deep into her soul then, his considerable men-

tal power as strong as hers, perhaps stronger in some ways. He held out his hand, and she emulated him. Briefly, they touched in the Khala, and thus reassured of her faith in her choice, Tassadar withdrew and nodded slightly.

"So be it."

Jake blinked awake, pain shooting through him. He felt Zamara trying to comfort him. *Eat,* she said. *Some things I must show you, for you need to understand them on more than an intellectual level. Other things, I can simply tell you and not tax you any more than is absolutely necessary.*

Jake loved the sharing of memories now. But he also loved the idea that somehow he might not die from brain tumors, and so he sent his agreement. Zamara had indeed figured out how to operate some of the dark templar equipment that had been left behind, and the news was good. The water was potable, clean and clear and refreshing, the creatures that lived in it—a cross between amphibian and insect and ugly as sin—edible, and fruits and roots from various plants added a little variety. At the very least he would not starve to death here. As he used his pocketknife to cut through the thick black peel that hid startlingly sweet white pulp and tiny red seeds, Zamara continued speaking to him.

On the planet Char, we discovered to our shock who it was who had been calling to Tassadar. She had once been a female human telepath named Sarah Kerrigan, a ghost, who was now infested by the zerg. She was crying out for aid at that moment—but soon enough became content with her lot. Later, with the death of the Overmind, she would become even greater than the being that had created her—she would become the queen of the zerg.

Startled, Jake cut himself with the knife and sucked on the nick. *Queen? Like . . . oh, God . . . Ethan talked about a queen. . . .*

Indeed he did, and you will recall I said I knew of her.

I do too, sort of. What hasn't been censored and regurgitated by the government. I just didn't put two and two together.

Bear in mind also—while many protoss encountered James Raynor, and thus discovered that human males could be staunch allies, Sarah Kerrigan was the only human female with whom we had any contact.

Oh great. That's not going to help Rosemary any.

She does have prejudice to overcome, yes. But my people are by and large rational. Rosemary will tell the truth. Do not despair yet, Jacob.

He sighed. He was trying not to. He urged her to continue.

But while the protoss were on Char, attempting to fight Kerrigan and the zerg, we met Prelate Zeratul and his soldiers. Tassadar sensed their presence almost immediately. He was sickened and horrified and angry. They met. . . . It did not go well.

But . . . oh, right. You weren't allowed to tell Tassadar about Raszagal and the others. That they weren't evil or even really rebellious.

Sorrow and regret washed through him along with

her affirmative. He thought that it must have been very difficult for her . . . to know that there was no real reason for hatred between these two factions, and be forbidden to do anything to heal the rift.

Fortunately, Tassadar did not need me to open his eyes to the truth. At first, they fought—how could they not? Tassadar had been taught that everything the dark templar represented was to be despised. Eventually, he agreed to speak with Zeratul. And along with James Raynor, Tassadar learned things about the dark templar that no one save the preservers knew. For a long time, I was not permitted to leave the Gantrithor, because of the possible danger from the dark templar. I did not see these things first hand . . . not at that time. Later, with Tassadar's death and regretfully those of many others, I knew and understood all that had transpired.

She showed him a little then, bits and pieces of images, nothing too intense that would tax him unduly. Jake marveled at what he beheld: two masters fighting with a grace almost inconceivable, the executor dealing what surely must have been a fatal blow, the prelate uncannily sidestepping the—no, no, not sidestepping, simply *not being there* when the glittering blue blade sliced, the clash and hiss of vaporous green warp blade contacting with the gleaming blue blade of the Aiur high templar.

Time passed and the images changed; the two protoss leaders sat, conversed, and Zeratul began to teach Tassadar. Jake was proud to see that much of the time, Jim Raynor, terran, was included in these conversations. Perhaps what was even more curious was he found himself being proud of Tassadar, almost as if Tassadar, like Raynor, was a member of his own species.

You are more than an ordinary terran now. You could not be closer to the protoss than if you had been raised as one. In a way, Jacob, you understand us better than we do ourselves.

Jake blushed.

And then it dawned on him what was happening.

Zeratul is telling Tassadar the real story—well, as much as he knows about it. And Tassadar's listening!

Yes.

Zamara . . . I know you are trying to spare me, but please—I want to do more than just see this.

Reluctance, then acceptance, and then Jake again was Zamara.

Once Tassadar realized he could fully trust the other protoss, the prelate was permitted aboard the Gantrithor. *Tassadar's warriors had learned to respect Zeratul almost as much as their leader did; there was no hostile thought turned toward the visitor as he made his way through the vessel to where Jake waited for him.*

Jake was nervous and excited. A dark templar . . . she had the memories of those who had known them, but meeting one herself was something she had never dreamed possible. She rose when the prelate entered, smoothing her robes and composing her thoughts.

Zeratul bowed deeply. "A preserver," he said. His mental

voice was dry, like scudding leaves, and bespoke age and wisdom. She liked him at once. "What a privilege, to meet one. I did not think I would live so long. Then again, I did not think our people would be reunited in my lifetime."

She caught a name, an image: Raszagal. "Raszagal . . . she is your leader now?"

"Indeed, she is our matriarch, a wise and just leader. She is old enough to remember the exile from Aiur. Few of my people still remember our brethren. Like myself, she desires that our people reunite."

Jake nodded slowly. Raszagal was ancient now, over a thousand years old. "I have within me the memories of your matriarch as a child. It would be interesting to meet her."

He looked at her, wistfully, almost hungrily. "The dark templar do not regret severing our nerve cords. We do not need the Khala as you do. But what you represent, Zamara . . . that I respect and wish we had."

"You have no way of keeping the knowledge of the past then?" Jake was appalled. To think of all that history, the journeys the dark templar had made, the things they had discovered, lost to time saddened her.

"Nothing so ideal as a preserver, no. But we have learned how to manipulate the khaydarin crystals to preserve memories. The solution is imperfect, and passionless, but the information is not lost to us."

"So that's how you knew!" exclaimed Jake. "You heard it from the horse's mouth."

"I . . . from the source, yes. Your human phrases are colorful indeed, Jacob."

• • •

Jake hesitated for a moment. "I . . . am pleased the two of you have learned to see past the lies. I would ask your forgiveness. I knew the truth that you, Tassadar, have only recently discovered. But I was and am forbidden to speak of it to those who do not know. Everything Zeratul has told you is true. Adun did not sacrifice himself to ensure that Aiur would be rid of some perceived evil influence. He did it to help the dark templar . . . in hopes that one day, they would again be accepted by us."

Tassadar was stunned. Zeratul seemed almost exultant. "We have a blessing among our people. 'Adun toridas . . . Adun give you sanctuary.' We knew he was our savior." He seemed about to say something more, then his thoughts were shuttered from both Aiur protoss. "In due time, I will share more of this. For now, I will content myself with training you—I will teach as much as you care to learn, Tassadar."

Tassadar straightened, and his eyes gleamed. "I will learn what you will teach to save all our people . . . my friend."

Jake shook his head in silent wonderment. "Remarkable. Both of them. As much as Khas or Adun. Tassadar—he died to save Aiur, right?"

"That is only the barest hint of his sacrifice and what it did for our people—the blow it struck against the zerg—but yes. Tassadar eventually turned against the Conclave, to the point where he engaged them in combat when they refused to listen to him. They were all slain."

"What? He killed the Conclave? All of them?"

"Yes. Members of the Judicator caste still survive, but there is no longer a Conclave. Tassadar did this with deep regret, but it was necessary. They would have imprisoned him at a time when his actions were desperately needed, and Aiur and the entire protoss race would have been destroyed. Tassadar learned what Zeratul had to teach him, about the energies and powers the dark templar had learned after centuries of exploring the mysteries of the Void. Alone, we could never have destroyed the zerg Overmind. Tassadar used both kinds of skills in order to defeat the Overmind and save our people. And it is because of his understanding and compassion to the dark templar—his befriending of Zeratul, and Zeratul's of him—that we were welcomed on Shakuras at all."

Tassadar was remarkable indeed. He had opened a mind that a millennia of lies had endeavored to seal shut, and not only accepted but actively embraced beings who were reputedly attempting to destroy what it meant to be protoss. He had chosen to see what was truly there, rather than what he thought was there, and had saved his people.

Perhaps even more extraordinary was Zeratul and the dark templar. Jake was pretty sure that if one branch of terrans had been rounded up, threatened with execution, and exiled into the unforgiving Void, they wouldn't feel all warm and fuzzy toward their oppressors.

I did not spend much time on Shakuras. I do not know what has happened over the last four years. But Zeratul and

*Tassadar have given me hope, that in my absence Aiur pro-
toss and dark templar have reunited, and we have become
one people once again. We will need to be if—*

Jake was instantly alert, but Zamara had shuttered
her mind to him again.

Are you ever going to tell me what's going on, Zamara?

*I hope to be able to, Jacob. You have earned the right to at
least know what it is you're being asked to perhaps die for.
But I must wait until we find Zeratul, or someone else who
can help us.*

That could be a long wait.

The mental blast that sang through his thoughts
almost caused Jake to black out.

Trespassers and thieves! Who dares violate my sanctuary?

Then again . . . it might not be such a long wait
after all.

CHAPTER 8

ZAMARA RESPONDED QUICKLY TO THE DISTANT
mindcall. "Zeratul, my old friend. It is I, Zamara. You
once told me of this world, though not its name, and I
have come, seeking your aid and wisdom."

Pain lanced through Jake as Zamara shared the
memory. He knew she needed to, knew she had to
make it crystal clear and unquestioning quickly if
Zeratul was to be mollified and help them. But still . . .

*Zeratul kicked at the dust beneath their feet, sending a lazy
gray puff of ash up in a little cloud. Jake looked around, curious
to finally see this place aptly named Char with her own eyes.*

*"Is it a burden, holding these memories? Does it tax you?"
Zeratul asked.*

*"It is an honor and a duty, and yes, occasionally a burden.
The memories themselves are easy to hold. It is only when—
when the memories are passed to me that there is pain."*

"Passed to you?"

*She regarded him evenly. "I receive a protoss's memories
when he or she dies. It is never pleasant, and if many die
somewhere at once . . . then it is painful to integrate."*

He nodded his comprehension. "That must be difficult indeed."

"Most of the conflict comes when I know something and am unable to share it. I am glad you and Tassadar found your own paths to peace with one another."

He regarded Jake thoughtfully. "How do you find your own peace, Zamara? Does it not threaten to overwhelm you, being the bearer of so very much?"

"As Tassadar has explained, we do not completely lose ourselves in the Khala. I am renewed and refreshed by contacting so many other minds in such a nurturing place. But because there are so many things I am not permitted to share freely, I find I must make time to meditate, channel my emotions and thoughts, and calm them with the crystals."

He half closed his eyes and tilted his head. Humor, at least, was conveyed identically whether one was an Aiur protoss or a dark templar, Jake thought with warmth. "Amusing and intriguing. Preservers are perhaps the epitome of what we turned against. You not only require the Khala to hold the memories, but you are even intimately joined with others via these memories. In a way, you become them. . . . They live through you. And yet you find comfort in pulling back from that, from being with the crystals, as we do."

Jake, too, titled her head, smiling at the accurate assessment. "Is that what you do, then? Surely you and your people have burdens of your own to bear, and you cannot share them with others in the Khala when they become too great."

"I meditate. I sit in the quiet stillness that is the Void. And there is a small world that no one else knows about. The hue of the sky, a comforting pink, soothes, as do the energies of a *certain place nestled in the mountains near rushing waters. It is there that I go when I am . . . uncertain or unhappy. The natural world heals."*

". . . Zamara . . . it is you . . . and yet it is not. There is another's mind—by the Void, it is . . . human?"

Jake whimpered then gritted his teeth against the weakness. Zeratul, for he knew now that it was that powerful individual, was still distant. Zamara was having to work hard to project her thoughts so far, and the strain was making his head throb.

"We are in the place you spoke of, so long ago, by the rushing water. Come to us and I will tell you more about why I am here, and what we seek from you."

". . . I would you had not come here, old friend." And with that cryptic message, Jake felt Zeratul withdraw from his mind. Zamara gentled her presence immediately and the pain eased. Jake gulped some of the delicious, refreshingly cool river water and splashed some on his flushed face. He despised his weakness, but it was both impossible and foolish to deny it.

Zamara—he will help us, won't he?

I have no doubt that he will. Zeratul is not one to run from the truth, no matter how unpleasant or difficult it may be to face. He was indirectly responsible for the destruction of Aiur, but he accepted his part in that and strove to do what he could to save the rest of his people.

Jake blinked, startled. *What? Zeratul destroyed Aiur? I thought it was the zerg.*

Zamara didn't respond, and Jake realized that he could now see the approaching ship. It was similar to the one he and Zamara had . . . borrowed, but it was larger and presumably capable of space flight as well as atmospheric travel. Still, it was obviously of dark templar design—purple-black with glowing green energies dancing around it, larger and bulkier than a comparable vessel of traditional protoss design. Jake got to his feet, both excited and uneasy and chafing at the fact that his question about the destruction of Aiur—a pretty major event—had not been answered. Zamara sent him calm, but no explanations.

The ship landed and the green, pulsating glow that danced about its hull subsided. A ramp unfurled and a door irised open, and there stood the first dark templar Jake had ever seen.

Zeratul was slightly stooped, and while he wore robes that were similar to what Zamara remembered, they looked a bit frayed around the edges, as if the wearer didn't much care for his appearance. His eyes, however, still glowed fiercely, and when he turned to regard Jake, the human thought he'd never felt as *seen* in his life. He felt positively naked under that piercing gaze.

"Why is it," Zeratul said mildly, "that recently I seem to become entangled with humans?"

"Maybe you need a little comic relief," Jake said deprecatingly. Zeratul half closed his eyes and tilted his head, and his laughter washed over Jake. The archaeologist gave a half-smile.

"I had thought Raynor a remarkable, perhaps unique, representative of the terran race," Zeratul continued, moving down the ramp with the same graceful stride that marked all of his species. "And yet behold, when I come to my secluded place to think and reflect, I am greeted by a human who holds a protoss preserver in his head." There was a hint of condescension in his mental voice, but more of admiration. And curiosity, but dulled somehow, as if it did not prick him as it ought to.

"Zamara," he continued, directing his speech to the preserver but including Jake in the conversation, "how is it I find you here?"

"My body is dead and decomposed," Zamara answered quietly. "But my will and spirit live on." She fell silent to Jake's mental hearing, but Zeratul listened intently, nodding. Jake realized she was quickly and efficiently filling the dark templar in on what had transpired.

Some of it, at least. There are things that would be best told by you, Jacob. And information I would reveal to you both at the same time.

Jake was oddly touched by Zamara's consideration. He had expected that he'd be the classic third wheel at this reunion, but Zamara seemed determined that he be an active part.

"Your will is admirable, Zamara," said Zeratul slowly.

Jake sensed a "but" in there.

". . . But I do not know that you have come to the right protoss for aid."

Zeratul turned his purple-hued face up to the sky and closed his eyes. There was weariness and something else in Zeratul's mental voice. More than simple tiredness or frustration. Something that—

I'll be damned, Jake said to Zamara. *Zeratul—he's soul sick.*

She did not respond, and he realized that she was as taken aback as he. Perhaps more so.

"Zeratul?" Jake said tentatively. "I don't know exactly what Zamara told you, but there's a lot at stake here. We really need your help."

"I did not come here to help you, human. And I do not know that I could even if I wished. Zamara knows." He turned and gazed at Jake, but it was Zamara he was looking for.

"This is my sanctuary. I did not ask you to invade it, and I am not pleased to see you, preserver. You bore witness to my failing once before, and it is now recorded in your memories for all generations to know. I, Prelate Zeratul, was the one who told the zerg where to find Aiur. The blood of all those who fell is on my hands."

Whoa! I thought he was one of the good guys!

He is, Zamara reassured him. There was no doubt in her mind.

"You destroyed a cerebrate, killing it permanently," Zamara said. "You used what the Void had taught your people—you did something we never could have done without you. You know it is not your fault that in that moment, your thoughts were made known to the Overmind, who plucked from them the location of our homeworld."

Jake felt a rush of sympathy. That burden of guilt had to be heavy.

Zeratul waved a hand, almost angrily. "I well know I would never have betrayed Aiur intentionally. And yet, betrayed it was, and so many died. I must live with that. That—and other things. Some of the things I have seen, and some of the deeds I have done, Zamara, are darker and colder than the Void itself, and all the rationality and reason in the universe cannot expunge the guilt."

Something as bad or worse than leading the zerg to an innocent planet? What the hell has this guy done?

Jake was shocked and more than a little worried, but Zamara was angry—angrier than perhaps he had ever seen her. "Perhaps you are right, Zeratul. I came seeking a protoss of wisdom, of insight. That is the Prelate Zeratul I sought. Instead, I find before me a shadow of that being. One who is more concerned with his own pain and guilt than the future of his people. I have seen arrogance in our people before, in the actions of the Conclave. I never thought to see it in the dark templar, least of all in the protoss I had come to admire as the best the dark templar had to offer."

Zeratul drew himself up to his full imposing height. Green fire blazed in his eyes. "Arrogance? You do not know of what you speak. Even with all that you have seen, preserver, I think if you had borne witness to what I have, you would be less judgmental."

"Perhaps," agreed Zamara. Jake stayed silent, utterly taken aback by this vehement confrontation between a protoss he knew to be rational and calm and one he'd been led to believe was the same. "But you are too consumed by your self-pity and what you have labeled your shame to confide in me. It is well you are here, Zeratul. I cannot think that in your present state you would be of any use to our people on Shakuras, or indeed, of use to Jacob or myself. Jacob and I have come from Aiur, where we watched others die protecting us and the information I bear. Our passage to Shakuras has been blocked. I know not where to turn now, but rest assured, until you can conduct yourself better, it shall not be to you."

For a dreadful moment, Jake was certain Zeratul was going to physically attack Zamara—and by extension, Jake and his terran body. With Zamara in control, he'd been able to defeat Ethan Stewart's pet assassin, Phillip Randall. But he knew with certainty that Zamara would not come off the victor in a fight with Zeratul, even if she had been equipped with psi blades. Though moody and emotionally shattered, Zeratul was still a force to be reckoned with.

Then to Jake's combined relief and disappointment, the blazing fire in Zeratul's eyes subsided to a dull ember.

"If anyone knows where to turn, Zamara, it is a preserver. You will find aid. But you will not find it here. Take the atmospheric vessel that brought you here. You have already stolen it from me. Take it to the gate and begone."

He moved toward them, brushing past them so close that Jake felt the whisper of the soft fabric of Zeratul's robe caress his bare arm. For an instant, Jake sensed astonishment, quickly contained, from Zamara. Obviously she hadn't expected the conversation to go this way.

"We shall depart," Zamara said, her mental voice cool and completely in control. "But this is a small world, Zeratul. If you will not deal with us now, you must do so later."

She borrowed Jake's body and bowed. Zeratul missed the gesture; he now stood next to his makeshift dwelling, his body stiff, his back to them. He was utterly silent, his powerful mind locking down on any telltale thought.

Jake and Zamara went to the atmospheric craft that they had, as Zeratul put it with brutal fact, stolen. Jake let Zamara operate the vessel while he sat in a corner of his own body, thoroughly stunned by the developments. Not even lifting off into the rosy sky cheered his spirits.

Zamara—I thought you were chasing a protoss hero. That guy down there—he's a total wreck.

. . . I am aware of that.

I . . . downloading your memories into a dark templar crystal was our last hope. If we don't do that I'm going to die here.

I am aware of that, too.

So what the hell are we going to do now?

Utter silence. Jake felt panic well up inside him for a moment, a bright frantic flame that was quickly snuffed out by the heavy darkness of complete despair.

They were stuck on a planet, the only other sentient being a protoss so far gone in trauma and self-pity that he was unreachable. The tumors in his brain were growing almost daily, and Zamara, the preserver, who had seen so much, who knew so much, who seemed to have all the answers, who had met every challenge with calm and aplomb, had no idea what to do about any of it.

CHAPTER 9

ROSEMARY WAS DOING HER DEAD LEVEL BEST TO keep from punching either the wall or her guard, and for the most part she was succeeding. But four days had ticked by—though the days here never got truly bright, there was a clear demarcation between night and day—and there was no sign of any movement.

She was naturally a headstrong woman, but she was also smart enough and experienced enough to know when to be calm and exercise patience and when to push.

She had been trying the former, but when the door opened and a protoss who was not her guard nor Selendis entered, she almost literally had to bite her tongue to keep from exploding at him.

"It is I, Vartanil," the protoss said, executing a deep bow. Rosemary still had difficulty distinguishing between individual protoss, but she was getting better at it. The fact that their mental "voices" were unique helped. Her impatience faded slightly as she realized she knew this protoss.

"You stood up for me when we came through the

warp gate," she said, remembering. "You tried to convince the guards to open the gate back up so Jake
could come through." He inclined his head, almost
shyly. She smiled at him, the first genuine smile she'd
had since setting foot on this obsessively blue planet.
"Thanks."

"I only wish I had been more convincing."

"Well, you tried at least. And honestly, I suppose I
can't blame them. To risk putting out a welcome mat
for the zerg on a story they couldn't verify—I guess I
understand."

She blinked as realization struck. "Hey . . . you're
here. They let you out. What happened?"

"They assisted me in clearing the Sundrop from my
system," Vartanil said. "Many sat with me, reached
their minds to mine, and when I was able, comforted me via the Khala. You, Rosemary Dahl, had
only Jacob and Zamara to aid you. You are strong
indeed."

Rosemary *was* strong, and she knew it, and the
knowing wasn't egotistical. She was always keenly
aware of both her strengths and weaknesses; an honest understanding of both was simply smart. But
somehow, Vartanil's praise made her feel uncomfortable.

"Yeah, well, maybe it didn't hit me as hard," she
said. "I'm glad you're all right though. Did they believe
you? About Jake and Zamara?"

He nodded. "Once I was purified of the drug, I spoke
with Executor Selendis herself." His mental voice held

tones of awe. "She also spoke with the others. We all verified your story. She believes us."

Rosemary's patience, stretched to the breaking point, now snapped. "Then where the hell is she? Why am I still in this damned prison?"

"It is not a prison."

"Where I come from, any place that you can't leave when you feel like it is a prison," Rosemary shot back.

"Selendis is the executor. She has a great deal of responsibility. When we linked in the Khala, I sensed part of her concern—over Jacob, over Ulrezaj, over the protoss left behind. There is much she needs to weigh, to consider, before she can make a wise decision."

Rosemary turned to him. She got the sensation that he was younger than many of the other protoss she had met, though she couldn't quite say why.

"Vartanil . . . Jake's sick. Really sick. Having Zamara inside him is *killing* him. And if he dies, she and all that information you protoss say is so valuable dies right along with him. This should be a top priority with your people."

Vartanil fidgeted, confirming Rosemary's theory that he was a younger individual. She'd never seen any of the other protoss fidget. They seemed totally disinclined to waste a single movement.

"When I was released," said Vartanil, "they said I was free to go. I came here. To you. I wanted to let you know as soon as possible what had happened. And . . . I wish to pledge my service to you."

"Huh? To me?" She stared at him, baffled.

He nodded eagerly. "To you—and Jacob, and Zamara. Alzadar believed in you. I fear he is dead for that belief."

Rosemary thought about the slaughterfest she'd escaped back on Aiur and shared Vartanil's fear. Anyone who didn't get through the gate was likely dead. She was pretty sure Jake made it through— the guards did say that someone was redirected—but the thought that it might be too late for him, that it might have been too late when she stepped foot on Shakuras, made her throat tighten.

"Alzadar chose to stay behind," she said, and cleared her throat. "He helped buy us time."

"And he died freely, a templar to the end. Rosemary Dahl—I am not a templar. I am of Furinax lineage, a member of the Khalai caste. Before the zerg came, I was a craftsman. I carved wooden objects. I was and am proud of my skills, but I deeply regret that I am not trained in warfare, to serve you better now. But what I can do, I will."

Yep, he was young all right, with that dreadful earnestness that only the young possessed. Still, it was oddly touching. Rosemary had had her share of admirers, but they usually all wanted something from her. What they wanted varied—money, position, or something more intimate—but it was still the same story. But this protoss—his thoughts were perhaps the purest thing she'd ever known. She shifted slightly, uncomfortable with the adulation, and decided that since it probably really wasn't directed at her but at Jake and even more so Zamara, it was okay.

"Uh . . . thanks."

He beamed at her, and she smiled back. They stood in silence, and then Rosemary said, "So . . . you just going to hang around then?"

"Until we depart to find Jacob and Zamara, yes."

She couldn't censor her thoughts well enough and he cocked his head. "You do not wish my company?"

"It's not that, it's just—I'm ready to be going. To be doing something. Do you have any idea when Selendis will make her decision?"

"I already have," came the thought, before the door even opened to admit the executor. She looked every bit as poised and in control as she had before. Rosemary squared her shoulders and regarded the protoss steadily.

"And it is?"

Selendis cocked her head and returned Rosemary's gaze. "The protoss who accompanied you have verified your story in the Khala. Even those who are not overly fond of you."

It was meant as a sort of rebuke, but it had the opposite effect. Rosemary grinned suddenly. She was used to being disliked, and somehow, it gave her hope.

"Well, that's good. So when do we leave?"

"I do not know if we will depart at all. We must convince Artanis and the others that this is a worthy mission, worth taking the risk."

Rosemary had thought that all she needed was to get this female on her side. But apparently, convincing Selendis was just the first step. Out of God knew how many.

"I regret if you got that impression," said Selendis, answering what hadn't even been asked yet. "The final decision on such a thing involves many more than I."

"Stop *doing* that!" Rosemary snapped. "Let me say my thoughts out loud, don't just barge in and read them!"

"I apologize," the executor said unexpectedly. "I am unused to not being able to freely peruse surface thoughts. I shall not intrude uninvited again, unless I feel the need warrants it."

"Uh . . . okay. Thanks." It was something, anyway. Rosemary composed herself. "I'm . . . glad you believe me." Beside her, Vartanil, who had no compunctions about his thoughts being read, was delighted.

"I have asked for an audience," Selendis continued. "I have hopes they will grant it."

"Can I get out of here?"

"They would prefer that you remain here, as our guest, until such time as you are given an audience."

"I'm a prisoner, not a guest."

"If you choose to view it as such, that is your prerogative."

And Rosemary had thought that Zamara was maddening. This implacable protoss, with her proud bearing, unblinking gaze, and graceful armor, seemed to her even more frustrating.

"Do you not get what is going on here? While you observe the protocols, Jake could be dying—could be dead! And Zamara and her precious secret right along with him. I don't get this. Do you simply not care? Is this what has happened to the protoss? Have you all devolved into a bunch of damned bureaucrats?"

"Rosemary!" Vartanil said, for her mind only. "She is the executor! You should not show such disrespect!"

"She and the others shouldn't show such disrespect to Zamara and Jake," Rosemary thought back.

For a long, tense moment, Selendis did not answer. She stayed silent, unmoving, her thoughts shielded from Rosemary. After a few moments, Rosemary shifted her weight. Was the executor ever going to say something?

"Four years ago, my world was beautiful, verdant, and safe. Tassadar was the executor of the templar, and I was his liaison with Artanis. We had order, harmony, a system that supported everyone and placed each where his or her talents, skills, and temperament best served the whole. The dark templar were little more to us than a part of our past, a cancer that we had vigorously cut out in order to protect everything it meant to be protoss. Our culture thrived. We were happy, and we were ignorant.

"Now my world is broken. What Aiur once was, what it stood for, is no more. Zerg wander its wounded surface. A darkness almost unimaginable has taken root in the sacred caverns that were created by the xel'naga. It has harmed my people, subjected them to the chains of addiction, and warped and twisted their minds. Where it failed to do so, it has slain them.

"I stand no longer in a verdant jungle world, with sun and moonlight on my skin, content in my naiveté. I stand now with all I know in turmoil and in question, on a world of blue sand and eternal twilight, united with the dark templar I once believed with every fiber of my being to be evil and corrupt. It is because of their mercy that I and my fellow protoss are even alive. And yet they threaten a heritage that I once vowed to preserve. You have heard our battle cry, Rosemary Dahl: My life for Aiur. I was not permitted to give my life for Aiur. I came with Artanis, and I stand by him still, and I protect what it means to be protoss. But I am not sure what that looks like anymore. Too much rested on my decision for me to decide lightly. I have chosen to champion you, a terran female, to those who are now the leaders of my people. The choice of what to do next rests in their hands. I cannot do more for you at this juncture."

Rosemary blinked. Anger flickered and died— a reaction born of a thousand moments before this, when she had been thwarted in one way or another from getting what she wanted. Selendis's words . . . shamed her. She had no right to be angry at the executor. Selendis was on her side. It was foolish—hell, it was wrong, Jake would be the first to say that—to lash out at someone who was trying to help.

"I'm sorry," Rosemary said. "I'm worried for my friend."

Selendis inclined her head. "I will continue to push for an audience soon. I am Artanis's protégée; I believe he will listen to me. Do not lose heart, Rosemary."

Selendis nodded to Vartanil, who bowed deeply, then turned and left. Rosemary gazed after her.

Do not lose heart.

An odd thing to say to someone who had frequently been accused of not having one.

Hang on, Jake. We're doing the best we can here.

Jake was still reeling the following morning. They'd made camp in a meadow next to a copse of trees by a small stream. Zamara was uncharacteristically silent when he asked her what they should do next, so he'd headed off on his own to forage. He'd found a tree that yielded a strange fruit that was at once utterly peculiar and quite satisfying. White, breadlike flesh was covered with small green scales that one could peel off. Jake sat in the pink-hued sunshine, scales the size of his thumbnail falling into his lap as he "shelled" the fruit, then took a bite of the creamy flesh.

We will return to Zeratul once you have eaten and cleansed yourself.

Jake almost choked. *What? He made it quite clear that he didn't want the company of either of us.*

Indeed. But nevertheless, we shall return until he orders

us away again. And then return the next day, and the day after that, until such time as he will listen to what I say.

Jake took another bite of the creamy-bready-strange fruit. *What if he snaps? He didn't strike me as someone who really had his act together.*

He will not "snap," as you phrase it. He is quite sane, Jacob. He is just lost in the maze of his own despair and guilt. Over what exactly, he would not permit me to see. But I glimpsed enough. Zeratul would never harm a preserver. We simply must continue to approach him. We have come this far. I have endured so very much to get here—and you, perhaps even more, for this was not your battle.

If this secret is as dire as you keep making it sound, then it is my battle. And— Jake hesitated. *And even if it wasn't . . . I've come to respect and like your people. I'll do what I can to help.*

Jake knew protoss could weep, after a fashion, anyway. He just . . . never thought Zamara did. But at the rush of commingled emotions that swept over him—gratitude, surprise, regret, guilt, apprehension—he realized that if Zamara had still been in her living body, she would be hunching over, her skin mottling with grief. If he could have hugged her, he would.

It is not self-pity, Jacob.

I know that.

But this information must be passed on. It must be preserved. And you must survive.

In that order, he thought wryly, but he agreed with it. He trusted Zamara, even though that information had yet to be shared with him.

It would have been so much easier had I not been killed.

Well, yeah, I'd think so too.

Jake finished the fruit, his hunger sated, and turned his face up to the rosy sun. Closing his eyes, he enjoyed the quiet moment of warmth on his face, then sighed and said, "All right. Let's go try and talk to that dark templar."

CHAPTER 10

THEY FOUND HIM SITTING ON A HUGE BOULDER so close to the waterfall that spray had dampened his skin. Zeratul had shed the heavy, dark robes and pieces of armor Jake had seen him in earlier and now wore merely a simple dark cloth wrapped around his groin. He was still, as still as the Aiur protoss Jake had gotten to know so well and missed so very much. Sitting in the familiar crouching position, his hands resting on his long, bony legs, Zeratul seemed made of stone. And Jake thought he must be, to resist Zamara's words.

Jake sat down beside the meditating protoss. Zeratul moved not a millimeter, though Jake knew that if he so desired, the dark templar prelate could spring into action and attack—and kill—the terran before Jake could blink. He let the preserver do the talking; she was the one who had known the guy, after all.

"Zeratul. My old friend. Together we survived the destruction of Aiur. We both loved the noble Tassadar, who gave his life to defeat the zerg and keep his people alive. You offered the sanctuary of your world when all seemed lost for—"

"I bid you silence, preserver."

Jake actually flinched at the iciness with which the mental words were spoken.

Wow, this guy is one coldhearted fish, isn't he?

Less so than he appears. Armor is not worn solely on the body.

Zamara returned her attention to Zeratul. He felt the longing to connect, the desperation in her thoughts as she continued talking.

"I will not, I cannot, be silent. I have the memories of so much horror. And yet so much courage—that of Tassadar and Adun chief among them. I know that you are great of spirit. You have made errors. All living beings do, Zeratul. It is arrogance of the highest degree for you to think that—"

"Again you reprimand me with charges of arrogance when you know nothing of what I have done!" With a speed that startled Jake, although he knew he should have known better, Zeratul was on his feet. He was ready to attack if Zamara pushed him too far.

"You will leave this place immediately! Leave me to my meditation and my pain. It is mine; it does not belong to you."

"No. We shall not leave."

Jake braced himself for the burst of outrage, the attack. Zeratul surprised him again by merely giving the protoss equivalent of a shrug.

"Be that as you wish, then. I shall go," he said. He rose from the crouching position, taller than most protoss and more imposing than any Jake had ever seen in the flesh or through Zamara's memories, and strode purposefully toward his vessel. A moment later, he was gone.

Well, that could have gone better.

Indeed. We will try again tomorrow.

And they did. And the day after that. Both times, Zeratul was implacable in his icy resistance to engaging in any sort of conversation. Finally, on the third day, Zamara said bluntly, "Are you not at all even curious as to how my essence ended up inside a terran body?"

Zeratul's head turned toward them at that, his eyes glowing. Jake tensed. He knew, of course, the basics—that Zamara had been evading Ulrezaj's assassins, that she had left a note in her own blood and clues as to how someone might find her. But the details she had not shared with him. He was not sure he wanted them.

"I . . . am curious," Zeratul admitted. The protoss had always struck Jake as catlike—not in how they looked in any way, but their grace, their power, and their overwhelming curiosity about first the world and then the universe around them. "I did not know that humans were capable of containing the essence of a preserver."

"He is not," Zamara said bluntly. "The duty is killing him."

Zeratul's eyes narrowed slightly, and as he regarded Jake, the archaeologist knew that this time, Zeratul was not seeing Zamara. He was looking at Jake.

"Did you undertake this duty freely, human?"

Jake shook his head uncomfortably. "No. But . . . I've learned to carry it freely."

Zeratul nodded, reading all of Jake's thoughts, catching all the subtle nuances and emotions, some of them conflicting, that surrounded his carrying a preserver. "I understand. I confess, your species is full of surprises. I have met one much like you. James Raynor."

Jake brightened. "Yeah! You said something about him before. You knew him?"

"Yes. I did." Zeratul volunteered nothing more.

"I know *about* him," Jake said. "He stood with the protoss on Aiur, helped Fenix to disable the warp gate. Zamara and Rosemary managed to get it working again. That's how we were able to come here."

This was the way to break through Zeratul's stony shell—curiosity. The tidbits Jake and Zamara were tossing out were simply too intriguing for Zeratul not to want to learn more.

"Shall I tell you, then, how it is that Jake and I share one body, but two spirits?"

Zeratul turned back to the waterfall. For a moment, Jake thought he was going to dismiss them again. But the prelate said nothing for a moment.

At last, he nodded. "Much I have learned in the Void. Much I have learned in the last four years. But this would be something I have not heard in all my long, long years. Tell me then, preserver, what skill you used to continue to preserve yourself and the memories you carry."

Jake closed her glowing eyes and hung on desperately with her four-fingered hands. It was something she had never expected—an attack by her own people . . . or by beings from another race who had commandeered protoss vessels. She didn't know which; none of the ships had responded to hails. They had only come out of nowhere, encircled the carrier, and with no explanation, opened fire.

The *Xa'lor* lurched and shuddered, evidence of the severity of the attack it was trying to withstand. Despite everything the skilled pilots could do, the valuable passenger was thrown to the metal plating of the ship. Before she could reach up to grasp the railing and pull herself to her feet, hands were there to assist her. She accepted the help with no arrogance, merely as something that was her due. She was a preserver, and she, more than anyone or anything else on this ship, had to be protected at all costs. Jake felt blood trickling from a cut on her head, right below the jeweled band that held back her nerve cords. She felt the concern of the crew wash over her in a warm wave, tinged with their own fears and the cold set of their determination.

Executor Amur's mind brushed Jake's. "Zamara, I can only think that this inexplicable attack has something to do with the knowledge you harbor."

Jake nodded, grieved but stoic; she agreed. It was the only possible explanation.

"We are outnumbered by our own ships," he continued. "I doubt there will be an escape for us. But you must survive. What you carry *must* endure. You know where the escape pods are; go there."

Jake felt the deep pain of sympathy wash through her as the words entered her mind. But she also knew that the executor was right. She, the individual named Zamara, was no more important than any other protoss aboard this vessel, but what she carried could not be permitted to die with her. It was ancient, it was secret, and it had to survive. It would be noble to die with her companions on this ship. It would be a good death—but she did not have that luxury. She would have to live . . . live long enough at the very least to transfer her precious burden to another. She had fled from similar encounters before; at least, she remembered doing so.

Jake sent back an affirmative, laced with subtle nuances of care, concern, and grief. Then she fully realized what he had said.

"Escape pods? Surely I would be safer in a shuttle."

"The shuttles are much more heavily armored, that is true, but they are also larger and will attract more notice."

"Yes . . . I understand. *En taro Tassadar*, Amur." The executor returned the blessing and war cry in one, then she felt his attention shift. It would soon be time.

Jake hastened down the corridor, her gossamer-fine lavender and white robes that marked her revered status as preserver billowing around her. She had no armor, no weapons; she was not expected to have to defend herself. There was now and always had been a line a hundred deep of those who would die for what she carried. And soon, those aboard the *Xa'lor* would die. But she would be alone.

I must stay alive! she thought fiercely as she reached the escape pod and eased herself into it. Her long fingers moved over the controls quickly and calmly, the absolute necessity of her survival overriding her instinctive urge to panic.

Soon now . . . be ready, Amur thought to her.

There was more, but it was not in words, but in images. Jake sensed the activity throughout the vessel. In other bays, the fighters would be soaring into space like golden, glowing insects, darting about quickly and powerfully. The *Xa'lor* itself, of course, was massively armored, but Jake had had no illusions that a single carrier would be the victor.

Jake knew what the executor was going to do, knew that the timing of the desperate attempt was crucial. She let her gaze go soft, the better to focus her powerful brain, to open her thoughts. Amur was going to let the attackers destroy them, and Jake was to depart mere seconds before the ship exploded. There would be scattered debris littering the area, and the enemy—fellow protoss, the enemy? The thought was agony—would have their hands full for a few precious moments attempting to locate her.

In those few seconds, with luck, Jake could make good her escape.

She waited for the instant when she would depart, and it came.

Now!

Jake thought with a stab of pain that Amur's thoughts had never been so focused, so *pure,* in all the time she had known him.

With a clarity and calmness that would have surprised her had she not been so secure in the serene confidence that what she was doing was necessary, Jake hit the controls. The little pod was propelled into space.

The pod, small but as beautiful and graceful and golden as any other protoss vessel—the khalai were proud of their handiwork and made everything aesthetically pleasing as well as highly functional—began moving swiftly forward. It had company; to cause further distraction, all of the escape pods had been launched.

A few seconds later, Jake's mind cried out and her hands flew to cover her glowing eyes as she felt the deaths of her crewmates, her colleagues, her friends. Their pain made her dizzy and ill. So many lifetimes of memories bombarding her was almost too much to handle. She summoned her will and with an effort got her thoughts under control. She chose not to look at the devastation behind her. She did not need to see it to know.

Her mind clearing, Jake determined where the

other escape pods were. Even these were beautiful, small, one- to two-protoss versions of the scouts, keeping that vessel's speed and maneuverability but lacking its weaponry. Carefully, so that the action would not look directed, Jake guided her pod in with the others and kept her mind closely shuttered. Just one of many bright golden dots in space.

Satisfied that she was not attracting undue attention, Jake called up a list of protoss vessels and the star charts of the area. She would need to either be rescued soon or find a world that had a warp gate. Her mission must not be delayed further.

Fortunately, she was on a well-traveled route. And she knew that Executor Amur had sent out a distress call. If she did not "drift" overly far, and if she eluded detection, there was a good chance she would be found in a short period of time.

If, if. Too many for her liking.

She was not as lucky with nearby planets, in case aid did not come. There was one planet two hours away, if she maintained this speed. She could reach it sooner than that, if she accelerated, but that would negate the current plan of deception. But it was far from an ideal choice, as it lacked a survivable atmosphere. No, waiting here was the best—

The little vessel suddenly rocked and Jake was almost thrown from her seat. It would seem she had not escaped detection after all. The crystal used for navigation was pulsing erratically, and a shrill, angry sound came from the console. Jake had no choice but to erect the shields full force—a sign that someone was alive in the escape pod.

Jake ascertained that only a single pursuer was after her, though doubtless he had informed his commander that he had found the prey they sought. With nothing to lose, Jake accelerated and headed for the inhospitable planet. Perhaps she could elude them yet.

Again the ship rocked, and despite the shields, Jake knew it had taken a solid hit. *Escape pod has sustained damage to the hull. Structural integrity failing. Damage irreparable and escalating. Estimated time to complete systems failure: twenty-eight minutes, fifty-one seconds.*

A quick check revealed that if the vessel survived the crash—unlikely at best, but a possibility—she would have enough oxygen to last for ten days. After that, she could use the protective suits; that would buy her another six hours. That was, of course, assuming that the assassin did not succeed in eliminating her and the threat she posed.

No! It must not be lost. The knowledge must not die with this protoss shell she wore. Jake refused to accept the cool mental voice coming from the crystal, telling her that she would die in less than an hour. The inhospitable planet was the only option left to her now. She sat back in the chair and reached for the khaydarin crystal she kept on a thin chain about her neck, her long fingers closing over it as she used its power to keep her mind calm and focused.

She did not know what she was searching for. Something to keep hope alive, perhaps.

And she found it. Her eyes flew open. There was a xel'naga artifact on this otherwise forsaken world. Was it a sign?

The assassin was no longer firing at her, but neither was he abandoning the chase. She realized that they wanted her alive if it could be conveniently managed, at least initially, so they could make certain of exactly what she knew, how she knew it, and whom she had told.

Unthinkable. Jake would take her own life before she would let the enemy have such knowledge.

Grimly determined, Jake headed for the planet, targeting the xel'naga temple. The world came into view, pale and unwelcoming. She flew closer, directing the glowing, graceful pod down into the atmosphere.

There. She could see the temple now. But even from this distance she could see that its exterior was dark brown, not the vibrant, living green a memory not her own told her it would have been had it still housed its treasure. The energy creature that had once dwelt inside it had departed for whatever glorious destiny awaited it—a destiny that not even she, who bore the knowledge of all protoss, could guess at. There was even a gaping, shattered hole in the top where it had emerged. It was for that aperture that Jake headed now. There was a good chance that, using the memories of others, she could navigate her way through the myriad corridors that were sure to comprise the chrysalis better than those who hunted her.

She focused all her attention on the jagged entrance. She thought she could glimpse a faint glowing from within. If it had crystals, perhaps she—

Another attack pounded her already battered ship. Clearly they were afraid they would lose her, and were trying to knock her off course. They succeeded. Jake crashed into the lip of the hole and knew no more.

Pain . . .

Sometime later, she blinked awake, pain stabbing her and a humming noise vibrating through her body almost to a cellular level. She was huddled beneath the console, and for a moment she didn't understand why. Then she realized what had happened. Her escape pod was tilted badly, almost vertically. She moved cautiously, aware that she was wounded, but not sure yet how bad it was. Her hand touched her slender torso and came away wet with blood, dark and thick and hot.

She was dying. She was dying and soon it would be lost, all lost. . . .

Jake craned her neck and her eyes widened. Where she had sat was now a huge, glowing crystal. It was so beautiful, its song—for now she realized it was crystals singing, as they had once sung to Khas and Temlaa and others—so exquisite she almost forgot to be shocked at its appearance. Her pod had impaled itself—and, she realized, her—upon it.

Somehow she reached the door, somehow it opened, and she fell down several feet and again lost consciousness as she struck hard. Impossibly, she revived a second time. Somehow she got to her feet and swayed for a moment, staring down at her bloody lavender and white robes.

There was no indication that her pursuers had followed her down, and she knew why. There had been no reason to. They had dealt her ship a crippling blow, and the area in which the pod had crashed would be far too difficult to navigate. There was no atmosphere here, and if they had taken any readings on her physical state, they would know she would be dead within hours. Indeed, she should be dead already. Her injuries were far too great. But in defiance of what should be, the wound was starting to close, and the lack of habitable atmosphere seemed to pose no threat. Something here was keeping her alive. But for how long?

She looked around, the pain receding in the face of the glories that met her eyes. This . . . cavern? . . . was filled with hundreds, if not thousands, of khaydarin crystals. Each one was singing, adding its own tune to the exquisite harmony that wrapped around her almost like a physical thing. They glowed blue, purple, and green, and she felt bathed in that light. Perhaps that was what was healing her and creating some sort of protective barrier against the lack of atmosphere, that, or the powerful residual life force that still thrummed throughout the now-abandoned chrysalis. There was definitely energy here; and Jake, with the memories of every protoss who had ever lived, thought she just might be able to put that energy to good use.

A hand on her lacerated abdomen, she moved carefully around the chambers, looking for an exit. There was none. In a way, that was good, if the plan that was starting to form in her mind was to be successful. But in a way, it was not, for success hinged on someone knowing what she knew—someone finding her.

The pain was returning, and she felt fresh wetness beneath her hand. She still lived, but not for long. Not in this broken body.

Jake threaded her way through the crystals, leaving drops of dark purple fluid as she went. Finally she reached a relatively flat wall and trailed her hand over it. A flash of memory—Temlaa and Savassan, touching the crystals in a precise order—the ara'dor, the perfect ratio. The ratio of the shell, of the hand, found again and again on all worlds the protoss had discovered. Such a pattern had opened doors that were otherwise hidden. Would it likewise permit her to create a door where none existed before?

Jake winced at the pain, but grimly pressed her clean hand to the wall. She could sense the energies in it still, feel it almost physically tingling on her skin. One to one point six, each print touching the other, making a beautiful but invisible spiral on the door. Then she drew the lines of the "door" she hoped to create, again measuring as best she could estimate, tracing a rectangular outline. She lifted her hand and waited.

The chrysalis and the creature it had sheltered had been of the xel'naga. And somehow, it remembered. Somehow, it recognized this timeless ratio. Before Jake's eyes, the spiral created by her hand, hitherto invisible, began to glow. There was a sudden brilliant flash of light, and then Jake realized she was peering into the dark depths of a corridor.

"Please," she whispered, to whom she did not know—the chrysalis, the souls of those whose memories she bore, the unknown protoss who would one day find this corridor. Jake looked around and found a small crystal she could conveniently break off. Holding the glowing source of purple-green illumination, she moved forward, following the corridor until it ended. She repeated the process on this wall. Again the spiral glowed and flared, and again a doorway she had created with nothing but the energies of this place and her own knowledge of the ara'dor's importance to the xel'naga opened for her. She stepped into the corner and turned around. How to close the door? Or rather, cause it to manifest again? On a hunch, she traced the ara'dor in the empty space and stepped back. Sure enough, the wall reappeared. She needed to leave a message, but also had to be cryptic. After all, there was a possibility that an enemy could find this place.

Jake turned to the wall opposite the doorway, dipped a long finger in her own blood, and began to write.

• • •

My brothers or sisters who have come this far—within, a secret lies preserved. To enter, think as the Wanderers from Afar would. Think of perfection.

She stumbled and blinked. Away from the energies of the heart of the temple, her wound was worsening. Fear shot through her that she might already have lingered too long. She opened the door, closed it again behind her, then hurried back as best she could to the innermost chamber.

She almost fell before she reached it. Faintness washed over her, gray and soothing; she fought it back determinedly. Not yet. Not just yet.

The energies from the hatchling from a similar chrysalis had turned Bhekar Ro, a harsh world, into a verdant field for kilometers around. Perhaps what was left here would do what Jake wanted it to do. And more than any other protoss, a preserver understood how to use one's thoughts.

She wasn't even able to reach the ship. She would have to do it here. Her body made the decision for her, her legs buckling as she fell hard. One hand reached out to grasp the nearest crystal, pulling its power and that of the temple itself into her.

Life energy was as real as any other kind. She knew that. And now she deliberately pulled it out of her poor violated body, shaping it into a cord, willing herself to live long enough to stop time in this place of deep, deep power. She twined the glowing, golden cord that was her life around the crystal. When the time came, if all went as she hoped it would, the cord would be found and held by another—another to whom she could pass on the vital information she bore.

Despite the emotions pumping through her system, the legacy of the primal protoss who had raged and slaughtered one another in millennia past, Jake calmed her thoughts and concentrated on the khaydarin crystal. It was warm where her hand rested on it, and she felt a slight tingling emanating from it.

I have done all that I could. I can only hope it will be enough.

She closed her eyes. The last thing she saw was a drop of her blood trickle down her hand and hang, poised to fall, from the tip of her finger.

CHAPTER 11

"I REMEMBER THAT BLOOD DROP," JAKE murmured softly. He'd seen Zamara's broken body and, moved by some deep-seated desire to show compassion even to the dead, he'd reached to touch that hand. The blood drop had stayed as perfectly formed as if it had been made out of a dark purple gemstone, then suddenly lost cohesion and spread across his palm—wet and fresh as if it had just been shed.

Zeratul saw both versions of the same incident then—Zamara's and Jake's, as both recalled the union. Jake censored nothing—not his panic, not his pain, not his wonder, not his pettiness. Zeratul was definitely paying close attention now.

"It is a marvel," he said finally. "That you were able to decipher the clues Zamara had left. Few would have thought that way. Few even among my people, let alone yours."

Jake shrugged, uncomfortable with the praise. "All that matters is that I did."

"And that you continue to cooperate, even though

what Zamara has done has cost the lives of many dear to you. And may in the end claim your own life."

"Yeah, well, the odds of that not happening will go up if you will just listen to what Zamara has to say."

Zeratul narrowed his eyes, and Jake suddenly held his breath. Had he really said that? He meant it, of course, but he wasn't usually so . . . blunt. That was more like something Rosemary would say. But despite the beauty of this environment, and all those negative ions Zamara assured him were charging the air, he was getting sicker and he knew it. The headaches were almost constant now, a dull, throbbing ache that shortened his temper and sharpened his tongue when they were not hot spikes of agony that made any movement other than clutching his head and whimpering impossible. Even so, he desperately hoped he hadn't blown everything with his comment.

Suddenly Zeratul laughed. It was a dry, yet warm and embracing sound that calmed him and somehow even made the headache more bearable.

"Indeed, you remind me of Raynor. He was a friend to our people, as you are." His eyes suddenly gleamed brighter, and Jake sensed that through the dark templar's heavy mantle of guilt and grief, there was yet a spark that could perhaps be fanned into a flame. "He thought of me as a storyteller of sorts. A riddler, a teacher who taught by asking questions and coaxing forth. I . . . have not felt like riddling, telling stories, or teaching, for some time now. The two of you have shared with me a profound story of the nobility of our people, and that of an entirely different species. Although I sense there is more to it than what you have shared, Zamara. Such as the identity of the ones who hunted you."

Jake felt Zamara smile. "Indeed there is. Although *I* sense you have something to say before I continue."

Zeratul nodded. "I should reciprocate with a story that is known only to the dark templar. A story of a hero. Only one, and yet more than one."

Riddles indeed. Was Zeratul finally going to tell them what had happened—why his outlook was so bleak?

Zeratul did not quite flinch, but the brightness in his eyes subsided for a moment. Of course, he had read Jake's thoughts.

"Nay. I would never call myself a hero, human. Not a villain, not quite, for I have ever acted for what I thought was best. But I am no hero. Nor would you think me one if—well." He turned his face to the soft, cooling spray of the waterfall and was silent for a moment.

"I will tell you of the Anakh Su'n—the Twilight Deliverer."

Jake felt unease for a moment. There was so very much at stake. He didn't want to hear some dark templar folktale, he wanted to *do* something. Zamara, despite her own driving needs, sent him calm. *Zeratul does not indulge in idle chatter. If he wishes to tell this story, you may rest assured there is a very good reason.*

Zeratul's eyes crinkled slightly. He definitely

had not forgotten humor. *Zamara is right, impatient youngling.*

The rebuke had no sting. Jake found himself grinning a little despite the direness of the situation and settled back on the grass to listen.

"Zamara has the memories of the Discord. When the dark templar were rounded up like beasts, forced into an ancient ship, and expelled from the only world we had ever known. One among the protoss defended us. Adun. He disobeyed the Conclave's orders to have us executed, and instead tried to teach us to find new mental abilities and ways to control them, for our own protection. Ways that did not involve linking in the Khala, which we chose not to follow. His disobedience was discovered, but even then, he chose to do what he could to protect us. The Conclave would not consider integrating us into their society, but Adun mitigated their orders from death to banishment."

Jake nodded. This much he knew—this much he had actually seen through the memories of Vetraas.

"Yet even as we were leaving, violence broke out. It was Adun, again, who saved us. He called upon both light and dark powers to protect us, so that we might survive. He gave his life to save us."

"That's not the spin the Aiur protoss put on it," Jake said. "They saw it quite the opposite way—that Adun died to protect the sanctity of the Khala, where the protoss could link and find unity and strength. What's the phrase—"

"*En taro Adun,*" Zamara replied.

"We dark templar also revere him in such a way. Except we say *Adun toridas . . .* commonly interpreted as 'May Adun give you sanctuary,' but literally and more bluntly, 'Adun hide you.' "

Jake thought about what Vetraas had seen, and rather agreed that the dark templar had the right of it. Adun had died protecting them.

"But did he die?" he blurted. "I mean—he vanished, certainly, and they couldn't sense him in the Khala. But no one is sure exactly what happened to him."

Zeratul was nodding. "That he was gone, is certain. But there was no body to give closure. No corpse to bear down the Road of Remembrance, to ritually bathe and sit with, and finally bury. Adun simply disappeared."

Jake stared at Zeratul. "You don't seem all that surprised. What do you think did happen to him then?"

Zamara remained silent, but Zeratul answered. "We believe he did not die. We believe he simply crossed to another plane of existence."

"Like Zamara."

"I am not Adun," Zamara demurred.

"No," Zeratul agreed. "But you have managed to live on in a fashion, through this terran."

"I could not have done this on my own. I used the energies of the temple to delay death until my memories could be transferred to another."

Zeratul gazed deep into Jake's eyes, seeing and speaking to both the human and the protoss who saw out of them. "True. It was a unique coinciding of need and opportunity. But you cannot argue that such another incarnation is impossible. You yourself, Zamara, are proof of that. Your spirit lives on . . . in another body. More than just your knowledge and memories are in Jacob's brain. *You* are."

Jake's stomach clenched at what Zeratul was implying. Somehow, once he'd gotten over the initial shock, the fact that he carried a protoss sentience in his head hadn't seemed all that weird. Jake was always the rational man. He understood that there were things like mental energies that could be scientifically explained. He hadn't used words like "soul" and "reincarnation." Now he wondered if he should. Despite all he had seen and experienced, with his own eyes or through the memories Zamara shared with him, he wasn't sure if he was ready to accept the ideas that Zeratul was tantalizingly putting forth.

"I had not thought of it in that fashion," Zamara said slowly. "It is intriguing. You are suggesting that something similar happened with Adun?"

"You survived, after a fashion, by using extremely powerful energies from a xel'naga temple. You were able to put your essence into Jacob. Adun was the first to wield both the mental energies traditional to the Aiur protoss, and the darker energies of the Void that we have wielded for over a thousand years. It is not illogical to assume that, for want of a better word, both you and Adun tapped into energies that had consequences far greater than anticipated."

The glowing eyes half closed and Zeratul tilted his

head in amusement. "Although for us, the story of the Anakh Su'n, the Twilight Deliverer, is a bit more mystical than something so prosaic. We saw him ascend before our very eyes—sacrificing this existence to achieve another, higher spiritual plane. A prophecy slowly began to take shape around this remarkable incident. We believed Adun was waiting until a similarly great need arose to return to us—to all of us, Aiur protoss and dark templar alike. Did he not use both powers? Did he not die protecting us—not because we were different, but because we were the same as those who would have seen us dead or cast out?"

Zeratul's eyes flashed as he spoke, and Jake saw he was sitting up straighter. He remembered the image Zamara had given him of the prelate, before the disappointment of actually meeting him. Zeratul had seemed to him powerful, controlled and yet passionate, an inspiring presence. For the first time since Jake had met him, Zeratul seemed like that protoss.

"I firmly believe that while Adun wanted to keep us safe, he also wanted to keep the Aiur protoss from committing an atrocity from which they could never recover. To have slaughtered all of us—the stain of such a thing could not have been removed. We could never be a united people, with so vast a river of blood flowing between us. It was to help them as much as us that he summoned the powers he did and made his sacrifice."

Jake boggled at the depth of compassion it took for Zeratul—and by implication, all the dark templar—to see the incident in such a light.

"Those who had such talents meditated on the prophecy. They were given visions, signs to look for, for the return of Adun. How he would return we did not know. But return he would, once these signs had come to pass."

"And . . . you think he has?" Jake asked. At the same time as his lips formed the words—old habits died hard, and he found himself still speaking to the protoss rather than just thinking at them—Zamara asked, "What are the signs?"

Zeratul chuckled. "Ah. So many questions. I think I have said enough. Zamara has told a story—a poignant and powerful one." He inclined his head respectfully. "I have told a story, a myth of my people that is not quite so fictional as it might seem to be at first. I think it is time that you, Jacob Jefferson Ramsey, told a story."

"Uh . . ." He was no raconteur. These two beings had lived much, much longer than he had, and had seen far more. They knew far more. What could he possibly say to interest them? Zamara already knew him practically down to the cells of the marrow of his bones. "I . . . really don't have a story. I'm just a digger in the dirt, honestly." Jake shrugged, slightly embarrassed.

"How did you come to find our friend Zamara, Jacob?" Zeratul asked. He had turned his full attention on Jake, and that intense regard was unsettling. "You are far away from the worlds of your people for one who is a mere digger in the dirt. Zamara crafted a puzzle that most protoss might not have been able to decipher, let alone terrans. How is it you were there to solve that puzzle? I am intrigued."

Jake knew that this was a key moment. He knew he was being analyzed by one of the shrewdest minds he had ever stumbled across. The members of the nominating committee for the Flinders Petrie Award for Archaeological Distinction had nothing on this guy. He suspected Valerian might—the young Heir Apparent was extremely intelligent and very canny—but even then, Jake would put his money on the dark templar prelate. Zamara's respect for him rivaled that which she had felt toward Adun and Tassadar.

He and Zamara had to get this guy on their side. Had to convince him to lend his aid, to get back in the game, to stop sitting here on this out-of-the-way planet nursing his pain. Zamara had hooked him, by playing to that most protoss of traits, a deep curiosity and a desire to know. It was up to Jake to reel him in, as it were, though it was nothing so manipulative as that. Zeratul might be persuaded to help Zamara. But Jake realized the dark templar also needed to be persuaded to help Jake. And therefore, Jake needed to be worthy in those glowing eyes that had seen so much.

"Okay, then. I'll tell you about how I got to Nemaka and found Zamara. It's pretty boring," he warned.

"That is for me to determine," Zeratul replied, reinforcing Jake's supposition that this was about a thousand times more important than any interview he'd ever had. Even the one with Valerian.

Jake sighed. *Here goes nothing,* he thought to Zamara, and began.

He spoke briefly about his career as an archaeologist under first the Confederacy and then the Dominion, letting a little pride creep into his thoughts and voice as he mentioned his work on Pegasus. "Unfortunately funding ran out before I could find anything to prove my theories that there was something more to the place besides what was immediately apparent, but it was those theories that started attracting attention—both good and bad. Lots of people started calling me a crackpot, but it was my work there and my publication of those theories that attracted the attention of Valerian Mengsk."

"Mengsk?" He had Zeratul's attention now, for sure.

"Yes. Emperor Arcturus's son. He sent me an invitation to work for him while I was on Gelgaris. Full funding, state-of-the-art equipment, and a promise of a great intellectual challenge—a very nice offer."

"I see," said Zeratul. "So the heir to the Terran Dominion plucks you out of obscurity with no warning. How very boring this story is." Sarcasm, it seemed, was something terrans and protoss both understood.

Jake continued, warming to the tale. He described his encounter with Valerian, the youth's passion and curiosity about ancient civilizations, the promise of a glorious and comfortable excavation. "It was only later that I found out that I wasn't Valerian's first choice. There had been other teams there already. Seems there was a hollow area in the temple, a chamber, that Valerian desperately wanted to get into. None of the other teams had figured it out. I did . . . but I started down that path by sheer luck, by quite literally falling on my ass."

Zeratul blinked . . . and then laughed with more warmth than Jake had yet seen from him. Jake grinned crookedly and chuckled slightly himself.

"Happy accidents have been responsible for more glorious discoveries than you can imagine, Jacob," Zamara told him. "And you achieved more than . . . falling on your ass."

Jake nodded. "That's how I found the doorway. Completely by accident. Fell through two tunnels and landed right at the door." Jake sobered slightly, remembering. "I saw the writing in blood. That's when I knew I was on to something. I realized that while I might not be the first to know about the chamber and try to break into it, I was the first to get a real crack at solving this puzzle."

"Zamara did not make it easy," Zeratul said.

"Indeed I did not. I assumed that only a protoss who was profoundly knowledgeable and spiritual would comprehend the message I had left. And yet, even though he could not read it, Jacob was able to open the door."

"I figured out that in the end, it wasn't about thinking like a human, or even like a protoss, that would get me anywhere. It was about thinking on a grander, more universal scale. And when I saw the spiral in the fossil, it came to me. Rosemary and I went through, found the wrecked ship and . . . Zamara."

He fell silent. "So . . . I guess that's it."

"What of the female?"

"Rosemary? She went through the gate before we did. She went with the other protoss to Shakuras. When we tried to get through, we found that we were redirected. Zamara guessed you might be here, and so here we are."

Zeratul's eyes narrowed. "Perhaps the female is responsible for your being unable to reach Shakuras."

"No," said Zamara. Jake was grateful, and surprised, at the rapidity with which Zamara came to Rosemary's defense. Then again, she had always maintained that the assassin would be useful to them, and she had been right. Still, he appreciated it. "Rosemary Dahl is not a traitor. Not all terran females are like Sarah Kerrigan, Zeratul. I would think you would know that. The dark templar have ever deemed females the equal to males. Was not your own leader a female? Matriarch Raszagal?"

"Raszagal!" Jake stared at Zeratul. "I know her! I mean . . . I saw her. In the memories. She was a rather lively girl. She's your leader? That's—"

The words died in his throat at Zeratul's reaction to Zamara's words. He had gone very, very still, and then suddenly leaped to his feet.

"Do not mention her name to me!" he cried. Jake gasped with pain at the power of the mental voice. At that instant, perhaps triggered by Zeratul's inexplicable outburst, perhaps just a horrible coincidence, Jake's world went white with agony and went away for a moment. Every muscle in his body tensed and when at last the torment began to fade, he gulped in air and found he was damp not with spray from the waterfall, but with cold sweat. He also found himself being supported by a pair of strong, sinewy arms that ended in hands with two fingers and two thumbs.

"This, then, is what you suffer from your joining with Zamara," Zeratul said. There was no pity in his mental voice, just an assessment of the facts. Jake started to nod, but that seemed to invite the pain to return, so he spoke instead.

"Yeah. Sometimes it's like this; most of the time it's just a dull ache." Jake was proud his voice didn't shake.

Zeratul released him. Jake could tell he was still angry for whatever reason, but Jake's episode had distracted him somewhat. Still not thinking clearly in the aftermath of the pain, Jake said, "Like I said, I know Raszagal. I'm sure she's an excellent leader."

Zeratul turned away, and this time, Jake saw him wince. "What is it?"

Zamara knew, but she remained oddly silent.

"Raszagal . . . *was* an excellent leader," Zeratul replied. The heaviness and pain that laced the mental words was almost physical.

"Was?" Jake said, picking up on the past tense. "I'm sorry. . . . What happened to her?"

Zeratul did not answer. At last, he turned to face Jake and straightened, slowly.

"I killed her."

CHAPTER 12

VARTANIL WAS SURPRISINGLY GOOD COMPANY.

Rosemary hadn't been at all sure about him when he chose to stay with her. He was young and very eager, and usually that particular combination annoyed the hell out of her. She suspected she disliked it so intensely because it was usually the young and eager who were the first to die in any combat situation, and that kind of waste pissed her off. But Vartanil had the fact that he was a protoss going for him, and that mitigated his zeal somewhat.

Besides, stuck in her "quarters," there was really nothing else for her to do. So they talked.

Vartanil was scrupulous about reading her thoughts only when invited to do so. She'd felt him catch himself frequently at first, and she supposed that was to be expected. After all, it would be like her trying to have a conversation by writing when the tendency would be to speak. But he quickly got the hang of it, and recently hadn't mentally trespassed at all.

His life, as he'd indicated earlier, had been an

uneventful and rather happy one until the coming of the zerg. Rosemary found herself smiling wistfully at his description of a family unit and a craftsman's trade. It had been a long, long time since she'd glimpsed that kind of peace. She supposed that was why she'd been so susceptible to the drugs—they gave her tranquility of a sort, even if it was a dearly-bought, short-lived lie.

When the conversation turned to her, she demurred. "Let's put it this way. Things were rough on me when I was younger, so as soon as I could, I made them rough on others."

He cocked his head, confused. Damn, she was starting to read their body language.

"You did not harm innocents though." He stated this so firmly she felt a twinge of guilt—another thing she hadn't felt in a long time.

"Sometimes I did. It was just—I did what I needed to to do the job." She shrugged her slender shoulders. It had always sounded logical. But now it sounded . . . well . . . wrong.

"I see." He didn't of course. And yet, he chose to stay with her. He chose to focus on the strength of will it had taken for her to kick the Sundrop. He chose to focus on how she had helped Jake, rather than how she had been happily willing to turn him over for a handful of credits. Okay, more than a handful, never let it be said that Rosemary Dahl could be bought cheaply. But she sure as hell could be bought.

Jake was a lot like these guys. More than he realized. Rosemary didn't think she and Zamara would have gotten three steps if Zamara had entered her brain. The clash of natures would have made her head explode. That line of thinking, of course, made her remember that Jake was in reality going through something similar and not at all wryly humorous, and that soured her temper even more.

So it was that when Selendis entered, Rosemary snapped at her, "What the hell do you want? Come back to interrogate me some more?"

Selendis didn't bat an eye. "No," she said. "I have come to inform you that Hierarch Artanis is willing to grant you an audience."

Crap. Rosemary wondered how many times she'd stick her boot in her mouth with these people, and if she'd ever get used to the metaphoric taste.

"Oh. That's great. Uh, thank you for your efforts on my behalf." The words felt unnatural, but the feeling behind them was heartfelt. She *was* grateful.

Selendis inclined her head. It was then that Rosemary realized that the executor was clad more elaborately than the terran had ever seen her. Her armor, always meticulous, now seemed to gleam even brighter. Beneath the armor, she wore a flowing robe of dark blue inlaid with tiny gems, probably khaydarin crystal fragments if Rosemary had to guess. The fabric was thick and almost cried out to be touched, so heavy and lush was it. The overall effect was that Selendis appeared to be draped in the night sky, with her almost-radiant golden armor a bright sun. Atop her head she wore a jeweled band to hold back her nerve cords.

"You look great," Rosemary said. She glanced down at her own body. They'd given her robes of a sort to wear as well, and had cleaned and mended the familiar leather outfit Rosemary had spent what felt like half her life in.

"If you so desire, I can arrange for more formal robes to be brought to you," Selendis said, watching Rosemary's eyes as they examined first the protoss and then the folded clothing on the bed. "You will no doubt wish to present yourself properly to the Hierarchy."

"Wait—I thought I was going to see Artanis."

Selendis made a quick movement—a slight twist of the head and a shrug of the shoulders, and Rosemary recognized it as a sign of slight irritation. "I had assumed that the audience would be private as well. But I was mistaken. With so much potentially at stake, all the representatives from the various tribal bloodlines wished to evaluate the situation and decide on the solution."

"Oh that's just great. Now I get to deal with a *committee* of protoss." Selendis regarded her steadily and Rosemary sighed. "Well, let's get this party started."

"Do you wish more formal robes to be brought to you?"

Again Rosemary looked at the leather outfit. Sure, Selendis looked great in the night-sky robe with her perfectly polished armor. Rosemary had no doubt that she, too, would look stunning in such a dress. There had been times when she would have dressed well for a meeting. Rosemary was a mercenary, and she used all tools in her arsenal, including her body if she had to. But she knew that a female human body, attractive though it might be by her standards, wouldn't matter at all to a bunch of protoss. And in the end, that leather outfit represented the essence of who she was far better than any borrowed and tailored robe. She wasn't a protoss. She was a human female with a very dubious past. They knew that already. They knew *everything* already.

She thought about that time, seemingly ages ago, when she'd walked into her room at Ethan's compound wearing nothing but a robe to find Jake waiting for her. Jake was convinced Ethan was planning to betray them. And of course, he'd been right. She'd chosen the comfortable, somewhat battered leather uniform over a sundress then. She would choose it over an exquisite protoss robe now. Much had happened between that decision and this one, but some things hadn't changed. Would never change.

She turned to face Selendis. "No thanks. I've got my familiar clothes here. That's who I am."

Rosemary felt a brush of admiration—reluctant, but real—touch her mind. She'd just risen a notch in the executor's esteem. An infinitesimal one, but a notch all the same.

As the two protoss left so she could dress in privacy, Rosemary thought she'd need every notch she could get.

• • •

A few moments later, Rosemary, clad in the supple leather that fit like a second skin, strode between two tall templar guards. They towered over her by more than half a meter, and they were dressed in no-nonsense armor.

"All this for little old me," she murmured to Vartanil.

"Do not flatter yourself, Rosemary," Selendis said, not even bothering to turn her head. She strode a few paces in front of Rosemary. "It is standard etiquette for a meeting of the Hierarchy."

"Whatever." They strode down a corridor, Rosemary hastening to keep up with the long-legged strides of her templar guards—whoops, it's etiquette, "escorts"—and up a ramp that led to a large oval door. It irised open to reveal a flight pad of sorts atop the building where Rosemary had been kept prisoner—whoops again, "guest." A small ship awaited them. Rosemary raised an eyebrow. Dark templar technology, it had to be. Protoss technology for sure—nothing humans made was so pretty, and while she didn't know much about what the zerg did, she was willing to bet it wasn't aesthetically pleasing—but there were no blues or golds here, just dark hues and a soft green glow. Perhaps the constant twilight hue of the planet made it seem darker than it was, but it was definitely a craft that had been made by a people who spent time in the shadows.

Rosemary had spent a lot of time in the shadows herself. She respected that.

She climbed in and sat down, watching the pilots as best she could, wishing that this was her vessel and that she and Jake were about to head somewhere and—

She blinked. Since when had her fantasies about open space and a ship to fly it in included Professor Jacob Jefferson Ramsey? It was an alarming thought.

Rosemary distracted herself by peering out the window. She could make out dim shapes in the purple-blue below her, spires and towers and smaller, shorter buildings in a variety of shapes and sizes. They were darker blue, with tiny dots of illumination flickering to show that living beings dwelt there. At one point, she passed over something looming and huge that did not resemble any of the architecture she'd seen before. Even she, who was seldom moved by art or architecture, found herself barely breathing, pressing her face to the window to gaze at the thing. It looked like an ancient pyramid, or ziggurat, made of several levels that climbed skyward. Each level was limned with glowing, pale blue and purple light. Khaydarin crystals. At the top, visible even from this distance, an enormous crystal hovered. It was very similar to the one she'd seen in the chambers beneath the surface of Aiur.

"That is the temple," Vartanil said reverently. He, too, was gazing almost hungrily out the window at the mammoth structure that was slowly moving out of their field of vision.

"Oh? Like what Jake found?"

"Yes and no," said Selendis. "Both bear the mark of the *Ihan-rii*'s, the xel'naga's, guidance. But the temple which you and Jacob explored is something quite different from this. Such a thing is more—organic. Wild." Something in the tone of Selendis's mental voice indicated she did not approve of wildness. "The temple you see below you is mathematically precise and orderly."

"Like the Golden Mean. One to one point six."

A flicker of surprise from Selendis. "You know of the ara'dor? The perfect ratio?"

"Jake did. That's how he found Zamara in the first place—she'd left a note, which of course we couldn't read, and sealed herself inside the temple somehow. So Jake was at even more of a disadvantage than a protoss would have been. But he made the connection. He . . . doesn't think like other people do."

"Obviously."

The temple and its flickering, oddly haunting lights was gone. Rosemary leaned back in the chair. "Selendis—can you tell me what I'll be facing when I go in there? I'm not really a people person, in case you hadn't noticed."

At that, Selendis ducked her head and half closed her eyes and laughed more heartily than Rosemary would have given her credit for. "Yes, Rosemary Dahl, this thing I had noticed." She sobered slightly. "Yes. I will prepare you, because I believe in this cause, if not the messenger of it."

That stung more than Rosemary expected, but she

brushed it aside. "All I want is for us to find and help Jake and Zamara."

"I know this now. And—they will know that as well. Be prepared to have your mind read immediately upon entering the hall. By everyone present. For the entire duration."

Rosemary's fists clenched and she almost literally growled.

"Rosemary . . . do you know about Matriarch Raszagal?"

"Raszagal . . . Jake met her through Zamara's memories. She was just an adolescent when she left Aiur. She's still alive?"

"No. And let me tell you why."

Jake stared at Zeratul. "You . . . you killed her?" *Zamara—why did you bring me to this guy? He betrayed his world and killed his leader! We're supposed to put my life and the fate of this secret of yours in those kind of hands?*

Patience, Jacob. To know all is to understand all.

Jake's voice revealed his shock, abhorrence, and trepidation. Zeratul did not cringe from it. He stood straight and nodded confirmation.

"Yes. By my own hand, I murdered our beloved matriarch."

"In God's name, why?"

"Because she asked it of me."

Jake's mind continued to reel, and Zamara continued to be silent. Jake thought about why someone might ask such a thing. "She . . . was she ill? Wounded beyond healing?"

"In a manner of speaking, yes. Raszagal . . . our beloved matriarch . . . powerful and wise . . . was being used. Used to betray her own people. Used by one so cunning and unscrupulous that to this day, I cannot fathom the depths of that mind."

Jake thought he'd gotten it. "Ulrezaj!"

"No." Glowing eyes bored into blue ones. "Though I am intrigued as to how you know that name. But that question is for another time. No, I do not refer to Ulrezaj, but to Sarah Kerrigan. The Queen of Blades. She who had once been human and is now the leader of the zerg."

Jake grimaced slightly. "Zamara and I were once discussing her. From what I understand, the zerg turned her into one of them."

Zeratul nodded. "They infested her, but somehow did not destroy her individuality. Kerrigan came to us seemingly in good faith, proposing a plan that would aid the protoss and Kerrigan both. But even before she arrived on our world, Kerrigan had gotten to Raszagal and perverted her to her will."

The words were flooding out of Zeratul now, as if a dam of some sort had been broken. Jake listened intently.

"It was all a trick. A ploy. Kerrigan planned to turn on us the moment she had gotten what she needed. We would never have listened to her at all, no matter how reasonable she sounded, had not our own matriarch urged us to do so. Kerrigan knew that was the only way to get what she wanted from us. She kidnapped Raszagal, and I managed to rescue her."

He looked away for a moment. Protoss facial muscles did not reveal much. It was through their thoughts, so much more nuanced and subtle than human thoughts, and the movements of their graceful and powerful bodies, that they communicated. While Zeratul's expression did not change, the pain and outrage of his thoughts and the slight hunching of his powerful form told Jake as much as—more than—if he had been a human speaking. Zeratul was in torment.

"It was only my matriarch's powerful will that enabled her to speak as herself in that moment," Zeratul continued. "In that moment . . . as she died. Kerrigan knew that I believed I could free her from the zerg queen's influence. And . . . so I had hoped, too."

He turned back to Jake. "But in the end, I was mistaken. I could not liberate her—at least, not that way. Death was the only freedom I could grant to one I respected with all my heart. And in that moment, she thanked me."

He bowed his head and shuttered his thoughts from Jake. But not, it would seem, from Zamara.

" 'You have freed me from her vile control at last,'" Zamara said softly, gently, and Jake knew she was quoting the ill-fated Raszagal's last words. " 'You have always served me with honor . . . Thus I must ask you—' "

"No!" Zeratul cried violently, spinning around to face Jake and Zamara. "You will not say those words!"

Oh crap, what the hell did Raszagal say? Jake thought, panicked that in his outrage and hurt Zeratul might forget that he wasn't supposed to kill preservers and throttle Jake right on the spot.

Zamara ignored him and implacably continued. " 'Thus I must ask you to watch over my tribe . . . Zeratul . . . *into your hands I give the future.*' That's what she asked of you."

The anger seemed to bleed out of Zeratul and he turned away again, hunching over, looking much smaller and more vulnerable.

"I thought Kerrigan would kill me. I expected it. I . . . planned on it. Instead, she *praised* me, calling me a worthy warrior." His eyes narrowed, and the anger—no, not anger, it was deeper, larger than that— the offense returned to him. "She said she had already taken my honor. She was going to let me live because my every waking moment would be torture. Because she knew that I would never be able to forgive myself for what she forced me to do. That, Kerrigan said, would be the best revenge she could imagine."

"You shouldn't let her win like that," Jake said softly.

The lambent eyes focused their full outrage on him. "Watch what you say, human."

"Kerrigan was wrong. She didn't take your honor," Jake continued, wondering where in the world this sudden rather reckless courage was coming from. "You let her take it."

Jacob—

Zamara was warning him to back off. Jake ignored her. "Kerrigan didn't force you to do what you did. Sure, she set up the situation, and it was a horrible one. But you decided what to do about it. You chose to kill Raszagal. Don't blame Kerrigan for that."

Jacob, I would advise you to cease this line of conversation.

Zamara, I don't have a lot of time left to me if we don't convince Zeratul to get off his ass and help us. He's wallowing in self-pity right now.

"You didn't lose your honor. You kept it. Raszagal was at peace with what you did."

Zeratul had been stunned into mental silence at Jake's words, but the mention of Raszagal startled him into erupting. "You did not know my matriarch! How dare you speak for her!"

"But I did know her, in a way." The words were spilling out of him now, as they earlier had from Zeratul himself. "I was Vetraas, and Vetraas knew Raszagal, and that girl, that gutsy little spitfire, was proud of who she was and what she believed in. I bet that didn't change when she got older and became the leader of the dark templar. I bet she just got smarter and wiser and stronger, developed a rational head to go along with that passionate heart. I bet she was a terrific matriarch and loathed every nanosecond of being under Kerrigan's control. You didn't kill your matriarch, Zeratul. Kerrigan did that the minute she forced her way into Raszagal's brain and used her as a puppet to betray her own people. All you did was cut the strings. Raszagal died free. If you don't think there's honor in helping her do that, then I gotta say, you are not the protoss Raszagal thought you were."

Zeratul jerked as if slapped.

"Her last words were a duty you're failing to discharge. You're letting her down, big time. She asked you to watch over her tribe. She put the future in your hands, and right now, you're just sitting on them. My individual future and that of your people— hell, if Zamara's hints are right, the entire universe—is ticking past while you sit here on this out-of-the-way planet and feel sorry for yourself. You want that to be Raszagal's legacy?"

Zeratul moved so fast that Jake didn't realize he'd gone just that extra smidge too far until he was flat on his back with the protoss's hands on his throat. Zamara took over at once, forcing herself into Jake's body and fighting back, flipping Zeratul over, wriggling free, and dropping into a crouching stance.

When she had done this before, Jake's body had been able to defeat a master assassin in hand-to-hand combat. He didn't underestimate Zamara's prowess— she knew every fighting technique every protoss had ever known, after all—but he knew the limits of his own body, and there was no way a human could win this particular fight. Not even a human with a protoss at the wheel.

After all this, I didn't think I'd die at the hands of a protoss, Jake sent wildly to Zamara.

But he didn't.

Exerting a mental control Jake could only marvel at, Zeratul regained his composure. Calm draped him like a cloak. That stillness, so profound as to be almost unreal, settled over him and he rose to his full intimidating height.

"Leave. Now. And do not return."

Rosemary whistled, soft and low. "Wow. So a human woman warped the matriarch of all the dark templar into serving her will and ultimately forced a loyal subject to kill her. Okay, I see your point. I'm surprised that this Hierarchy of yours is even willing to talk to me after that. I'd heard some about Kerrigan. But not that."

"You do have a great prejudice to overcome," Selendis agreed. "The amount of pain Kerrigan has caused my people cannot be underestimated. Bear in mind also that protoss are unfamiliar with your culture. It may well have been that all females of your species are untrustworthy, and only the males are capable of actions of merit and compassion."

"Well, that's not true. We're all individuals."

"Your past does not exactly lend itself to our believing that."

Rosemary sighed. "I know. But there's nothing I can do about it. I can't and won't deny it or pretend it didn't happen."

Selendis eyed her, and yet again Rosemary felt her measure was being taken. The protoss continued.

"As I said, your thoughts will all be read. That is one thing you must be prepared for. The other thing is, they will do their best to unsettle you, to keep you off balance. Do not permit yourself to be intimidated, and if you do, in Tassadar's name do not become adversarial. Yet also, do not be overly meek. If you win their respect, they will be more likely to give credence to your request."

"Great. Diplomacy. I'm not good at it."

"They will know that too. There are those who will be ready to take your side and those who will be ready to oppose you. We are . . . not quite yet the united people Adun and Tassadar had hoped we would become." The executor's thoughts were laced with just the barest hint of pain and regret, quickly covered. "But even the dark templar respect preservers. You have an advantage in that the truth of what you say can be verified. Engage them, do not alienate them, and I am hopeful of the outcome."

Engage, but don't alienate. Rosemary made a wry face. Much, much easier said—or in this case thought—than done. She settled back in the overlarge chair, still facing the window but no longer seeing the images that passed below her.

She'd been before the Heir Apparent to the Terran Dominion and stood her ground. She'd killed—or at least thought she'd killed—a man she'd loved in cold blood. She'd lobbed grenades at zerg, piloted a ship under attack, and done any number of other things that required nerves of paristeel.

Why, then, did anticipating this audience make her stomach knot?

She realized it was because before, the only thing that had been at stake was herself. Her life, her fortunes, her feelings. But this time, more—much more—than that rested on how she'd impress this High Muckety-Muck Hierarchy. This time, maybe the whole universe rested on her shoulders.

And even more than that . . . Jake's life rested on that.

"Fighting zerg was easier," she muttered.

CHAPTER 13

ROSEMARY PACED IN THE ANTECHAMBER OF what Selendis had told her was the dark templar's citadel. It had been fascinating to watch the ship maneuver in for a landing—the entire citadel was erected atop a gigantic hovering disk. She'd been shunted off to this room, and had been told to wait. And wait.

Vartanil watched her in sympathetic silence. "Protoss protocol moves at a glacial pace," she muttered.

"I must agree with you, Rosemary," Vartanil said. "I have spent the last four years on Aiur, where sometimes a fraction of a second meant life or death. There was no option for hesitancy or slow deliberation. Not even among the Tal'darim, where we were somewhat safer than our brethren on the surface." He added, "Safer, of course, being a relative term. We did not need to fear the zerg, only our own Xava'tor."

She nodded absently, wondering if she'd made the right decision in coming in her worn, stained leather outfit rather than the graceful protoss clothing. She shook her head at herself, her silky, gleaming black hair flying with the gesture. It wasn't like her to second-guess her decisions. This whole situation had put her off her stride. It was time to pull herself together. Too much was at stake for her to walk into that hall rattled and fretting about clothing choices.

"Rosemary Dahl, they will see you now." The mental voice belonged to one of Selendis's templar who had accompanied her in the ship. Rosemary turned and nodded. She took a deep breath and forced composure on herself as she had so many times in the past.

"Let's do this thing."

The templar turned to the Furinax. "Vartanil, you also are requested to appear."

"I?" Vartanil's hands fluttered in agitation. "But . . . I am no one important! Why do they want to see me?"

"Because you know firsthand what Ulrezaj did to those who followed him. And because you have chosen to support Rosemary. Your experience is important in their decision."

Vartanil turned lambent eyes to Rosemary. For her mind alone, he sent, "It is my greatest hope that nothing I bring to this meeting jeopardizes your chances of recovering Professor Ramsey."

"I know," Rosemary said. She couldn't hide her own worry, and unfortunately that did nothing but add to Vartanil's agitation. "But hey, you could be a great help too. Let's just go find out, okay?"

Vartanil nodded. The templar beckoned, and Rosemary and the former Tal'darim followed him.

They strode down a long corridor that was wide and yet somehow confining. Little décor was on the walls here; this was a purely functional route, merely an entrance to the chambers. Wide but oddly cramped feeling, the design of the corridor was a security measure, she realized. Petitioners or perhaps even honored guests would be monitored every step of the way.

When they emerged, Rosemary blinked at the sight that met her eyes.

She had seen displays of wealth and power before, and she was not one to be easily intimidated by such things. Ethan's compound had dripped wealth on lavish display, and Valerian's private study, while more tasteful and understated, was filled with items that were actually even more valuable than anything Ethan possessed.

But this . . .

The door, deceptively modest and undecorated on this side, opened onto something straight out of a dream. The dark templar obviously fostered craftsmen every bit as talented as the khalai. She couldn't take a guess at how old this building was, nor how long it had taken to erect, but it was magnificent. Where the corridor had felt narrow, this room was cavernous. Soft black carpeting rendered her footfalls silent as she moved forward, not breaking stride despite the shock of the place's grandeur.

The enormous room, large enough to be a building on its own, was circular. Above arched a dome made of faceted crystals. Unlike most of the crystals Rosemary had seen so far, these were not opaque and radiant but translucent, to let in as much natural light as possible. More illumination was provided by the more familiar crystals, scattered throughout the hall on intricately crafted metal stands. Alcoves ran the entirety of the circular hall, and in each one sat a protoss on a huge chair, surrounded by several attendants. Rosemary's eyes darted around, finally coming to rest on a figure at the far end on a dais. Standing beside him was Selendis, who turned to Rosemary. Though she appeared tiny because the place was so damn big, Rosemary recognized her immediately; her armor was distinctive, and she was the only female present in any position of authority.

Selendis's thoughts brushed hers. "They will not read your thoughts until you are formally introduced. Do not be afraid, Rosemary Dahl. All here are aware of the situation, and many are already sympathetic toward your goal."

"And some aren't."

"Yes. But you knew that. The truth is your ally in this case. Present it calmly, and I have high hopes they will listen to you."

Present it calmly. That was the trick, wasn't it?

Selendis stepped lithely down from her position and strode to the center of the chamber. Her thoughts rang out as loudly and clearly as if she had shouted them.

"Templar, judicators, khalai, dark templar—thank you for assembling here today to acknowledge the petitioner. She has traveled far and endured much, and stands before you to respectfully ask you to pay heed to her requests. She is terran, and female, but beside her stands a protoss who has willingly chosen to stay with her, based entirely upon what he has endured. What they know, you will soon know. I believe their request to be a true and honorable one."

Rosemary felt a tickle in her mind and turned toward the one who was sending it.

"Come forward, human. And you, Vartanil." The mental voice was almost kind, and Rosemary obliged, striding forward and looking up at the speaker. Vartanil followed.

The protoss's seat was at once more beautiful and more humble than the others in this vast hall. Simply crafted, it did not drip with gems or crystals, nor were there elaborate swirls in its design. And yet it was exquisite, clean, its plain lines eloquent and harmonious. On each side stood a protoss standard-bearer, and swathes of purple covered the walls of the alcove. For such a formal place, this protoss was simply, almost staidly clad in a few pieces of armor and something that looked like an apron. Like the throne, if one could use such a word to describe something so plain, it was very well crafted and well worn. The glowing eyes squinted and the protoss hunched his shoulders, using his body language to smile reassuringly at her.

"I am Tabrenus of the Furinax lineage. I see one of my own stands with you. That speaks well of you."

Rosemary felt Vartanil's pride and humility at the words. Not sure what to do, she bowed respectfully. That seemed appropriate, for Tabrenus nodded and settled back.

"Cross the hall to Urun of the Auriga," came Selendis's thoughts in her mind. "Their ancestral tribal color is orange. Continue to alternate until you reach Artanis at the end. Remember . . . from this moment, all your thoughts are clear to us."

The advice was welcome, and Rosemary shot back a quick thanks. She backed away a bit from Tabrenus, then turned and approached the leader of the Auriga.

His armor reminded her of Selendis's, but it was more elaborate. Rosemary wondered at that—she'd thought Selendis the highest ranking military officer. Perhaps it was simple personal choice. An elaborate headpiece and large shoulders should have looked oversized and ridiculous, but this protoss had the physical frame and the presence to support it.

"You came from Aiur," Urun stated bluntly. Rosemary nodded, unsure if she should speak.

"Only if asked a direct question," Selendis whispered in her mind. Again, Rosemary was grateful.

"Our people fought well." He nodded, satisfied. "I am not surprised. But you do not come here proposing to return and take back our world from the zerg . . . or Ulrezaj."

The amount of loathing with which Urun infused

the dark archon's name was almost painful. Slowly, Rosemary shook her head. "No. That's not my idea to suggest. I'm here to ask you to help Jake and Zamara."

Urun's discontent washed over her. This was an impatient one, eager to fight back and reclaim the honor of the protoss people. Only if she could persuade him that that cause would eventually be served by recovering Zamara would she sway him.

He dismissed her with a wave of his hand, and the gesture annoyed Rosemary. Urun's eyes narrowed slightly.

"Watch your thoughts," Selendis reminded her.

"It's damn hard to do when you're not a telepath," Rosemary shot back, but instead focused on what she'd come here to do. Following Selendis's instructions, she crossed the hall again, to stand in front of Nahaan of the Ara. If Urun was ceremonial, almost ostentatious, this protoss tribal leader—it was the best word she could think of; she knew that the protoss had long ago adopted caste intead of tribal distinctions, but clearly the bloodlines and heritages were remembered and valued—was almost monkish. Although the color that adorned his alcove was red, his clothing was dark, almost somber, and a hood hid his eyes until he moved it back with a deliberate gesture to regard Rosemary thoughtfully.

"You and the problem you present have brought me back to Shakuras," Nahaan informed her. She got a distinct impression of a dislike of Shakuras and all that it represented. "Rest assured, I will pay close attention to your plight."

The words were not comforting. She'd known she was going to be under tight scrutiny, but Nahaan seemed particularly interested in how things would turn out. Rosemary bowed. Sweat was starting to gather at her hairline and armpits. She wished she could just get this over with.

Three down, three to go.

Zekrath certainly seemed like the kindest of the leaders, a slender protoss whose blue-gray skin seemed paler than most. His garb, bright yellow and orange, seemed even brighter against the white backdrop of his alcove and draped his body simply. He looked tranquil, calm, and Rosemary found her gaze drawn and held by several small crystals that whirled about Zekrath's head, creating the illusion of a crown. Or a halo.

Even more than the others, Zekrath of the Shelak spoke less in words than in sensations. There was a feeling of pity for all Rosemary had undergone, and sympathy for her cause. Rosemary found herself smiling at Zekrath, thinking that maybe she'd found an ally. She bowed, just a little more deeply than she had to the others, and turned to face the next to last tribal leader.

His name and allegiance came into her head as she regarded him. He was Mohandar of the—no, she had been thinking "dark templar" but now was corrected; not the dark templar, they had taken a new name,

Nerazim, for a new tribe that had arisen from the original group that had been exiled from Aiur.

If Zekrath had been bright colors and gleaming white, this being was shadows and darkness. His eyes glowed green in this light, visible even through a veil that obscured much of his face, and his features were more irregular and sharp. There were jutting protrusions on his brow and cheekbones that made him look almost lizardlike compared to the protoss she was familiar with. While both Zekrath and Mohandar were clearly old, they showed it quite differently. Zekrath had that timeless look that Rosemary had sometimes seen in elderly humans—an inner energy, a radiance, that belied any external signs of aging. She had no idea how old Mohandar was, but he bore every year in his face and his bearing. Even his clothing struck her as old; it was strangely tattered and ragged, and twined about his wizened form in a way that reminded her of mummies from ancient Earth.

Yet Mohandar was most definitely not enfeebled with age. The tribal color the Nerazim had adopted was a verdant green, which at first struck her as strange, but then as completely right. She felt her mind being probed and assessed, and then Mohandar withdrew without a single comment.

It rattled her.

"Rosemary Dahl." The mental voice was young and perhaps had once been enthusiastic, but now seemed tempered. She turned toward Artanis, leader of the Akilae and now hierarch of all the protoss. He was clad in armor almost virtually identical to that which Selendis wore, and struck her as the quintessential protoss. Gold and blue draped his alcove, and his dais was slightly higher than the others. His eyes were a calm sky-blue in the light. "It has been some time since the protoss encountered your people. You are only the third terran to visit Shakuras."

Thrown into a comfy prison and forced to wait—some welcome. Rosemary winced; she couldn't stop the thought, and she felt their displeasure rumbling around her. Artanis held up a hand.

"I understand Executor Selendis has informed you of the last time we encountered a terran female," he said mildly.

"Yeah," Rosemary said. Her voice echoed with startling clarity in the hall; for a people who didn't speak, they constructed their buildings with fantastic acoustics. "I know about Kerrigan. May I respectfully remind the hierarch, however, that the first time humans encountered the protoss, you guys incinerated one of our worlds without so much as a by-your-leave, and yet my friend may die trying to help you."

More rumblings, but some admiration was laced in with it. To her surprise, Rosemary felt humor coming from Mohandar. "The female has a point."

"Selendis has informed us all of what she has obtained with speaking to you and those who accompanied you." Artanis was striving to keep the meeting on track. "Yet we would know this directly from you."

Rosemary swallowed hard. So many thoughts crowded her mind at once. Where to begin? Images came—the cave where she and Jake had found Zamara, her betrayal of the archaeologist, his horror at having been used to turn a madman loose on his friends, the stories of Temlaa and Vetraas and Khas and Adun, the Sundrop—oh, God, the Sundrop—the whirling radiant darkness—what an oxymoron *that* was—that was Ulrezaj, the sudden and unexpected pain in her chest when Jake said he was dying, the living carpet of zerg that just came on and on and *on*, Ethan's betrayal and resurrection as a tool of this Kerrigan who—

She opened her mouth to speak, to try to begin the linear, calm telling of the tale, when Selendis touched her mind: "Well done, Rosemary."

Well done? She hadn't even started—

"Thoughts are richer and swifter than words. And your thoughts are vibrant," Selendis replied. "You were more eloquent than I—or many others—expected."

"Well, I guess that's good," Rosemary replied.

Artanis leaned forward a little, his bright eyes on Rosemary. "A preserver is precious to us," he said. "All of us. Even the dark templar can appreciate the knowledge she houses. We are a people still reeling from what transpired four years past. A preserver in our midst now could only be a boon."

"Wait—don't you have preservers here?" Rosemary blurted.

"They were ever rare," said Urun. Rosemary turned to look at the martial leader of the Auriga. "When the zerg overran our world, much was lost. Millions of protoss died. Doubtless, among them were preservers. Some may have been killed when the Conclave was destroyed. Others are likely scattered. Do you think that every protoss in the universe is gathered here on Shakuras now, Rosemary Dahl?"

She realized she had been thinking precisely that. "So you don't know where the other preservers are?"

Artanis shook his head sadly. "Always, there was at least one with the Conclave. To have one by my side now would be invaluable."

"Zamara died fleeing Ulrezaj's assassins," Rosemary said heatedly. "That her essence is even around at all is sheer good luck and entirely due to Jake. She said she was one of the last. What if Ulrezaj got to all the others?"

She paused, and looked around the vast chamber.

"Good God, people—*What if she's the last one?*"

CHAPTER 14

THE HORROR THAT RIPPLED THROUGH THE crowd was most satisfactory to Rosemary. Maybe at last she'd gotten their attention.

"Do not grow insolent, human," Selendis warned.

"Listen," Rosemary said, forging forward, "I know you all don't want zerg here, or Ulrezaj, or anyone else who might cause harm to the protoss. I fought the zerg myself. I know what they are. I saw what they did to your world. But you *have* to find Zamara. She knows too much that can help you right now for you not to. And—I would ask you—to help Jake. It's because of him that Zamara's survived this long. He's earned your help."

Some of them were leaning toward her side, though for their own reasons. Urun—he was burning to take the fight to Aiur, just as Rosemary knew Selendis was. Artanis struck her as someone who could appreciate the power of ancient knowledge, as well as such an important link with the past. Too, he had met this Jim Raynor, and she sensed from him a liking toward her people. Tabrenus seemed almost disinterested; he represented a group of artisans and craftsmen, not politicians. Zekrath of the Shelak was utterly inscrutable to her, and there was something about the Ara and their leader that chilled her on some level she couldn't quite articulate.

As for Mohandar, he was as unreadable as Zekrath. She didn't expect aid from that quarter—it had been made clear to her that dark templar couldn't have preservers, because they chose to separate themselves from the Khala. Likely as not, this guy might even be against them as a symbol of the "bad old Aiur" they sought to disconnect themselves from. And yet he was eyeing her steadily. She faced forward to Artanis, trying not to feel her skin crawl under that unblinking gaze.

"Vartanil," Artanis said, "Your thoughts are welcome here. You stand by this human, and support her request to seek Zamara and the being who houses her. Speak now of this . . . and of the nightmare that is our old enemy Ulrezaj."

Both Vartanil and Rosemary started at that. "Whoa, wait a minute . . . you all already know about Ulrezaj?" yelped Rosemary.

"We do indeed," Artanis answered, his thoughts grimmer than any she had yet sensed from him. "Shortly after we scoured the zerg from Shakuras, we encountered him for the first time. He was not nearly as strong then. From what you have told us, he now has the unheard-of power of seven dark templar assassins."

"So Zamara told us," Vartanil replied.

"He attempted to attack Shakuras by positioning an orbital space station that emitted powerful energy waves. They disrupted our communication and drained Shakuras's energy shields. Zeratul, a friend to the Aiur protoss and the one who offered us sanctuary on Shakuras, tried to convince Ulrezaj that old hatreds were best laid aside. But by then, Ulrezaj had already merged with three other protoss and had become the most powerful dark archon the dark templar had ever known."

Rosemary snorted. "Four . . . you guys had it easy."

"So it seems," Artanis acknowledged. "And that is grievous knowledge. Unfortunately, at the end, he eluded us. And now we know where he has been hiding, and at least some of what he has been doing."

Rosemary became aware that her mouth was hanging open and closed it with a snap.

"This monster . . . our Benefactor," Vartanil said, his heart sick. "Attacking his own people, in a time of war . . . how could we have been so misled?"

"Do not berate yourself one moment longer," said Artanis kindly. "Ulrezaj was clever and strong enough to escape us when he was but four dark templar. That he was clever enough to create the Sundrop and dupe those who remained on Aiur when he had the brilliance and power of seven beings in him, is no surprise. Once the zerg overran our beloved Aiur, we again permitted dark archons to be created. They are devastating weapons, certainly. Their wildness and uncontrollability was the price paid for the damage they caused our foes. But ordinary dark archons do not exist for long. They do not become what this Ulrezaj has. To learn that he has grown yet more powerful is horrifying—what dark knowledge has he obtained, and from whence, that he is able to continue and not be ripped apart by the very power that made him?"

Rosemary couldn't help it; she turned to look at Mohandar, and as she did so, she knew others were as well. The ancient being who represented the dark templar in this assembly seemed completely unruffled by the scrutiny. There was still fear of the dark templar, the shadow hunters, old and stubborn, lurking in the back of many minds here.

Artanis shook his head. "No, Vartanil. Be at peace. All that truly matters is that once you understood what he was, you had the strength of will to forsake him."

Vartanil nodded slowly. "Rosemary was the first of anyone to break free of the Sundrop. She has proven herself to me, and Jacob Ramsey should be remembered in protoss history as one of the greatest allies we have ever had."

Rosemary's eyes widened a little at that.

Artanis's indecision was palpable. On the one hand, a preserver was a rare treasure. On the other hand, in the end she was one person, and her fate was tangled up with the dreadfully dangerous dark archon.

Going after her could cost innocent protoss lives. Was it worth it?

"Zamara thought so. She was willing to let an awful lot of people die for this secret she harbors. Some of those people were friends of mine."

And some were friends of Jake's . . . and he loved his friends. Mine were business associates.

"And," she continued, "unless your preservers have a history of being selfish and egotistical to an insane degree, which I don't think is the case, then yeah—I *do* think the risk would be worth it."

"How dare you tell us what to think?" Urun's mental voice cracked like a whip, and Rosemary winced from the pain of it in her head. "You are in no position to demand anything!"

"Peace, Urun," Artanis said, holding up a hand. "The terran female merely states her opinion."

"Which should carry no weight whatsoever in this council," said Nahaan. "There are too many opinions already. We are like beasts trying to pull a vehicle in several different directions. We will get nowhere!"

Someone else had a snappy retort, and Nahaan rose to it, and Rosemary slumped slightly. In a way, Nahaan was right. They would get nowhere, arguing like this.

"Rosemary Dahl, I am so very sorry," Vartanil said in her mind. "We are a people who strive so hard for unity and yet it seems it is forever eluding us."

They'll just send me back to my comfortable cell until they've argued over it some more, Rosemary thought.

She tried to direct her thoughts privately to Vartanil, and had no clue if she'd succeeded. "Jake and Zamara could be dead by then."

"Hierarch! May I address the council?"

Rosemary's dark head whipped up in surprise. That clear, strong mental voice belonged to Selendis. The slender but still powerful protoss stepped forward, moving with a graceful stride toward the human woman. Rosemary wasn't alone in her shock; apparently no one else had expected Selendis to speak.

"Of course, Selendis," said Artanis. Rosemary got a brief hit, quickly smothered, of other protoss not being quite so willing to have the executor share her thoughts.

"I was the first in a position of authority to be informed of the human's arrival, along with the other evacuees of our homeworld," Selendis began. "I have never attempted to hide my feelings; on the contrary I am proud of them. None here assembled can question my devotion to my people, nor my desire to fight and protect them."

Her gaze swept the hall, almost as if daring anyone to challenge her. No one did.

"It is said that nothing can be forever hidden, if it wishes to be found; that lessons not learned the first time they appear will come again until we accept them. So it is with this situation now. The lesson craves to be understood and embraced; and the secret once unspoken strains to be shared. Those who knew it kept their silence, truly believing that it would serve nothing and harm much to speak of it. At the time, that might have been true—but no longer. Hierarch, I will tell them."

Everyone in the room strained forward. Mental murmurs of surprise pattered softly on Rosemary's brain. She'd already had a profound shock in discovering that the Hierarchy, at least, knew about Ulrezaj and she braced herself for another. What kind of bomb was Selendis about to drop?

Judging from Artanis's reaction and the sudden stillness that meant they were communicating privately, it was a big one. Artanis sat back, looking unhappy but resigned, and Selendis turned to address the hall.

"The attack on Shakuras," she said solemnly, "was not the first time we had encountered Ulrezaj. We found him and his cohorts shortly before then . . . when we sent a small fleet of protoss on a rescue mission to Aiur."

Rosemary gritted her teeth and clutched her head at the mental pain this revelation caused.

"You knew there were survivors on Aiur?"

"Why did we not send a larger fleet?"

"So many could have been saved!"

Selendis held up a hand. "We were investigating what we thought was a slim chance to recover a handful of individuals," she said. "We came expecting to find only the three templar who had survived because they were in stasis cells. When we saw the reality on Aiur . . ."

"Zeratul and I agreed that it would serve us nothing to mount a larger rescue mission," Artanis interrupted. Selendis turned to him. "In the end, it was my decision, Selendis. To not rescue our brethren . . . and to keep word of it silent."

Rosemary stared. "Why, you heartless—"

Urun let out a mental roar so intense Rosemary almost passed out. Vartanil reached to steady her, doing what he could to shield her from the telepathic bombardment, even though he himself was reeling from the news that he could have been rescued four years ago.

"Our people are *dying* there!" Urun thundered. "You have told us that we did not have the strength to fight the zerg, to recover our world. . . . You let us believe that there were no survivors to save!"

"We expected only to find those who had been in the stasis cells," Artanis repeated. "We were shocked and stunned to discover more had survived on the planet. And yet even while we were there, we could see that the zerg were still rampaging across Aiur, overwhelming them . . . slaughtering even as we watched, too few in number to save them. Even if we had sent a rescue mission, we had no reason to believe that by the time it reached Aiur, there would be anyone left to rescue."

"It is true," said Vartanil unexpectedly. All eyes turned to him. "No one could have known that the zerg would stop targeting us. . . . No one could have known that we would find a Benefactor." He lifted his head and looked at Artanis.

"To discover that there were so many left, and that they had endured so much these four years—I do not think there is one among us who was unmoved by that. Particularly those of us who had known some survived, and believed you to simply be walking dead," said Selendis. Her emotion was obvious.

Vartanil nodded. "I . . . understand your decision, Hierarch."

Others still did not, Urun among them, but they could not continue protesting when Vartanil, the one among them most wronged by the choice, was willing to forgive.

Artanis rose and bowed deeply to the young Furinax, who suddenly looked rather endearingly embarrassed.

"We must focus on the present, for the past cannot be changed," Selendis said. "Though I greatly wish it could be. Ulrezaj has resurfaced, to prey upon the remnants of those left behind on Aiur. But to what end? And what does he want with a preserver? What does she know that has shaken so vastly powerful a being? Our only clue so far is what Vartanil and Rosemary can tell us. And that, my fellow protoss, is insufficient. It is as clear to me as the stars were when glimpsed from Aiur on a cloudless night what we must do. Ulrezaj may have indeed fallen upon Aiur, under the combined attack of the Dominion, the protoss, and the zerg. Or, he may not have, and he may continue to hunt Zamara and every other protoss down, to silence them forever."

Selendis's eyes glowed fiercely. "We must not let him succeed. He has murdered many protoss, used them for his own unknown ends. Shall we sit idly by and let him do the same to a preserver? Put an end to a line that has existed since the arrival of the xel'naga? Permit that song to be forever silenced, all that knowledge eternally lost?"

That hit home with Zekrath. Out of the corner of her eye, Rosemary saw him physically jerk as if struck. His thoughts, however, were tightly lidded.

"And perhaps worse still—shall we permit a terran male, who did not ask for this burden, and yet who has done all that he could to support the preserver, to die alone and in pain because we are too afraid to go to his aid?"

"The protoss are afraid of nothing!" The angry retort came from Urun, who had actually leaped to his feet and fairly bristled with offense. "You know as well as I that the Auriga have stood and stand ready to mount an assault to reclaim our world." Rosemary had thought he disliked her, but apparently when it came to showing that the protoss, and particularly the Auriga, could kick serious ass, Rosemary and Urun were on the same side. She guessed she'd take it.

"This is not a question of fear or of pride, but of practicality," said Tabrenus. Vartanil, still so very young, gave his tribal leader a wounded look. "Even if we were to agree that this Jacob Ramsey and the preserver he hosts are to be rescued, how would we find them? What horrors would we risk loosing upon this world by opening doors and searching? I admire your courage, Selendis, and your enthusiasm, Urun. And Vartanil, your thoughts shine only with the purest of intentions. But Aiur is in ruins, and Shakuras almost became so, through trusting terrans."

Back to that damn Kerrigan again. Rosemary vowed if she ever met the woman, she'd get in at least one blow that hurt like hell before she went down.

"I agree with Tabrenus," said Nahaan, his mental voice deep. "There is too much at stake. And we only have this human's belief that Zamara's secret is so important. For all we know, Zamara could have gone mad and this entire thing is some insane rambling."

"You did not touch Zamara's mind, as I did," Vartanil blurted. "Otherwise, you would not say such a thing."

Disapproval lowered from almost all the alcoves at Vartanil's outburst.

"Vartanil, you were not in the Khala when you touched Zamara's mind," Tabrenus reminded the younger protoss gently. "You could have been fooled. And humans are not protoss. Rosemary could easily have been duped."

Embarrassment wafted from Vartanil, and even Rosemary, though she was annoyed at the comment, had to concede that Nahaan had a point.

Selendis, however, seemed completely unruffled. "If this were madness, then surely so powerful a being as Ulrezaj would pay it no credence."

Aha! thought Rosemary, almost gleefully. *You tell him, sister.*

Selendis granted Rosemary a brief, baffled thought, then returned her attention to the protoss tribal leaders.

Artanis called for calm, and turned to those who had not yet spoken. "The decision is mine, but I have always striven for unity among our people. Mohandar, Zekrath—do you wish to speak?"

Zekrath inclined his head. "I yield to what our hierarch chooses. There are points to be argued on both sides. The Shelak, in the end, attend to the past, not the present or future."

It was a curious thing to say, though Rosemary suspected it was true, as far as it went. She was a little disappointed; she had thought the Shelak would be more anxious to help something that was so linked to the past.

"Duly noted," Artanis replied. "Mohandar? What say you?"

For a moment, the leader of the Nerazim did not speak. Rosemary felt her brain all but being bored into, her thoughts analyzed, sifted, then discarded. She had to admit, that if this guy was a typical example of the dark templar, she could understand why they unnerved the Aiur protoss.

"Curiously enough, I agree with my esteemed colleague Zekrath," said Mohandar. "I would know what the hierarch would do."

Selendis was silent, but her gaze was locked with

that of Artanis. Rosemary knew that she was the hierarch's protégée and as such might be expected to be
shown a bit of favoritism. But Rosemary also got the
feeling that although it was clear that Artanis was
fond of, and proud of, his pupil, he was also smarter
than to let his personal feelings get in the way of so
important a decision.

Artanis lifted his gaze from Selendis to Rosemary.
She felt his thoughts, for her alone.

"Rosemary Dahl, Selendis, whose judgment I have
learned to respect, sides openly with your cause. Let
me ask you this, and I will know if the answer comes
from your heart or your head: Do you truly believe
that this quest is worth the deaths of more of my people? For such I fear it may come to."

She couldn't shut out her personal feelings for
Jake, and didn't even bother. She wanted him back,
alive, happy, wanted to hear that unique combination
of brilliance and goofiness that was his alone as he
spoke and thought and acted. So she let Artanis see
all that, and then let him see the urgency in Zamara's
words. The single-mindedness of Ulrezaj, who was
somehow bound up in all this. And what he'd done
to the Forged.

Artanis nodded, once, and respectfully withdrew.
He got to his feet. "I have listened to all sides. I have
touched this human's mind, and that of young Vartanil.
Even before Rosemary came here today, I had been listening to the evidence gathered by Selendis. After all
this, it is my decision that we do everything we can to

locate and retrieve the terran, Jacob Jefferson Ramsey, and Zamara, the preserver."

Rosemary closed her eyes and almost sagged in relief.

"Further, we shall immediately attempt to extract Zamara from Jacob's mind, so that what she knows may be safely kept, and that he may survive once he is no longer carrying her. We will do all in our power to save them both."

It had to be exhaustion that stung Rosemary's eyes at this announcement. She blinked hard and glanced over at Selendis.

"Thanks," she said.

"I did not do it for you," Selendis replied. "I did it because I believe it is what is best for the protoss." She hesitated. "Nonetheless, if we can indeed save your friend who has endured so much for our people . . . That is good."

"Rosemary, I am so very pleased!" It was Vartanil, and his delight was palpable. "Your truth was heard today. Surely we will recover Jacob and Zamara quickly now that all understand how important it is!"

Rosemary smiled and impulsively squeezed Vartanil's arm. She was glad someone was enthusiastic about this. While she was pleased that the decision had been made in her favor, there still remained the problem—how were they going to find him?

"That is the challenge," Artanis said in response to her unvoiced question. "I will speak with those who attended the gate when you came through. We will see if there is a record of where Jacob was sent."

"Even if that is the case, we may not find him there," Selendis warned. "He and Zamara may have left whatever world they ended up on, in an effort to continue their quest. They may well be trying on their own to link up with dark templar, to extract Zamara's essence from Jacob's mind. The need seems to be immediate, rather than something that can be delayed indefinitely."

Damn right, Rosemary thought fiercely. "We need to move soon."

Those who had opposed the idea were now silent, settled in their chairs, cloaked in their displeasure like something physical. But thankfully it didn't look as though they were going to undermine the attempt.

"Perhaps those left on Aiur had some idea of where Zamara wished to go," said Urun. "We could send our forces there and rescue those who yet remain."

"Urun," said Selendis, bowing deeply, "if only it were that easy. But you will recall that Zamara wanted to come here—and that if anyone knew of a secondary place where she intended to go, it would doubtless be Rosemary Dahl rather than one of our people. If she does not know, they would not."

"Then perhaps Jacob Ramsey is still on Aiur, awaiting rescue," Urun persisted. Rosemary felt for him. She'd seen what Aiur was like, had heard about what it had been before. Urun and others would take any excuse to return and try to heal that wound. She felt Selendis yearning to agree with him, but the executor gave the protoss equivalent of a sigh as she spoke.

"He was redirected. We have confirmed that much. I suppose the best place to start is to determine where they went, and from there . . . make our best guess."

Selendis didn't like guessing. Selendis liked facts, things that were concrete, things that one could move on immediately. Despite their clash, Rosemary found herself realizing she and the executor had a lot in common.

"And what might that be?" asked Nahaan. "I think I need not explain to you, Executor, that every gate opens onto every other gate, unless it is blocked."

That was for my benefit. Got it, bud.

"There are thousands of worlds this Jacob might have fled to, and each place is vast. It could take us months—years—to find him, and waste valuable resources doing so. Hierarch, you need a better plan than this!"

This guy really seemed to enjoy pushing Artanis's buttons. If Urun had his own agenda, then clearly all the others did too. Urun simply seemed less inclined to hide his—and why should he? It was a noble one. Rosemary wasn't so sure about Nahaan's. Come to think of it, she wasn't sure about anyone's except for her own. And maybe Selendis's. Maybe.

As if on cue, Selendis spoke. "It is indeed a daunting task, but when have the protoss ever shirked such?" She turned to Artanis and to Rosemary's surprise, knelt. "With the hierarch's permission, and that of the Hierarchy, I will lead the search for Jacob Jefferson Ramsey and Zamara."

Artanis blinked. "I—yes. I trust you as I trust myself, Executor, and you have earned the respect of all here."

Rosemary realized that was true. Even those who were clearly opposing Artanis and the plan did not raise objections.

Selendis rose and nodded. "I will begin by determining where the human and the preserver went first. After that, I will begin winnowing down our options. I will try to think like a preserver—a daunting task, no doubt, but I will do my best. Rosemary will doubtless be able to assist me in this, as she knows both Jacob and Zamara."

"I believe," came the raspy mental voice of the ancient Mohandar, "I can save you a little time, Executor."

Startled, Rosemary turned to the dark templar. His eyes crinkled slightly, and she realized he was amused.

"I think I know exactly where Zamara wishes to go. And I can tell you how to get there."

CHAPTER 15

ULREZAJ WAS MORE THAN FLESH NOW. HE WAS energy, powerful and strong, unable to be wounded by such simple things as bullets or spears. But other creations of energy, mental or physical, could and had wounded him. And had done so more severely than he had anticipated.

He had come close to victory over Shakuras, over the despised Aiur protoss and the inexplicably passive dark templar he had once called his "people." He could not fathom why they had embraced the very beings who would have slain them, who drove them to exile. Zeratul—once a brother, now a more despised foe than even the weakling hierarch they had put in charge. He expected the Aiur protoss to be dishonorable and vile; he had not expected so respected a dark templar as Prelate Zeratul to be a traitor.

They had come to embattled Aiur, to rescue so-called "heroes." Ulrezaj and his allies had slain two of the three, but had been captured. But Ulrezaj had had allies; and Ulrezaj had had plans upon plans. He had escaped, taking with him a precious khaydarin crystal, creating five twisted copies of it. He had used ancient knowledge to become not just a dark archon, but the mightiest dark archon the universe had seen by combining his essence with those of his three comrades. He had taken the fight and the five warped crystals to Shakuras, where he planned to use an extraordinarily powerful electromagnetic pulse generator to create chaos and drive out the despised refugees. Let them know the terror of being hunted; let them perish as they should have on Aiur, ripped to pieces by zerg.

But he had been defeated . . . temporarily. He had withdrawn to the hidden place where he replenished his unheard-of power, and where he thought how best he could retaliate. He had drawn to him others willing to subsume themselves into the glory that was Ulrezaj, in order to be on the side that would eventually triumph.

And so his path had led him back to Aiur. It became clear that the protoss were too cowardly to save their embattled brethren, even though they now did not have the excuse of ignorance. Heartless, pathetic fools. They would turn their back on their homeworld, the world that the dark templar had mourned with their very souls when forced to leave it. Those that were forsaken deserved no kindness.

It had seemed to him so very easy to gather to himself the worried, frightened refugees who had been abandoned on their devastated homeworld. To convince them to follow him, to soothe and control them with the fabricated drug that penetrated their skins and bloodstreams and freed them from the invasiveness of the Khala.

He had not expected them to turn against him, even when confronted with the truth—or at least part of it—of what their benefactor truly was. Curse the terrans. The male, strong enough to bear for at least a while the vastness of what it meant to be a preserver. The female, strong enough to resist the drug and by doing so, demonstrate that it could be done. The ingratitude and betrayal stunned him. He had rescued them, and they had repaid him with hatred, loathing, and rebellion.

Ulrezaj was slightly mollified as he recollected how vastly he had been outnumbered. The onslaught of the Dominion vessels and the zerg, combined with the psionic storms the protoss had somehow pulled themselves together sufficiently to create—there was no shame in retreating from that. Wisdom often necessitated retreat, regrouping, and planning.

But regardless of how he justified it, he had been wounded. Much of his energy had been drained. He might have been able to recover had he been able to rest, even for a few days, in the chambers of the xel'naga. But they had dogged him even there, the zerg; the humans had given up and the protoss had either fled or died where they stood. Like a beast gone to ground unwillingly flushed, Ulrezaj had been forced to run.

The thought galled him.

Even as he maneuvered himself into one of the xel'naga vessels he simmered with resentment. At full strength, he could teleport the distance. But he was weak.

Ulrezaj despised weakness, even in himself.

They were following, and he knew it. Yet they did not attack.

We all wish the preserver, one part of him put forth. *They wish to capture her, to determine what she knows. I wish to destroy her and render her silent.*

They think I know where to find her, and therefore, they follow me, another part concluded.

It was undoubtedly so. And Ulrezaj did know where the preserver would flee. Perhaps not immediately, no, perhaps it would take a while for her and the human she was using to discover their destination.

But Ulrezaj knew. He knew and he would be there when Zamara and Jacob Jefferson Ramsey arrived. He would be the spider, sitting quietly, his web subtle and sensitive and lethal.

Would the zerg that followed him try to kill him upon his arrival? Perhaps. Although he thought their queen wiser than that; for they did not know this was the destination. What if their quarry had come to this place merely to heal? Ah, what then if they slew him before they knew for certain the preserver would come? That would be a fool's choice, and Sarah Kerrigan was no fool.

His followers had pursued Zamara once before.

Had blasted apart a carrier in search of her, had driven her small vessel to crash in a dead xel'naga temple. Their reports had been accurate, so far as they went. They had told him that she was either dead on impact or soon would be; she could not live long on so inhospitable a planet. And they were correct. Zamara, the protoss preserver, had not lived long.

Not in that body at least.

But she had found another body, and like a parasite had attached herself to the first host that had had the misfortune to stumble across her. And so she, and the secret she carried, still existed and could possibly ruin everything.

Ulrezaj would not permit that to happen. Zerg or no, he would travel to the place where he knew she would come. He would rest, and heal, and think.

Zamara had eluded him once. She would not do so again.

All heads turned to the dark templar.

"You do? You can?" The exclamation came from Artanis. Even he, apparently, was startled by this statement. Thus taken by surprise, Artanis inadvertently seemed very young in his reaction.

A dry raspy chuckle came from Mohandar. "We have shared much with our brethren from whom we were separated so long ago. But we dark templar have a thousand years of history separate from you. Not all can be explained or revealed in a mere handful of years. Especially when the present and the future seem more dire than the past."

Rosemary watched him closely, her eyes narrowing. That much was true, yes—but she suspected this canny elder would not play his hand before he had to. She was willing to bet there was a great deal the dark templar still kept to themselves. After all, that was the great lesson, wasn't it—to hide in the shadows, to keep themselves secret and therefore be safe? That, too, wasn't going to change in a mere handful of years.

"Speak now, then," said Selendis. For all her counsel to Rosemary on patience and always having time to do things the right way, she clearly was more than ready to depart. "Where is this place?"

"I said that I believe that I knew where Zamara would wish to go. It is possible though that Zamara herself does not know this. Preservers know a great deal, but it is unlikely she is aware of the existence of this place. This is dark templar knowledge—profound, and powerful, and sacred."

The old bastard's enjoying this, Rosemary realized.

"Yes," came Selendis's private thought, obviously annoyed. "He is."

Mohandar sat back in his chair, surveying the protoss who were all gazing at him with rapt attention. His eyes crinkled in a smile. "When we were cast out of Aiur, we traveled for centuries. We became nomads, explorers, finding and investigating many worlds. Some we stayed on only temporarily. Others, we built structures upon, and they became anchors of a sort. But nothing permanent. Nothing we could truly feel in our souls as home, until we found Shakuras and its temple.

"The site I mention, though, is still an important place to my people. It is called the Alys'aril, the Sanctuary of Wisdom. The little moon upon which it was built is called Ehlna. It means 'Haven' in our language," he added for Rosemary's benefit. "It was one of the first places we settled, and we stayed there for well over a century before we decided to move on. Still, it was not abandoned. It could never be abandoned. Many stayed behind, to tend the Sanctuary of Wisdom. And to this day, those of us who left to find our true home return there on pilgrimage toward the end of our days, if such a thing is at all possible."

Like creatures that returned to the place they were born to reproduce—or die, Rosemary thought. But why? Just for nostalgia's sake?

"There is a nexus of energy there that alters the khaydarin crystals," Mohandar continued. "I will not say 'refines' them, for that is not truly accurate. I think even our terran friend here knows that the crystals serve us in many ways. They can calm us, channel and focus our energies. We even use them in our technology. One use of the crystals is data storage. The energies on Ehlna render them uniquely fit for this specific task, less so for others." Mohandar turned and looked squarely at Rosemary. "Therefore, it is a library of the greatest sort. A collection of as much knowledge as the dark templar can assemble—taken from the very minds and memories of our people to be recorded forever."

Rosemary gasped. "Yeah, that would be where Zamara would want to go all right," she agreed. "She knew you guys had the ability to do something like this, but she had to find a dark templar to find out where. That's why she wanted to come to Shakuras."

"Friend Mohandar," said Artanis reproachfully, "why have you not told us of such a place as this before?"

"Friend Artanis," replied Mohandar, not using Artanis's formal title, "you had no need of such information. After all, your people have preservers. You have living embodiments of memories who advised your Conclave. We dark templar utilize a technological substitute—one that maintains our individuality. Why would we need to tell you of our Sanctuary of Wisdom when such 'sanctuaries' walked among you?"

A good enough explanation, but Rosemary realized—as did everyone present—that the leader of the Nerazim was cannier than this simple, self-effacing explanation would convey him as. He didn't tell because he had had an ace in the hole. But now the need had arisen, and he had revealed the existence of this place.

"The tenders of this place, the Keepers of Wisdom, will likely be able to assist Jacob and Zamara with the process of transferring Zamara's essence to a crystal.

Rosemary, you spoke of a crystal that you and Jacob found in the chambers beneath the surface of Aiur?"

Rosemary nodded, sensing a renewal of interest in her from Zekrath and also from Selendis. "Yeah. Zamara seemed to think we'd need that crystal."

"She may find all that she needs at the Alys'aril, but perhaps not. The alysaar are trained to extract memories from ordinary dark templar, one at a time. We keep them in the Chalice of Memories. A preserver, however, has literally billions of memories. Perhaps Zamara was wise to bring a crystal from so powerful and ancient a place. Regardless, eventually her path will lead her and Jacob there. I am surprised she even knew about our abilities to do this thing."

"She's a preserver," Rosemary said. "She knows a lot."

"Mohandar, I am deeply grateful you have chosen to tell us of this place," said Selendis. "Otherwise I fear we would not have been in time. We can only hope that Zamara learns of its existence as well. In the meantime I will travel there with Rosemary and see if the preserver awaits us. If she does not, we will have to take other measures to—"

"No." Mohandar's blunt response silenced Selendis in midthought. "It is a sacred place to the dark templar. We alone will travel there."

Ah, crap, thought Rosemary. *We were finally going to do it and now it's going to get all tied up in the "who gets to go" issue.* She didn't bother to even try to censor her thoughts. She'd had it about up to here with protoss red tape and chafed for action.

"The Shelak have long tended the things of the Wanderers from Afar," murmured Zekrath. "And yet we share them with all protoss—even your tribe, shadow hunter."

Mohandar's eyes flashed. Rosemary had sudden confirmation, as if there was any doubt, that this ancient being was far from nonthreatening.

"The xel'naga created us all, Zekrath. All protoss, including the dark templar. To forbid any of us entry to such things would be indefensible and foolish. But this is not of the xel'naga's doing, or of any Aiur protoss. This place *we* built, we, the exiles, banished from our home that we loved so dearly. It arose from *our* experiences, to serve *our* needs. It is nothing of yours. For me to even speak of it, to encourage a preserver to travel there, to aid her—so much is already a great gesture on our part."

"We understand and appreciate the place this holds in dark templar history," Artanis began.

"I am far from certain that you do," Mohandar replied dryly.

"Then come with us," said Selendis. Rosemary whirled to stare at her. She'd have thought the executor would argue this point. "Come with us, Mohandar. Let this be more than a gesture. Let this be a healing, a new beginning. The knowledge a preserver has can serve us all. You have the ability to keep that knowledge from vanishing. You know full well no one in this hall will reach agreement on this if you insist on being the sole protoss to oversee it. If you truly mean what you say, if you truly wish to aid Zamara and Jacob and bring an end to the malice that is Ulrezaj once and for all, then withdraw your sole claim to this expedition."

Utter mental silence fell in the chamber. Everyone was waiting on Mohandar's reply. There was no way to force his hand; he alone knew where this mysterious library was. Rosemary knew that Selendis was right. There was no way in hell this council would agree to let this be handled as a dark templar matter. Mohandar was no fool, he had to know this too.

Mohandar was still for a long time, his thoughts sealed away from them. Finally his eyes half-closed and his shoulders hunched in amusement.

"Well played, Executor. Well played indeed. All right. I would ask you to remember that this place is very important to us. I will tolerate no disrespect."

Selendis stood utterly straight. "My templar will be so informed. There will be no disrespect."

Mohandar turned his gaze to Rosemary, and his thoughts were for her alone.

"I have little love for your people, terran. If I could exclude you, I would. But it appears that you are inextricably involved in this situation. Know this—you may be leaving Shakuras, but you are still being evaluated by the protoss. Your actions may confirm our opinion of terran females as established by Kerrigan, or give us pause for thought."

"Yeah, I've figured that one out by now," Rosemary retorted. "Let's just get this show on the road, shall we?"

Anger, irritation, and amusement all vied within Mohandar for a moment, then he withdrew from her mind.

"It is agreed then," said Artanis. "Selendis may choose whatever templar she sees fit to accompany her. Rosemary, you will yet be of help, I think. Mohandar, we will take whomever you appoint to represent you in this matter. I—"

Vartanil flung himself on his knees before the hierarch. "Artanis, I beg you, permit me to attend as well!"

Artanis blinked. "You have already endured much, Vartanil. Surely you would prefer to remain here, to find friends and family and recover from your ordeal."

"I have grown to respect not only Zamara but the humans she has deemed worthy to accompany her," Vartanil said. "I have done much harm under the influence of Ulrezaj, our enemy. I was his tool. I would redeem myself by acting now for the right cause. Hierarch—I gave my word to Rosemary that I would not leave her side until Jacob and Zamara had been safely recovered. You would not have me be forsworn?"

Artanis was at a loss and looked at Selendis. Both templar were still for a moment, and Rosemary realized that a private conversation was taking place. Finally Artanis nodded.

"Very well. You will have a chance for your redemption. Your desire for such does you credit. But you must swear to obey the executor. Your fondness for the humans must not override your loyalty as a protoss."

Vartanil got to his feet, his eyes shining, his body straight and tall. Rosemary thought that at this moment he looked every bit as noble as any of the templar she'd seen.

"The two are not in opposition. You will see. Serving one serves the other. But yes, Hierarch, I do swear."

"Then go. Make haste. Executor Selendis, while your group ventures forth to Ehlna and the Alys'aril, others will be investigating other worlds. We will prepare for the arrival of the preserver."

Selendis bowed deeply, respectfully. "It shall be done. *En taro Tassadar*, Hierarch."

"*En taro Tassadar*, Executor."

And heaven help us all, added Rosemary. They were going to need it.

CHAPTER 16

JAKE MUNCHED ON SOME FRUIT AND THOUGHT longingly of a steak. He sighed when he realized he was also thinking longingly of rations.

When do we go back to Zeratul? he asked.

. . . We do not.

What? What do you mean?

He will either come to us now, or else we depart. We have pushed him as far as we can.

Jake bit his lower lip. *I went too far, huh?*

So I thought, at first. But perhaps it is what he needed. Zeratul carries more than one burden of guilt, of bringing tremendous harm to those he only sought to protect. Compassion is necessary, yes. But we do not have the luxury of days or months for him to heal from this. He must decide to join us, or we must press on.

Press on to where?

She was silent within him. Her stalwart spirit was close to despair. It rattled Jake and upset him more than he would have thought, and he was desperate to comfort her. More than just his life was at stake here, and Zamara had always been rock-solid.

He's not the only dark templar, Zamara.

We cannot go to Shakuras. He is the only dark templar I know of who is not on that world.

But . . . well . . . the protoss are on a lot of different worlds, aren't they?

The protoss of Aiur are not the protoss who were banished from Aiur. The dark templar, to the best of my knowledge, stayed together. I knew of only two sources. One is closed to me by technology; the other has closed himself to me by choice.

Then we just go. We go somewhere that sounds logical and we eliminate places one by one.

Humor that was painful and sad moved through him. *Jacob, there are quite literally hundreds of worlds. And each world is wide.*

"Needle in a haystack," Jake muttered. "I understand."

She sent back a thought of utter bafflement until he explained the reference. Jake finished the fruit and tossed the rind and core into the little pool. He buried his face in his hands for a moment.

"Even if it is a needle in a haystack," he muttered, "we can't give up. We'll just keep trying, and trying, and if we fall down, we'll get back up."

"That," came a thought that was not Zamara's, "is the lesson of the humans."

Startled, Jake looked up. He saw nothing. He got to his feet, looking around. The mental voice belonged to Zeratul, but where was he?

And then, right where Jake was staring, something

shifted. A ripple, a blur, then again nothing. And then there, over in the shadow of the large tree, there was a darker shadow, and then there was Zeratul.

Jake realized with a start that he had seen this before—he knew what to look for. His mind went back to the memories Zamara had shared with him: "The fugitives need to be able to cover themselves. To . . . hide," Adun had said.

And Raszagal's promise: "We will put our knowledge toward keeping ourselves safe. To merging with the shadows, unseen." And later, "We have studied hard, as I told you we would. Now we can bend light to hide ourselves."

"*Adun toridas,*" Jake whispered. Zeratul nodded.

"We learn, we dark templar. It is what has kept us alive," he said quietly. "We learned much when we were on Aiur, and we never forgot who we were. We learned from Adun that shadow and light are illusions, and how to clothe ourselves in them so that others see what we wish them to see. We learned from the cold darkness of the very Void itself knowledge and skills that we have mastered, skills that enabled us to work against the zerg in a way that other protoss could not. We learned from the zerg and their queen the price of trust too lightly given."

He stepped forward. Jake found him an imposing figure, dark and green and powerful in a way that the Aiur protoss, straight, gleaming, and sunlit beings that they were, were not. But there was nothing to fear from Zeratul. He knew that. There never had been, not even in the moments of his blackest despair or his hottest rage. And now there was a calmness about Zeratul that eased the tension in Jake's chest as the protoss drew within three feet of him.

Zeratul bowed. Deeply. Jake blinked. The gesture wasn't meant for Zamara—it was meant for him.

"From the humans, I have learned that it is possible to be willing to die for others. Others who are not friends, as might be expected, nor even of one's own race. James Raynor was willing to die to protect Shakuras from the zerg. He knew he would be stranded on the deadly side of the gate, and yet he willingly undertook that risk. And you stand here, Jacob Jefferson Ramsey, bearing Zamara. You do not even know her secret, yet I have touched your mind, and if it came to it, you, too, would give your very life for it."

He shook his head, and two emotions brushed Jake: hope . . . and shame.

"You were correct. I do not serve my people by retreating to this pleasant place, to nurse my wounds and indulge my guilt. To brood helps nothing and may indeed invite harm to the very people I have sworn to protect. I must not give up, not even in the face of utter despair. Not even against odds so dreadful I tremble to think of them, or beings so powerful and alien to me that I am but an insect to be squashed. As you said, I must just keep trying, and trying, and if I fall down—why then, I get back up. I am not proud that it took a human to teach me such an important lesson. But I am glad that at least I am not too old to have learned it."

Jake didn't know what to say, so he said nothing. But a smile stretched his face, and hope rekindled inside him.

"Humans are a remarkable race, though still young," Zamara said. "I, too, have learned from Jacob. And it has become important to me that he survive."

Zeratul nodded, then squared his shoulders. "I have heard you speak of your death, Zamara," he said. "And you and Jake now know of the burdens I carry that caused me to shirk my duties to the protoss people. I am ready to shoulder those burdens again. We began with a story. I would hear more of it. But before you speak of Ulrezaj, let me tell you what I know of him."

Jake listened attentively, for he realized that even he didn't know everything that Zamara did about Ulrezaj. Zeratul told him about the first time he and Ulrezaj had met. Under Zeratul's command, a handful of ships had landed on Aiur, investigating a rumor that three particularly powerful individuals survived in stasis cells.

"And of course, once we reached orbit, we realized how many were still alive on Aiur itself. That revelation, and my agreement to stay silent about it, is yet another burden of guilt I carry," Zeratul said heavily as the story unfolded. "We three—Selendis, Artanis, and I—decided that it was wiser to not plant false hope. We assumed, given how the zerg were rampaging across the surface of Aiur, that by the time a rescue mission of sufficient strength could be mounted, there would be no one left on Aiur to save."

Jake nodded slowly. "I remember that the protoss themselves were surprised when the targeted slaughter just stopped," he said. He felt pity for Zeratul. The guy had a lot to handle.

The dark templar prelate continued. "Ulrezaj and his followers attacked, destroying two of the three stasis cells and the templar within them. He was physically a dark templar then, one of the deadliest in our history. I know not how he learned to merge with more than one other, nor how he continues to exist. The dark archons are powerful weapons, but until Ulrezaj, they were finite beings. He must have some source of energy to replenish himself, and to continue to bring more dark templar into his madness."

"Maybe it was something he learned from the chambers," Jake offered. "Some long-forgotten xel'naga technology. If he was on Aiur's moon, maybe he'd already begun exploring the caverns."

"That is a likely theory. But how he learned this does not matter. What matters is that Zamara knows something he wishes kept hidden. And I believe that it is time she shares this with us."

Jake was barely breathing. Finally, he was going to learn what Darius and Kendra and Teresa and all his other friends had died for. What Ulrezaj was willing to kill for; what he, Jacob Jefferson Ramsey, might still die for.

Zamara was silent for a time, then began to speak, her mental voice soft but intense. "We know already that the xel'naga shaped and altered us, encouraging certain aspects of our development. And we know that the zerg were also . . . experiments of the xel'naga. At least," she amended, "those are the terms we have always used before. In all the memories I bear, I have learned the truth of the situation—a truth that has been shared with only a select handful throughout our long history."

Puzzle master that he was, few things excited Jake more than a mystery, and he knew from the tenor of Zamara's thoughts that he was on to a humdinger of one. Zeratul as well leaned forward eagerly, giving his catlike protoss curiosity free reign now that he had broken the shackles of his self-imposed guilt.

"We thought we and the zerg were experiments— perhaps trial and error. We thought that we were flawed in some way, and that is why we were abandoned. But the truth is, the xel'naga were simply done with us. They needed a second species . . . the zerg. This was no trial-and-error experimentation. The xel'naga knew exactly what they were doing. They had done this uncountable times before, throughout millennia so numerous our minds can barely stretch to comprehend it. They were not *inventing* us; they were *preparing* us."

"Preparing us for what?"

"For themselves."

Jake frowned. "I don't get it."

"Nothing lasts forever, Jacob. Not even the xel'naga. At least—not in that incarnation."

Zeratul's eyes widened. "Hosts," he said. "They were preparing host bodies!"

"Less crude than that, my old friend. The xel'naga have a cyclical lifestyle. Their lives are almost unfathomably long as we reckon such things, but they are finite beings. When the time comes that their existence is to end, they seek out two other species. Over time, they manipulate and alter these species so that they, separately, form two halves of a whole. They seek purity—purity of form, purity of essence. This time, they chose the protoss and the zerg."

Jake ran a trembling hand through his hair. "They . . . are going to destroy you?"

"No. Not destroy. Simply place two aspects of their essences into our people and the zerg. And again, over time so vast that we can barely grasp it, we would change and evolve . . . and come together again, naturally, harmoniously, and the xel'naga would be reborn."

Gooseflesh prickled Jake's arms as he listened, despite the balminess of the day. "The chambers," he breathed. "That's where they worked on the protoss."

"They were not entirely selfless protectors, as was first thought before the Aeon of Strife, certainly," Zamara said. Beside Jake, Zeratul sat still and silent, listening, absorbing. "But neither were they monsters. They wanted us to become great and glorious. They would not suddenly descend, to possess our bodies; rather we would evolve so that we . . . became them."

Zamara floundered. "It is even less invasive than that. Forgive me. . . . The concept is difficult to explain or even for minds that are as limited as ours to grasp. And since I cannot link with either of you in the Khala, I cannot fully share my understanding of it exactly. What I can say is this; it is a cycle that is as natural to them as breathing is to you, Jacob, or as gathering nutrients is to us, Zeratul. It has existed for so long and has shaped so much of the cosmos that it is, perhaps, as natural and right a thing, universally, as life and death, the spin of planets, and the formation and cessation of stars. I do not know that I can say it is wrong."

"You are more forgiving than I," said Zeratul, shock and anger simmering beneath his calm surface. "I cannot help but wonder if I, too, have glimpsed some part of this—this directed evolution in progress. This, then, is your secret?"

"Partially. But as I say, I do not think the rebirth of the xel'naga will be harmful to us. It is not how it was intended."

"If it is so much a part of the order of the cosmos then," said Zeratul, "why should we be concerned?"

"What I have told you is the way things had always unfolded before," said Zamara. "Had it been permitted to continue uninterrupted, I am not even sure the protoss as we are now would have been harmed. But this time, something went very wrong. The xel'naga were eliminated before they had completed their preparations by their own creations—the zerg. Their careful plans—eons in the unfolding—were thrown into turmoil. Zeratul . . . you have seen what has arisen in the vacuum."

Zeratul nodded slowly. "Although I freely admit that I was bowed down with the weight of my guilt, that is not the sole reason why I have not returned to Shakuras. It is because I glimpsed something at once so perplexing and so abhorrent that my mind reeled from it. I came here to try to make sense of something utterly senseless . . . but now I believe that I can grasp some of it."

Zeratul spoke then, in his calm mental voice, of investigating protoss power signatures emanating from a dark moon. "It was shortly after Raszagal's death," he said. "We had no records of a protoss settlement in that quadrant. What we found . . ."

Jake wished he could simply link up with Zeratul's mind the way he could with Zamara's, but it was not possible. Zeratul was his own self, not entwined with Jake's mind as Zamara was, and he realized how cumbersome simple speaking could be. Though even if he could connect so intimately with Zeratul, Jake got the impression that the prelate would rather keep this particular story as unemotional and distant as possible.

Which, of course, was even more unsettling.

"We were surprised to discover a terran settlement, with a protoss pylon powering rather makeshift stasis cells. Our horror and revulsion increased when we realized that there were protoss held captive inside some of these cells, and zerg in yet others. All, zerg and protoss alike, were deep in cryo-hibernation. But the most shocking revelation was that someone was experimenting on our people and the zerg." He looked at Jake levelly. "They were experimenting with their DNA . . . splicing together zerg and protoss genes to create hybrids so foul and revolting that even now, I can barely speak of it calmly."

Indeed, Zeratul's body was trembling perceptibly. Not with fear—with outrage. Jake didn't blame him one damn bit. His mind went back to the images of the desiccated bodies in the chambers beneath Aiur, the ones he'd seen with his own eyes, and the ones Temlaa had seen. And then he thought of the mysterious, inky-black vats and the horrible feeling he'd gotten from them—a feeling so intense Zamara had had to erect a barrier to protect him.

His stomach churned. "Those . . . whatever they were . . . that's the new xel'naga? A genetic combination of protoss and zerg?"

"No," Zamara answered swiftly, and Jake closed his eyes in relief. "No. Those—things—are truly abominations. There is nothing in them of the natural cycle of the xel'naga. I grieve for the protoss who were so violated. The xel'naga are implacable in their way, but not to that extreme. What you saw, Zeratul, and what perhaps we also beheld in the caverns is something else entirely. Something very wrong, something that should not be."

Zeratul as well seemed somewhat relieved, though still trembling slightly with outrage at what he'd witnessed. "There was a human coordinating this. Or at least something that appeared human. It claimed to have existed for millennia, and gone by many names. The only clue I have of his true identity is the name he chose to reveal to me—Samir Duran."

It meant nothing to Jake, but it clearly did to Zamara. "Duran . . . that was the name of Sarah Kerrigan's consort."

"Wait, whoa, I thought Ethan was her consort?" Jake asked, confused.

"He left Kerrigan," Zeratul responded. "Duran claimed to be superior to her, a servant of a far greater power."

Jake tried to take this all in. Somehow, according to xel'naga physiology, zerg and protoss were to be combined. But the hybrid that Zeratul had seen wasn't that.

That meant it had to be someone else. And *that* meant . . .

"Someone has got the arrogance—or the stupidity—to try to mess with the xel'naga," Jake breathed. "And if they succeed—"

"The xel'naga will not be reborn. Instead, a monstrous and powerful perversion of both protoss and zerg will be set loose upon the universe, and all that we know and cherish will fall in their wake."

CHAPTER 17

THEY WERE DIRE WORDS, EXTREME WORDS, BUT Jake felt they barely scratched the surface. Zeratul had been almost motionless, save for his furious trembling. Now he unfolded himself from his squatting position so quickly it startled Jake.

"We have lingered here long enough. We have told the stories that need telling. It is time for action. We do not know who or what is behind these events; but we know that Ulrezaj and Samir Duran are involved to some degree." He turned his glowing eyes to Jake, speaking to both him and Zamara. "Our prophecy states that the Twilight Deliverer's reappearance heralds a great crisis. A time when things that seem to be in opposition must join together if we are to triumph. We saw it in Adun—the first to use the energies of both Aiur protoss and dark templar to protect the dark templar and save the Aiur protoss from making a tragic error from which they could never recover. We saw it in Tassadar, when he began to listen to me and what I had to teach. No teacher has ever been prouder of his pupil than I of him. And he taught me much as well. Things that until recently, I have forgotten."

A hint of Zeratul's shame brushed Jake again, but there was no self-pity, just acknowledgment, acceptance, and the resolve to move forward.

"I thought the prophecy fulfilled when Tassadar brought us together—when we joined to fight the zerg and do what we could to save our people. He sacrificed himself to destroy the Overmind. And yet, this crisis that faces us now is even more atrocious, more abhorrent, than losing our homeworld. It could mean losing . . . everything."

His eyes glowed brightly. "I think perhaps the Anakh Su'n has yet one more manifestation before all is said and done. But first, we must take care of you— both of you. There is a place, one of the first settled by the dark templar soon after we were exiled from Aiur. Though we have spent many hundreds of years exploring the Void since we found Ehlna, we have not forgotten it. It is a place of lore and knowledge. Indeed, our term for it, 'Alys'aril,' means Sanctuary of Wisdom."

Zeratul hesitated. "I once considered traveling there myself, on pilgrimage. It is instilled in us that we should do so, as we have no preservers to keep the memories for us."

"I remember, you once spoke of such a method of preserving knowledge among your people, but you did not tell me where," Zamara replied. "That is why I sought you out."

Zeratul nodded. "You have a crystal? From the chambers that lie beneath the surface of Aiur?"

"Yes," Jake answered. "Zamara seemed to think a crystal from there would give us a better chance of success in downloading her knowledge."

"May I see it?"

Jake smiled. "Of course." He fished in his pockets for the precious shard, his hand closing on it gently. Even to him, a non-telepath, it felt powerful. Warm and smooth in his hand, it seemed to have a vibration that was not physical, that one sensed with the soul rather than the body. He knew from experience that the sensation, now pleasant, would increase to the point of discomfort, and he let it drop into Zeratul's outstretched hand. Zeratul's eyes widened the instant it touched his palm. Two thumbs and two fingers closed over the precious item.

"Powerful indeed," he said softly. "I have never felt the like. Not even in the Alys'aril, not even in the Uraj and Khalis crystals. Truly, this is special—I will not say unique, for as you have said, many more crystals exist in those chambers. What a powerful force for good or ill they would be." He peered at the gem, cupping it carefully, reverently. "I am even more distressed to learn that Ulrezaj has commandeered the chambers now that I can sense for myself the power he controls."

Reluctantly, he extended his hand to Jake. "You are the best custodian of this for the moment, Jacob. You would not be tempted to use it, as I would. Save this for yourself—for Zamara."

Jake nodded and slipped the crystal back into his vest.

Zeratul hesitated. "Zamara . . . Jacob. Surely you must be aware that what you ask has never been attempted. We are able to capture memories of ordinary dark templar. A preserver is something else entirely. And to retrieve those memories from a human brain . . . could prove to be impossible. One or the other, or both of you, could die."

"We know," Jake said before Zamara could speak. "But honestly—is there even an option? If I don't get Zamara out of my head, I'm definitely going to die, and if I die, all her memories die with me. There might be a chance to transfer Zamara's memories to another preserver, but it'd be even harder to find one of those than get to Ehlna, especially now that we know Ulrezaj has been trying to kill them all. We've got this," and he patted the crystal in his pocket. "And we've got you. If anyone can convince the Keepers of Wisdom that this is an important task, it's you, Zeratul. I'm willing to take the risk because, hell . . . it beats sitting here and dying on a pink planet."

Zeratul half closed his eyes and hunched his shoulders, laughing.

"Then let us go to Ehlna, where the Keepers of Wisdom will do all they can to preserve a preserver, and save a human life."

Jake had, for some reason, gotten the impression that this was going to be a long journey. But as he rose to join Zeratul and said, "We should probably lay in some supplies—I'm going to need food and water for however long it takes," Zeratul only chuckled.

"If you are hungry, eat now. Otherwise, I am certain food will be found at the Alys'aril for you. Ehlna is not the most congenial of worlds, but it has clean water, and there is life upon it."

"Oh . . . I thought this place was pretty far from here."

"Not via warp gate," Zeratul replied. Jake followed him into his small atmospheric craft and settled in, blushing a little. "Remember, Jacob, the gates are not protoss technology. They are creations of the xel'naga. And there is one on Ehlna. It is why we are still able to return, most of us, on pilgrimage, to have our memories recorded for future generations."

"Those on Aiur could have found you any time they wanted to then."

"Not if they did not know the gate's coordinates. But if they did, yes, they certainly could. And if they ever had, I think my people would have looked on it as an act of destiny."

It was a short trip to the warp gate, and Jake looked out the window at the pink sky and purple-hued landscape. He would miss it. Zeratul had been right—it was a soothing and calming place. Even his headaches had seemed less frequent here. Absently he rubbed his temple, where he realized another monster of a headache was waiting, like a coiled serpent. He bit his lip and willed it back.

Soon, Jacob, this will be over, Zamara said, offering comfort.

One way or another, right?

She chuckled, sadly. *One way or another.*

And three minutes later, right as the small dark templar vessel sped through the gate, the pain hit. And this time, Jake blacked out.

Jake came to to discover himself lying on his back on something cool and hard and looking up at a dark, polished ceiling. It was inlaid with a dazzling display of glowing, singing crystals. They were beautiful, but blurry and wavy. He blinked hard, and then suddenly panicked.

Powerful, nonhuman hands grasped him to steady him, and he flailed, staring wildly at the purple-skinned protoss. Who was this person? Where the hell was he? The caverns beneath Aiur, with Savassan—or in the temple where that dead protoss was—

Jacob. Listen to me. Remember.

The voice in his head terrified him for half a second, and then he remembered. Zamara. He was probably in the ancient library Zeratul had spoken of on . . . Ehlna. The Alys'aril. The protoss sitting over him, keeping vigil while he slept, was Zeratul.

"Are you all right now?" Zeratul asked. Jake nodded shakily. Zeratul released him and sank back on his haunches. Jake closed his eyes for a moment, breathing deeply, and when he opened them again his vision had cleared.

More symptoms, he thought to Zamara. First headaches, then seizures, and now blurred vision and memory loss.

Yes. But we are here now. At the end of our long journey together.

"Are you well enough to speak with the alysaar'vah?"

Jake guessed that was the supervisor of the library and nodded again. "Yeah. I'm not going to get any better just sitting here. How long was I out for?"

"We had barely laid you down when you awoke. I explained a little to the alysaar about our situation."

"Yeah, I'm sure he was wondering what you were doing bringing me here." The ice pick in his brain had been removed, leaving behind only dull pain. He got to his feet, taking his time, realizing that his legs felt weak. Yet another symptom. Zeratul watched him closely, ready to aid him if it was needed, letting him keep his dignity if it wasn't.

Damn, Jake liked the protoss.

"Indeed, some information was necessary. But I also felt much needed to be explained by you and Zamara, and she was unreachable while you were unconscious. Krythkal has been here for several centuries," Zeratul continued. "He is now the alysaar'vah, the head of the alysaar. He oversees the work done here and sees to it that the traditions and the level of care are kept."

Jake followed Zeratul out of what he assumed was the sleeping quarters and into a cavernous hall. He stopped dead in his tracks.

He'd thought the crystals in the temple were impressive, but compared to the sight that greeted him in this room, they were a candle next to a sun. Obsidian walls arched far, far above his head, pocked every foot or so by a small alcove that held a crystal. Some were larger than others, some less radiant, some were more beautifully prismed, but to his eye, they were all glorious. They seemed to him to have a slightly different hue than the ones he'd seen on Aiur and in the temple where he'd encountered Zamara. He rubbed the palms of his hands on his eyes and looked again.

"So is it the brain tumors or are these crystals different from others?" he asked Zeratul, his eyes roving over the countless crystals nestled in their alcoves, each one a unique little star.

"You are quite observant for a non-protoss," came a pleasant mental voice. Jake turned to behold a protoss so old that he made Zeratul look like a capering youngster. So they, too, showed physical signs of aging, though subtler than a human's white hair or wrinkled skin. A slightly brittle fragility to this dark templar's skin and build indicated that he had been around for a long, long time.

His eyes, which also seemed paler to Jake than Zeratul's, crinkled and he hunched in laughter. Jake felt heat rise in his face.

"Yes, Jacob Jefferson Ramsey, I remember the expulsion from our homeworld. I was even older than Raszagal, and I do not anticipate my life to extend overmuch longer. But glad I am to have lived this long, to see our people reunite, to meet a non-protoss who honors our knowledge as we do, and to give my aid to a preserver. You are right about the crystals. There is a rare combination of energies here that alters the crystals on a deep level. There are two such places where the energies converge. One is in the ocean depths, the other is beneath our feet. It is why we chose to stay and create the Alys'aril on this precise location."

He shifted slightly, and Jake could no longer hear his thoughts. Jake assumed he was talking privately with Zamara. Something Zamara said affected the old protoss profoundly—Jake saw his eyes widen and his body stiffen, then settle sadly into the closest thing to a slump he'd ever seen a protoss display. At length, Krythkal nodded.

"Dark times indeed are upon us, that it comes to this," he said. "Zamara, here in the Alys'aril we have ever sought to preserve memories in our own way. That does not mean we do not respect the way our brothers kept their wisdom—through protoss such as you."

"I know this," Zamara said. "I am grateful beyond expression that the dark templar used their skills to such ends. Now information vital to the survival of not just the protoss as a united race, but perhaps many other species as well, can be passed on."

He nodded, but something else concerned him. "You speak of Ulrezaj. Do you know if he was defeated on Aiur or if he survived?"

"I couldn't stay long enough to determine whether or not we'd brought him down," Jake said. "I had to get through the warp gate before it was too late—I'd lingered long enough to miss the boat to Shakuras as it was. But he was definitely being weakened, that much is for sure."

He expected Krythkal to express at least some pleasure in the news, if not exactly delight. Ulrezaj, after all, was originally a dark templar, albeit a misguided one. But even the dark templar feared the power of the dark archons, and the horrors Ulrezaj had perpetrated on the protoss would move all but the hardest heart. So he was surprised when Krythkal seemed genuinely saddened.

"I am glad that his evil was stopped, but I will mourn him," he said.

Jake blinked. "Come again? I know he was one of your people once, but I don't think anyone should weep over the death of something so awful."

"Some*thing*? No. A dark archon of such tremendous power and malice—no. That I do not mourn. But I will mourn Ulrezaj."

He regarded Jake steadily. "I will mourn my student."

Jake stared. His student? "Ulrezaj—used to be a Keeper of Wisdom?"

Krythkal nodded. "Many centuries past, he studied these crystals. He was passionate about the cause of our people, as we all were then, with the wound still so very fresh. His was a sharp mind, an eager mind, not content with merely cataloguing memories and transferring them from one crystal to another. He hungered for knowledge, and we foolishly granted it to him."

The dark templar looked, if such a thing were possible, even older as he spoke. "We let him rise in our ranks, for he proved an able student. We took great care to allow him only limited access, for much of what is recorded in the Wall of Knowledge is forbidden lore. We understand that, and while we preserve it because all knowledge is precious, we do not access it. No one living in the Alys'aril, not even I, knows most of the secrets contained in the Wall."

"Ulrezaj did not confine himself to the areas that he was permitted to explore, did he?" It was a rhetorical question from Zeratul; he, Jake, and Zamara already knew the answer.

Krythkal nodded again. "No, he did not. Secretly, he was rising in the night, and studying the darkest, most forbidden knowledge the dark templar possessed."

"That's how he did it," Jake breathed. "*That's* how he figured out how to become a dark archon that's greater than just two dark templar joining!"

"We caught him one night," Krythkal continued, his mental voice laced with pain. "I confronted him, begged him to tell us why he had so betrayed our trust. I thought I could reason with him, but by then, he was too far gone in his zealotry. Anything that advanced the dark templar cause, he claimed, was worth doing. No matter whom it harmed, no matter the cost, even to our own people. We would have our vengeance on the protoss who had banished us, and he would be the weapon of their downfall."

He lifted his eyes to Zeratul and Jake. "I barely recognized him then, as he stood here raging. I could see no trace of the scholar, the bright youth I had been so proud of. All that was left was burning anger and hatred, and a firm conviction that however abominable the means, the end—revenge on the protoss of Aiur—was worth it. We begged him to tell us what he had discovered, but he refused. We implored him to let us erase what he had learned, so that he could again return to us as an alysaar, one who tends the knowledge but does not abuse it. Again, he refused. He left us that night, seething with rage and a hatred that was at once so dark and so pure as to astound the mind. I did not think to see or hear from him again. To discover that he used the Alys'aril—to become this . . . this monstrous entity . . ."

Krythkal was overcome and quickly shuttered his thoughts. Zeratul reached out a hand and laid it on the old protoss's shoulder. "Your remorse is understandable, but no one could have foreseen this. Do not overburden yourself with guilt. What is done is done. That Ulrezaj chose to steal knowledge for such reasons was his own decision."

The elderly alysaar'vah nodded, but it was clear that he did not quite believe Zeratul. "You speak wisdom, yet the doing is not so easy. But I will do what I can to make amends. You are aware, Jacob and Zamara, that I cannot guarantee a positive outcome."

"We know," Zamara said.

"But we have to try," Jake added.

"I think you must, and all the skills we have are offered to you. I understand you have a crystal from the chambers beneath Aiur, where the Wanderers from Afar kept knowledge of their own, safe and secret."

Jake nodded and fished in his pocket for the fragment of the crystal. Krythkal suddenly froze, his head cocked, listening. "Excuse me," he said. "I will be right back. There is some kind of commotion—"

He strode down the long stone hallway. Zeratul and Jake exchanged glances. They did not even need to touch thoughts to realize they were both thinking the same thing, and as one, turned and followed their host. Despite his age, Krythkal, like every protoss Jake had yet seen, could move very quickly when he so chose, and Jake had to break into a lope to keep up with him and Zeratul.

Several alysaar were hastening to them, their robes fluttering, every line in their bodies speaking of their agitation. A silent conversation that was clearly of great importance went on, and Jake chafed at being left out of it.

I, too, am not being included, Zamara said.

"Zeratul?" Jake asked, because clearly the dark templar prelate was part of the conversation. Zeratul's gaze was fastened on Krythkal and he did not respond away. All at once he hunched his shoulders and half closed his eyes. Jake frowned slightly—why was Zeratul laughing? And then Zamara was laughing too, and in the silent chambers of this ancient temple a strong, assertive, and quite definitely female voice rang out:

"I don't *care* if he's in a meeting, I don't *care* if I don't have clearance, and I *really* don't care if I step on your strange-shaped protoss toes. You're going to take me to him right now or else I'll—"

"Rosemary!" Jake cried, delight filling him and chasing away for the moment even the lingering throbbing ache in his temples. He pushed through the little throng, straining to see past the tall bodies of the protoss acolytes blocking his view. Down there, a group of alysaar clustered around several newcomers, including a tall, strangely-clad dark templar and a female templar in glittering gold and blue armor. And in the center, as they milled about, he caught just a glimpse of a sleek black head.

She, too, pushed her way through and they hurried toward each other. He slowed and stopped, and so did she. They stared at each other for a moment. Jake wanted to hug her, and he thought maybe she wanted that too, but just as he stepped forward she shoved her hands in her back pockets and grinned up at him.

"About time you got here," Jake said softly. He drank her in—the short, glossy black hair, the large blue eyes, the Cupid's bow mouth, the petite but, God help him, gorgeous figure that was snugly wrapped in formfitting leather.

"Yeah," she said. "When this is all over, remind me to never, ever get caught up in protoss red tape again."

Jake's smile broadened. He realized with a hitch in his chest that he hadn't honestly thought he'd ever see her again. He couldn't help it. He closed the short but enormous gap between them, and swept Rosemary Dahl, assassin, traitor, drug addict, trusted ally, and holder of his heart, into his arms and embraced her tightly.

And to his astonishment and delight, she didn't resist.

CHAPTER 18

AFTER NOT NEARLY LONG ENOUGH, ROSEMARY drew back. Jake released her at once, feeling his face grow hot, and distracted himself by regarding the newcomers.

"Jacob Jefferson Ramsey," the dark templar said in a voice that was as dry as the strips of fabrics with which he had chosen to wrap himself. "Your journey has brought you here to the Alys'aril, the holiest of holies among my people. I am sure you and Zamara are properly grateful. I am Mohandar, and I, Selendis, Razturul, and Vartanil have accompanied Rosemary Dahl on her journey to locate you and the preserver who has chosen you for her host. I thought to arrive before you, but clearly, Zeratul is a step ahead of me."

Zeratul smiled slightly and inclined his head. "It is not I, but Zamara who is a step ahead of *all* of us, my old friend. She sought *me* out. She and Jacob have roused me from my lethargy. We only arrived ourselves a short time ago."

"Indeed?" Something flickered in the depths of

Mohandar's eyes. He turned to Jake. "I have been informed that you possess knowledge vital to the safety of our people, preserver. It is because of that information that I have revealed this site to Selendis and the other Aiur protoss. I hope I did not give that secret away too lightly."

Jake's legs trembled. They started to buckle as the headache hit. He hissed at the sharp pain, reaching out and grasping Zeratul's arm for support. Selendis's eyes narrowed; she hadn't missed the gesture.

"You spoke truly," Selendis said. Her mental voice was strong and yet soothing, definitely female but one used to command. It reminded him of Rosemary's. She read the thought and he sensed she didn't like the comparison, but she continued on. "The host is unwell. Have you determined whether or not you can successfully transfer Zamara's essence before it is too late?"

"The *host* has a name," Rosemary growled.

"Indeed he does," said Zamara, and her possessiveness and care for Jake couldn't be mistaken. "He is Jacob Jefferson Ramsey, and regardless of the outcome today, his name should be remembered by all protoss—not just preservers. He has sacrificed much in the bearing of me. We must hurry. I have no wish to see him suffer a moment more than is necessary."

"I agree. And I will take my leave of you now, so that you may attend to this."

Jake stared up at Zeratul. "You're leaving?"

Zeratul nodded. His eyes were kind. "I must. My

lingering here will help nothing—I cannot be part of this transference. If it fails, I cannot help; if it succeeds, I cannot better that outcome."

Mohandar was nodding. "You will best serve on Shakuras, Zeratul. We need your wisdom in the Hierarchy—you are respected by all."

Zeratul shook his head. "I will not be returning to Shakuras, either. Soon, I give you my word—but not yet. There are some things, too long pushed aside, that I must investigate in order to help strengthen Zamara's statements. I can add verification of some of her assumptions, I believe. And the more we know, the better armed we are."

Mohandar was disappointed but nodded. "You know what I do not . . . yet. If this is what you must do, then go. *Adun toridas.*"

Zamara agreed with Zeratul's statement, but Jake was sad to see Zeratul go. The dark templar hesitated, then spoke for Jake's mind only.

"I owe you a debt, human," he said quietly. "Who knows how long I would have sat alone, staring at the waterfall and pink skies, wrapped in my misery as in a blanket. That is not who I am, and you helped remind me of that. Your kind is a young race yet, but already, a handful of individuals have proven to me and to others that you are a force to be reckoned with—and one that has inherent wisdom and potential. I was proud to call James Raynor a friend. I would be proud to call you that also."

His legs all but useless, his head pounding, Jake

gazed up at the prelate. "I . . . would be proud as well," he said.

"Zeratul," said Zamara, "in case the transference is not successful, let me share with you one last thing. I think it may be of great importance. Jake—I am sorry, this will hurt."

"Go for it," Jake said, bracing himself.

The image filled his mind and Zeratul's. It was a distant, dusty world, like a hundred other worlds but for the strange rock formations that seemed too lovely to be coincidental. But nature did that; it was why humans could see rabbits in clouds and the faces of holy figures in frost patterns. Jake, the scientist, knew that. He knew it as he beheld the landscape, his gaze traveling across the swirls and whorls and formations, one of which dominated the landscape and looked to his scholarly eyes like a beast out of legend—a white, winged horse—

"Hey!" he exclaimed in his mind to Zamara and Zeratul. "I know this place—this is Pegasus! I led a dig there. . . ."

He watched as the guided vision bore his gaze away from the natural Pegasus statue and gasped slightly. There, gleaming and bright and green and vibrant, and God help him, *alive,* was a xel'naga temple.

It had most definitely *not* been there when Jake was leading the expedition. It had to have recently been unearthed—by an earthquake, perhaps, or storms, or perhaps it just simply decided it was tired of lying undiscovered and unappreciated and shoved its way through the earth under its own energies. With all that Jake had learned in the last several weeks, nothing would surprise him.

He pressed a hand to his temple, breathing through his nose to try to will away the pain of sharing the vision. Out of the corner of his eye, he saw Rosemary watching him worriedly. He wished she didn't have to see this.

"I am sorry you were not able to investigate the site, Jacob, but at least you can tell us exactly where to find it. That this has come to light so recently seems to be of great importance," Zamara said.

Jake easily shared the information with Zeratul, absurdly pleased as, for the first time, he had something real and concrete from his own field of expertise to contribute. Zeratul bowed deeply to him.

"Perhaps we will meet again, when the crisis is over, and we have protected our worlds and those we love. But for now, I must act." The glowing eyes crinkled slightly. "It is, after all, what my friend Tassadar would have wished me to do."

He turned to the others. "Mohandar, Selendis . . . I believe that a battle which will need us both—need us all—is shortly to begin. I will return to Shakuras as soon as I may."

"We will await your return, Prelate," Selendis said, and Mohandar nodded.

"Krythkal . . . Zamara and Jake both are precious. Take the utmost care in what you must do."

"I shall bring to bear all my centuries of skill. And," he said, chiding gently, "perhaps soon you will return here so that we may have your memories as well. *Adun toridas*, Zeratul."

"*En taro Tassadar*," said Zeratul, and then he was gone without a backward glance, moving forward purposefully. Jake was glad of it. This was the Zeratul that Zamara had known, whose integrity and strength of purpose had convinced Tassadar that he was worthy of trust.

Whatever happens to me, Zamara said for Jake alone, *my people know as much as I can tell them.*

The ice pick in his head returned and Jake felt the blood drain from his face. Someone was there, holding his arm firmly, not letting him fall. He glanced up, assuming it was Krythkal or another protoss, and then down. Rosemary gazed back up at him.

"Whatever it is you're going to do to him, Krythkal," Rosemary said steadily, "you better do it soon."

Krythkal nodded, troubled. "Agreed. I shall assemble my best students to help me, and we will begin at once."

Jake looked at the little group that surrounded him as he followed Krythkal. By anyone's estimate, it was an odd assembly. Two ancient dark templar and a younger one, one executor—female at that, which Jake knew was rare—a rather enthusiastic youngster that he understood was a Furinax, a craftsman, and two humans, one of whom had a preserver in his head.

He chuckled softly. "Bet you never thought you'd see this," he said, directing the comment to everyone.

"Truer words were never thought," Mohandar said. "The ways of fate are strange indeed."

He felt Vartanil's gaze boring into him and turned to regard the young protoss who had slowed his long-legged pace to Jake's. "Jacob, it pleases me so greatly to be here with you and Rosemary. To lend my support, however weak it might be, to your cause."

"Vartanil was a strong voice in the Hierarchy," Selendis said, looking over her shoulder as she strode ahead of them. "I do not think Rosemary alone could have persuaded them. At least not in time. You were of more aid than you suspect, Vartanil."

Vartanil ducked his head. If protoss could blush, Jake thought the Furinax would be scarlet by now.

"Thank you," Jake said quietly. Vartanil turned radiant eyes upon him.

"It didn't help that the only human female they'd met was Sarah Kerrigan," Rosemary said. "Nothing like a mountain of prejudice to climb over."

"Your sincerity and concern for Jacob was a great factor in our decision as well," Selendis said. "We did not expect to see such ferocious dedication in one of your species."

Rosemary didn't look at him, but her cheeks were more traitorous than Vartanil's. "Yeah," she said, "whatever. So, how does this thing you're going to do to separate Jake and Zamara work?"

Krythkal turned expectantly to Jake. "Oh, right," Jake said. He slipped his hand into his pocket, feeling again the tingling sensation as his fingers closed around the crystal, and handed it to Krythkal. The pro-toss started as the crystal settled in his long-fingered palm. Jake felt his surprise and pleasure wash over them all.

"It is . . . astonishingly pure," Krythkal said, in slight awe. Recovering, he added, "The alysaar have, over the centuries, developed a technique for the joining of thoughts that enables us to transfer them to certain khaydarin crystals that have been specifically attuned for the task. It is a recording device. It stores the memories as images and information that can then be accessed later by anyone who has been trained in the proper technique, which is very simple."

"Like a hologram," Rosemary said, nodding. "Gotcha. But Zamara's kind of . . . a super memory holder, right?"

Krythkal was clearly worried. "Yes," he said. "We have never attempted anything this ambitious. Also, we are used to probing protoss minds, not ter-ran minds. I will do the best I can, but I fear I cannot promise anything."

It would have to do.

A few moments later, Jake found himself in a narrow chamber. He, Krythkal, Selendis, Mohandar, Razturul, Rosemary, and Vartanil crowded the tiny space, and when two more alysaar approached, it got positively cramped. He glanced down at the small raised table in the center of the room, made of the same black polished stone that comprised the rest of the temple. It didn't look very comfortable.

Krythkal turned to them. "The fewer present, the better. We will need to concentrate quite intently."

Selendis nodded and inclined her head. "We will wait outside then."

"No," said Rosemary.

Selendis turned to her, slightly annoyed. "You wish to be a distraction in this delicate operation?"

"I—of course not. But I thought maybe I could help."

Jake's hand shot out, almost of its own volition, and grabbed Rosemary's. Startled, she glanced up at him, and he felt her start to pull back.

Stay with me.

Her eyes widened slightly as he sent the thought, lacing it with everything he felt for her. Her lips curved in a slight smile and she nodded. He wanted then, so badly, to read her thoughts—to know exactly how she felt, as he had let her see. But he wouldn't do that. He'd promised.

Selendis was looking at them both. "Perhaps your presence would be a positive thing," she allowed. "If it strengthens Jacob's spirit." She turned to Jake.

"I have every confidence that this will be a success, Jacob Jefferson Ramsey. I look forward to when we will speak again."

He nodded. She shifted her gaze, and he knew she was speaking with Zamara. With a brief, brusque nod, Selendis left. Vartanil lingered.

"Go on," Rosemary said. "He and Zamara are gonna be fine." As if she actually could foretell the future,

Vartanil executed a low bow and left as well. Mohandar said nothing to Jake, but he knew that the old protoss and the preserver had exchanged a few words.

The door closed quietly behind them. Jake, Rosemary, Krythkal, and his two attendants were alone in the little chamber. He looked at the flat slab and suddenly a shiver went up his spine.

It reminds me of what we saw in the chambers, he sent to Zamara.

I know. But there is a world of difference between what Ulrezaj did and what is about to happen to us.

Are we sure? Ulrezaj used to be one of these guys, after all. And they are dark templar . . . maybe this Krythkal secretly hates preservers, because you do naturally what he can't ever hope to accomplish.

Perhaps, she agreed, and he was totally unnerved. *Although I doubt this. Jacob—there is no other choice. It is your life at stake, and my knowledge. They cannot continue together any longer.*

He nodded and lay down on the cold stone slab, shivering a little where it touched his bare skin. "You might at least offer a guy a blanket," he joked.

Krythkal regarded him steadily. "You will shortly be in a mental state such that you will be completely unaware of your physical body," he replied. Like that was any kind of reassurance.

Jake sighed and stretched out, folding his arms, prickling with gooseflesh, across his chest. "Okay, let's get this over—"

Her lips were soft and warm on his, but not gentle.

As he'd imagined far too many times than was good for his sanity, Rosemary's kiss was as fierce and passionate as she was, and after the initial shock had passed Jake responded. His arms wrapped around her small frame and pulled her close for a moment that was both long and timeless and far, far too short.

When she pulled back, he was shaking. She seemed completely composed, of course. She smiled and gave him a wink.

"You. Don't. Die," she said.

"Okay," he stammered. The grin was stupid and as unstoppable as the rotation of a planet. He sensed the protoss's confusion, annoyance, and humor, but none of that mattered.

We're surviving this, Zamara.

I had no idea that a terran gesture of affection was such a powerful force, Zamara said wryly, but she was pleased for him. As Jake lay back and closed his eyes, he felt her wrap her essence around him like a cat curling up for a nap, and in the midst of his giddiness, he knew sorrow. Even if this attempt was completely successful, she would never be in his mind as she was now.

I will miss it too, she said, reading his thoughts even as he formed them. *I had not expected to become so fond of you.*

Me neither.

The slab beneath him was firm and cold, and then, all sensation of it was gone.

Jake opened his eyes to a scene of bright sunlight, steamy warmth, and an overabundance of green. He realized that he was on Aiur, but Aiur before its devastation and fall to the zerg. He turned and knew whom he would see, and smiled at Zamara.

She was clad in the clothing her corpse had worn: purple and white robes, shining and soft and suiting her admirably. She tilted her head and half closed her eyes, but he did not need to see her in order to feel her smile. They sat as they had done so many times before as Jake had watched the unfolding of one of the myriad memories Zamara kept. But this time, while this image of an untouched Aiur was a memory, Jake knew that he would not see anything else. This was how Zamara wanted their separation to occur.

He sensed Krythkal's thoughts, wafting to his mind like the scent of flowers on a breeze.

"The crystal is astoundingly pure. I think it will successfully contain all the memories."

"What about Jake?" Rosemary demanded. It was good that they would get whatever it was that Zamara was so insistent was important, of course, but her concern was Jake. He lay alarmingly still on the dark stone slab; she wasn't even sure he was breathing.

"I do not understand human anatomy, child," Krythkal chided her. "All I can do is remove Zamara's influence from him. You will have to turn to your terran physicians after that. Now be silent, and let us complete this."

Rosemary frowned. She hadn't expected that. Somehow she'd thought that if they could extract Zamara, Jake would suddenly be right as rain. But his symptoms were physical, too, weren't they? Brain tumors didn't just disappear.

Krythkal extended his right arm and placed the crystal in midair as if he were setting it on a shelf. It hovered there, a miniature version of the huge crystal she'd seen in the caverns. Krythkal gave a signal, probably telepathic, and as one, each protoss extended his right hand and held it a centimeter from Jake's body. Their left hands, they raised, palms out, facing the crystal chip.

Rosemary hissed as they seemed to suddenly be pulling cool blue light from Jake's inert body. A moment later, a thin, glowing line extended from each alysaar's palm into the crystal. So that was how they did it. They physically took the energy of memories from the subject and transferred it into the crystal, like siphoning blood into a jar.

She didn't say anything, but couldn't help wondering if this was hurting Jake.

"No," came the thought from Krythkal. "He feels nothing."

Rosemary bit her lip. She had no idea how long this would take . . . but one thing she did know: Zamara had a *lot* of memories to transfer into that tiny little crystal.

"Beginning transference," came the implacable mental voice of Krythkal. Zamara's body jerked slightly, as if something were tugging at her. It was going to work after all! Jake started to grin at Zamara, but instead of pleasure and relief he sensed shock and grief rolling off her. In that place that was not real but seemed very much so, he grasped her hand, touching her, making contact as he had once done before with her physical shell.

"Zamara, what is it? What's wrong?"

"I—should have anticipated this," she said. She squeezed his hand, trying to reassure him. "But at least the knowledge will survive."

Coldness filled his gut. "What do you mean?"

She looked at him sadly. "What the dark templar have been able to do is admirable. It is important and worthy, and they record the memories as best they can. But the way they do it is different. Preservers are organic beings; they are not technology, which is what the dark templar utilize."

"I'm not following you."

"Do you remember how the memories unfolded when I shared them with you?"

He nodded. "I don't think I'll ever forget. It was like I was the person whose memories you were sharing. It was as if it was happening to me right at that moment."

"They lived, then," she said softly. "Through you. Through me. Through all preservers, when they delve into the waters of the memories we carry. Those who have gone before us do not cease to exist. We don't just remember them—we *preserve* them."

He nodded, still not seeing why this was so—

His eyes widened as understanding struck him. "Oh God . . . Zamara . . . you won't be preserved, will you?"

She shook her head. "No, Jacob. The memories I hold that the dead have experienced—all preservers have those memories. So they will live on, which is a relief to me—provided I am truly not the last preserver. But I and my memories . . . the knowledge will be saved, and that is important. But . . . *I* will not be saved. When others activate this crystal, it will be as if they are reading a history. It will be facts, and figures, and information. But they will not know *me*. It will be as if I had never existed."

The entire time he had known Zamara, she had been pragmatic and courageous. She had let slip frustration and worry from time to time, and as his condition had worsened, her affection for him had come through. But he had never seen her so vulnerable, so grieved. And he understood completely.

She would be erased. The information, blunt and lifeless, would survive, but all that was Zamara—her stubbornness, her dry humor, her love for her people, the depth of compassion and understanding that only a preserver could have experienced—would be lost to her people.

Zamara would be no more.

This was taking a long time. Rosemary began to fidget after she suspected only an hour had passed. Into the second hour, she could stand it no longer and rose as quietly as possible. Their eyes closed, their bodies as motionless as they had been since they had started, the protoss took no notice of her. With silent steps Rosemary moved toward the door. It opened and she slipped out.

Selendis, Vartanil, Razturul, and Mohandar were there. As one, they turned toward her.

"Is it complete? Was it successful?"

"They're not done yet," Rosemary said. "I had to get out and move a bit. They said they thought it was going to work, though."

"Ah, that is good! And the professor? He will be all right?" asked Vartanil.

"We'll need to get him to a doctor right away. The tumors won't be aggravated anymore, but apparently they won't disappear either. I'm not sure how we're going to find a human doctor, but I guess we'll cross that bridge when we come to it."

"I would offer the skills of our people, but we do not understand your physiology," Selendis said. "Yet . . . perhaps we may be of some help regardless. The tumors were created by exposure to protoss mental energy, which—"

She froze. Her head whipped around. Before Rosemary could blink, Selendis had clenched her fists and summoned two brightly glowing blades from the bracers that encircled her wrists. Razturul emulated her, his blade glowing a bright green rather than a cool blue. Mohandar and Vartanil, too, had tensed, all four protoss staring down the corridor.

"What the hell's going on?" cried Rosemary. They had returned her weapons to her, and now she reached for the rifle she carried strapped to her back.

"The Alys'aril is under attack," said Selendis.

CHAPTER 19

AS IF IT WERE FATE, ALTHOUGH ZERATUL WAS not certain he believed in such a fixed concept, the planet that Jacob had named "Pegasus" was located in the same sector as Ehlna. He realized that the dark templar had even visited the planet briefly in ages past, assessing and then dismissing it as of no real importance. Ah, if those earlier explorers of this world had only known.

Moving swiftly into orbit in the *Void Seeker*, Zeratul was glad of the closeness of his destination. Experienced as he was, he knew both the necessity of careful consideration and swift, decisive action. What burned inside him was neither. It was a strange sensation of urgency, almost anxiety, that sang in his blood now. Was it simply that finally, after too long spent brooding in isolation, he was again engaged in action? Perhaps.

Perhaps not.

Surely some of this sensation was due to the fact that Zamara had clung so tenaciously to life, of a sort; what she had to impart was vital indeed. Combined with what Zeratul already knew, it was logical to fear and to wish to do something, anything, quickly. But he wondered if it was more than that.

He took the ship through the atmosphere, his fingers moving lightly over the crystal that carried his mental instructions to the vessel. A holographic image of Pegasus's surface appeared. It was exactly as it had appeared in Zamara and Jake's mind. There was the enormous rock formation, looking like a hooved beast with wings. And there—

The xel'naga temple. Zeratul forced himself to remain calm as he looked at it. He felt privileged in this moment, to behold such a thing. Luminous, glowing green, this was a wild temple, not a planned, structured, organized one such as the one on Shakuras. And yet Zeratul realized, temple indeed it was. Something marvelous and sacred and wonderful was to be found here.

He gazed at it a moment longer, drinking in the sight as he might absorb nutrients from the cosmos, and feeling as nourished by the act. Then he mentally directed the ship to move closer. He would land and approach on foot. Answers were here, he knew it in his bones. He would—

A bright white zigzag suddenly danced across the top of the temple, and with a thought Zeratul swerved away from it. What was going on? From a distance he watched unblinking as the crack spread across the surface, which was glowing even brighter than it had before. Zeratul suddenly recalled Zamara sharing the story of her death with him and Jacob. She had crashed her vessel into such a temple—but one that was a dull green-brown, not this radiant, vibrant green. Zamara had known by the color that—

The energy creature. These temples were eggs—chrysalises. And Zeratul had arrived just in time to bear witness to the hatching of the being housed within. Perhaps that was what he had sensed—the urgency, the need to arrive soon before it was too late.

He watched, enraptured, as the surface of the temple-chrysalis seemed to bow, straining against the white zigzag crack. Suddenly, it shattered, and Zeratul stared at something that was as far beyond his ken as his people must have been to the humans upon first contact.

Beautiful. It was exquisitely, radiantly, gloriously *beautiful*. It burst through its shell as if propelled, this white, glowing entity of pure light and energy. It should have appeared hideous, displaying as it did tentacles, odd feathery wings, and enormous eyes that shone with a light so bright that Zeratul was forced to turn his head and close his own. But it was not hideous. It hovered over its discarded shell that even now was starting to dim and turn greenish brown, dancing in the air for a moment. Turning back to look at it through slitted eyes, Zeratul's spirit soared. It was powerful; it was potentially lethal, and if it turned its terrible, wonderful attention upon him and destroyed him now, he would die in happiness.

But the energy being, so new and fresh, had no

concern for Zeratul. It hovered for a moment longer, then shot upward as if propelled, moving with a clear sense of purpose. For a precious second Zeratul was too startled to do anything, but he recovered swiftly and began to follow it.

Home.

More than something so simple, this moon was the site where Ulrezaj had first embraced his destiny. But like all things that birth one's fate, this world had a hold upon him, and he had returned many times ere now.

The unique manifestation of energies that had enabled Ulrezaj to begin his transformation, his becoming, had also necessitated that he return here when he was depleted. And so he had done over the last four years, a silent shadow slipping unnoticed into the deep waters of Ehlna's ocean, settling downward until the surface light faded to darkness, only to find brightness again in the illumination of a cluster of glowing crystals.

She was here already, the clever prey he hunted; somehow she had learned of Ehlna, of the Alys'aril, of the memories that could be housed here by means of research, skill, and intellect rather than a disturbing accident of birth. How Zamara had learned of the site he neither knew nor cared. In the end, it did not matter. The freakish preserver and the uncountable memories not her own would die, and the secret would be safe.

If he could have closed his eyes in pleasure, he

would have, at the sweet sensation of gathering strength and restoring himself. He would not be able to fully regain the energy that he had expended in the recent battle; he lacked the time. His enemies were right behind him. Ulrezaj knew well that it was not for him that the zerg had come, but for the same prey he himself sought. He could afford to linger only the barest amount of time, so that he could fight and destroy both Zamara and the zerg. Once that sweet goal had been achieved, then he could rest and enjoy the healing and peace a full restoration would bring.

But ah, it was good, to begin to shed the weakness as he had shed his physical form. He would enjoy this.

Thoughts were exchanged between the protoss so swiftly that Rosemary didn't even have time to process them on a conscious level, but she got the gist of it. The Alys'aril was pretty much defenseless, at least to her and Selendis's way of thinking. There was an energy shield that could be erected to protect the building and its precious contents from the devastation of weather or other environmental dangers, and in a pinch—which *gosh*, Rosemary supposed this was—the alysaar could augment the shield with their own mental abilities. Thoughts on how this would be accomplished were flying, and Rosemary winced from the speed and intensity of them.

"Who's attacking? What's going on?" Rosemary demanded, trying to get at something she could understand.

Selendis favored her with a quick glance. "Zerg."

Rosemary swore. "Same crew we fought on Aiur?"

"It appears to be, yes."

"Can't you call for help through the Khala?"

"I have tried to do so. For some reason, I am unable to enter the Khala here." Her mental voice betrayed some of the strain and frustration she was feeling.

Several of the alysaar raced up to them, their robes fluttering as they ran. Terror poured off them, and their thoughts assaulted Rosemary: zerg, lots of them, and their leader wanted to speak to whoever was in charge.

Mohandar was obviously outraged; fury roiled off him so thick Rosemary could almost see it. "Zerg. Here. Our most sacred space." His eyes fell upon Rosemary, and there was accusation in that gaze. "You brought them here, human."

"We made the decision as a united people to come here, Mohandar," Selendis said. Her words were quiet, but firm. "Even you agreed, knowing what might happen."

Rosemary couldn't tell if Mohandar agreed. He had shuttered his thoughts from her, but she could tell he still seethed with anger.

"This is your world," Selendis continued quietly, permitting them all to hear the mental conversation. "Your people who are in danger. But I am the executor. With your permission, I will go to the zerg's leader and speak for all our people."

Mohandar composed himself with a visible effort.

"Go," he said, surprising Rosemary and apparently also Selendis. "Razturul and I will see what can be done to protect this practically defenseless place. We will be in contact."

Selendis bowed and then began to race outside, to the courtyard that encircled the temple and the steep stone steps that led down from it. Rosemary followed her; Selendis did not protest. A heartbeat later, Vartanil followed them as well. Rosemary had to run flat out to keep up with Selendis's long strides, then came to an abrupt stop and swung her rifle up in a single smooth motion.

She had known there would be a lot of zerg, but here, pressed in so close around them and yet not attacking, there seemed to be an infinite number of them. But she had eyes only for one being—a humanoid, sitting astride what looked like an enormous flying serpent.

Ethan.

"Protoss!" came a strong masculine voice. Rosemary jerked as if stung. It was not a mental voice, not this time, and the sound of it shivered along her blood. "My queen does not desire your blood. We have come only for the preserver. Hand her over to us and we will leave you unharmed."

"Oh, come *on*," Rosemary retorted. "We didn't fall for that the last time; what makes you think we will now? There's no way in hell you'll just take what you want and go away."

Ethan turned and fixed his gaze on her, a slight

smile, sickening in its familiarity, turning up his lips as he regarded her.

"Actually, I'm not lying, Trouble," Ethan drawled. "I really don't care about anyone or anything that is here. I've come for Zamara. And I will have her, one way or another."

Rosemary closed one eye and peered through the sight on the rifle in response. She tightened her finger on the trigger. If they were all going to perish here, at least she'd take Ethan down with her this time.

"No, Rosemary!" Selendis's mental shout was so powerful that Rosemary gasped slightly. "There may be another way."

Slowly, Rosemary lowered the weapon and shot a glance at Selendis. She stood straight and tall, holding out her hand, palm up, toward the hovering figure.

"I am Selendis, executor of the templar. And I tell you truly, if you attack this temple now, Zamara will perish!"

Ethan was silent for a moment. Rosemary looked at the thousands of unblinking zerg eyes riveted on her. "Go on," Ethan said at last. "And I will know if you are lying."

Rosemary wondered if that was true and thought it might be.

"Zamara's presence in Jacob's body is killing him," Selendis continued. "We are in the middle of a delicate attempt to extract her essence from him. If we succeed and can transfer Zamara's essence to a specially prepared crystal, both Jacob and Zamara's knowledge will survive. If you interrupt the ritual now, both will die and the information your queen seeks will be forever lost. I do not think you wish that."

Rosemary smothered a smirk. From Ethan's silence, he most certainly did not wish that.

"You are hopelessly outnumbered, Executor Selendis," he said at last, his voice laced with contempt. "And even if these . . . monks who have been cloistered here for God knows how long can actually put up a fight, we will still triumph. You must know this."

"I do," Selendis said quietly. Rosemary turned to look at her, narrowing her eyes slightly. She was familiar enough by now with how protoss mental abilities worked to recognize that Selendis had tightly shuttered her thoughts. Nothing was coming in or going out that she did not want to hear or be heard.

I know as little as you, Rosemary Dahl, came Vartanil's baffled thoughts.

Ethan laughed harshly. "You will hand Zamara's essence over to me then without a fight? How disappointing. My zerg want sport."

"They were given enough sport on our homeworld," Selendis snapped, her glowing eyes flashing. "We desire no more bloodshed."

Rosemary frowned. What the hell was Selendis playing at? She knew that the knowledge harbored at the Alys'aril was invaluable to the protoss. Maybe it was more important than the information Zamara bore. While Rosemary would be quite happy if her life and Jake's were spared, she wasn't sure she thought this was a good trade. Selendis turned to regard her, but with her thoughts so closed, Rosemary could not read the glance.

Was Selendis really going to sell Zamara out?

Ethan waved a hand airily. One of his extra scythe-arms emulated the gesture. "I will wait. I can kill you later as easily as now, if it comes to that."

Selendis inclined her head. "Thank you," she said. "Rosemary—Vartanil—let us return to Krythkal and see how he progresses."

"On one condition," Ethan continued.

Here it comes, Rosemary thought, and tensed.

"Your story sounds plausible and feels true. I believe you about the ritual. But what's to stop you from suddenly changing your mind and absconding with both of them once it's completed? No, I think I need verification along with my trust."

Selendis was still, even now, radiating calm. "What do you need to be satisfied?"

"I'd like to have one of my zerg watch this little ritual you describe. And when it's complete, you will give it the crystal that contains Zamara."

Rosemary bit back a retort quite literally, chomping down on her lower lip rather than snapping "Like hell" or another such comment. She couldn't give the game away—whatever the game was. She had to trust Selendis now.

"I cannot think that having a zerg present while a

sacred protoss ritual is transpiring will help us achieve the desired result," Selendis said sharply.

Ethan shrugged. "It will not attack unless attacked first. And come now, Executor, you would do the same in my position. A witness, to prove what you say is true and take delivery of something you have agreed to provide. Surely that's not too much to ask."

Selendis nodded. "It is an understandable precaution on your part, yes. But your creature must do nothing to interfere, or Zamara and Jake will be forever lost to both of us."

"Agreed. He'll be a good boy. Or girl. I'm not sure exactly which. Oh . . . and if you double-cross me . . . well, Trouble, you'll be the first to die."

Ethan made no gesture, but suddenly one of the creatures waiting silently began to undulate toward them, slithering up the steps, its scythe-arms bobbing in front of it as it moved. Rosemary fought the impulse to shoot the hydralisk on the spot, instead feeling a rare wave of fear wash over her at its approach. It towered over her, slaver dripping from its jaws, then came to a halt in front of Selendis, utterly obedient to its master.

Confused, alarmed, and furious, Rosemary gave Ethan another glance. He met her gaze, and the face that was still recognizable as his twisted into a smirk of victory. She ground her teeth and forced herself to accompany Selendis and the zerg inside.

"What the hell are you doing?" she asked as they hastened up the long, broad steps to the heart of the temple.

Selendis favored her with a brief glance. *I am buying us time.* The thought was for her only, and Rosemary closed her mouth and tried to "speak" only with her own thoughts in turn.

That bit about Jake and Zamara dying—that was a lie?

No. It is my understanding that the ritual cannot be stopped at this juncture without the loss of both parties. Krythkal must be permitted to complete his task.

What about our new best friend here?

Selendis glanced back at the zerg, which slithered along behind them, its silent pacifism almost more chilling than an outright attack. *There was no alternative. Ethan was correct—I would have done the same thing. For the moment, there is no harm in it watching. And even now, no one is certain that the ritual will be successful.*

Rosemary didn't need to be reminded of that. Oddly, though, despite the peril they were all in at this point, she felt relieved at being able to do something rather than simply sit around and wait.

It is difficult, to feel helpless, Selendis agreed. *I would prefer that Ethan had not come . . . but yes. I understand how you feel.*

Rosemary shot the executor a quick glance. For all their differences, for all her alienness, Selendis did share that same pleasure at being finally able to act.

A few moments later, Rosemary, Selendis, Vartanil, Mohandar, and Razturul were cloistered with Ataldis, the alysaar who was in charge while Krythkal was conducting the separation rite. They all stared at the hydralisk, who turned its hideous head to first one of them then the next, peering at them with yellow eyes through which Rosemary assumed Ethan saw. None of them seemed surprised, although they seemed frightened and unhappy; Rosemary assumed Selendis had warned everyone that they were bringing a friend along.

Selendis was brutally blunt—another thing Rosemary liked about her. "We cannot hope to win an out-and-out battle against the zerg," she said the moment she had everyone's attention. Again, Rosemary knew she was directing her thoughts so that the eavesdropping hydralisk wouldn't understand. "We are outnumbered quite literally a hundred to one. Nor do we have superior technology on hand that might even the odds. It is distasteful to me to say this, as a warrior, but if we fight, we will die, and they will take Zamara."

Vartanil thought the protoss equivalent of swallowing hard and turning pale. Rosemary frowned slightly, but nodded. "So—we're not going to fight?"

Selendis turned fiercely glowing eyes upon the terran. "Some of us will. And we who choose to fight, will die. But others, and the knowledge of this sacred place, may be able to continue on."

A flicker of approval from Mohandar. "You have at least one vessel that can bear some of us to safety," he said. "Is this your plan?"

"Partially. Some protoss, and as many of the memory crystals as can be salvaged. But first, I must know. Are there other vessels we can utilize?" Selendis asked, turning to Ataldis.

The alysaar hesitated. "We do not leave the Alys'aril, we who tend to it," he said. "Others come to us. We do not go to them."

"So that's a no?" Rosemary asked.

"Not precisely. We do have vessels, from the time when Ehlna was first settled. I do not know if they are even functional anymore. There is no one here who has the knowledge of repairing the vessels."

"I think I could."

"You? You are not even protoss!"

"I helped Zamara repair the warp gate on Aiur," Rosemary shot back. "She was in my thoughts. I know a lot about the simple physical mechanics of things and more than a little now about how your technology works. At least give me a crack at it."

"You shall have a chance to examine it," Selendis said. When Ataldis bridled slightly, she added, "The hour is desperate, Ataldis. If Rosemary can help us, more lives and more knowledge can be saved. We must allow her to try."

Ataldis nodded, though he was still obviously unhappy. "Come then," he said. "I will take you to the vessels."

"I will accompany you," said Mohandar.

As Rosemary, Ataldis, and Mohandar started to leave, the hitherto silent zerg snarled and whipped out a scythe-arm, blocking their path. Rosemary looked up—and up, the thing was enormous—and stared into its baleful yellow eyes.

"You've got your eyewitness, Ethan," she growled.

"I'm leaving this room. You tell it to kill me, they kill it and you don't get Zamara. You can either send it to follow me around or go watch the separation ritual like you wanted it to. Either way, I'm going."

The thing hesitated, the eyes narrowing. Rosemary stood stock still as the zerg extended a hooked appendage and, very gently, stroked her cheek before turning back to gaze at Selendis. The executor pivoted and moved purposefully toward the room where Krythkal was conducting the ritual. The zerg followed.

Rosemary shivered as she watched it, not with fear, not this time, but with hatred. She hoped she'd have a chance to kill Ethan Stewart herself.

At any other time, Rosemary would have been ecstatic to get her hands on such antique alien vessels. She'd have spent many pleasant hours tinkering with them and learning, trying this, adjusting that.

She didn't have hours. She wasn't sure she even had *an* hour, and stared, simultaneously enraptured and horrified, at the ancient ship before her. There were only three of them total, and only one that was capable of anything other than atmospheric travel. They were oddly huge and clunky-looking compared to every other protoss vessel she'd seen before, even the bulkier dark templar ones. They had been kept in a special room below the main grounds of the temple, and Rosemary was willing to bet a million credits that no one had been down here in the last century. They had been covered, at least, for which she was grateful, but even so they were dusty and ominously still-looking.

"When we were exiled from Aiur," Mohandar said, "the Conclave initially resisted giving us any vessels at all other than the single xel'naga ship. Adun insisted that we have some, that we might be able to travel and explore any worlds we happened upon. Fortunately it seems as though our ancestors left a few here with us when the majority departed for other worlds."

"Yeah, fortunately," said Rosemary hesitantly. She took a step up to one and touched it, feeling the cool metal beneath her fingers. She peered inside. Yes, there was a crystal there, but it was dark.

"What do you think, Rosemary?" asked Vartanil, slipping up beside her and looking down at her hopefully. "You can repair it, can't you?"

"I'm not sure. Is there a protoss who can assist me on this?"

Vartanil ducked his head shyly. "I am a Furinax," he said. "I have not personally constructed any vessels, but I do understand the mechanisms of how such things work."

Rosemary smiled at him. He was not a warrior, like Selendis, nor a politician, like Mohandar, nor a priest, like Krythkal. Vartanil was a humble craftsman—a worker. And that was exactly what was needed now. She was very glad he was here. She again looked at the console, remembering how she had manipulated things when she had shared thoughts with Zamara.

"Then get in the driver's seat and we'll see if this thing has any juice left in it at all," Rosemary said.

He nodded, touching the metal cautiously with his four-fingered hand. It had done nothing when Rosemary had done so earlier, but now, under the hand of a protoss, the door lurched slightly, then with a series of jerks slid open. Rosemary and Vartanil exchanged triumphant glances. The young Furinax slipped inside and touched the crystal.

Nothing.

Rosemary mentally swore. "Try it again," she said. Vartanil hesitated, then obeyed. And this time, suddenly, the crystal came to life for a brief second. Purple illumination chased itself around the console and she *felt*—there was no other way to explain it—the ancient ship come to life for just a moment.

"Well done, Rosemary," came Selendis's mental voice.

Rosemary turned to Selendis, pleased that the executor had witnessed her triumph, confused as to why she was here. "I thought you were with Ethan's little friend?"

"I escorted it to the room, but it does not need to be watched. Ethan would not be foolish enough to permit the hydralisk to kill anyone. He has too much at stake."

Rosemary was forced to agree. Ethan ever looked out for himself.

"I think the crystal might need to be replaced," she continued, "but from what I know about how your ships function, everything else I can get up and running. I'm sure of it."

She let herself enjoy the sensations of pleasure wafting off the protoss for a moment, but then Selendis was all business again.

"This is very good news. We will soon have a second operative vessel. While it is true that Ethan has many zerg here under his command, their number is not infinite. If we can reach Shakuras in time, we can bring in reinforcements, and they will certainly fall beneath a protoss assault."

That much was inarguably true. Also true was the fact that in order to get to the warp gate, whoever took that ship would have to get past zerg piled six thick all around the Alys'aril, both on the ground and in the air. Which was pretty much suicide.

"I will take the vessel we arrived in and—"

"No." Razturul's interruption was blunt, almost rude. "I will go, Executor. I am a skilled pilot, and you are needed here."

"I am a trained warrior," Selendis protested. "It is my duty—"

"Let us not pretend that this attempt to gather reinforcements is likely to succeed," said Razturul evenly. "You are more necessary to the survival of our people than I, Executor. Too . . . the Alys'aril is a sacred site to the dark templar. Long have we revered and striven to keep it safe and secret. I would ask for the honor of attempting to defend it at what may be its final hour."

Rosemary peered at Razturul. She hadn't been overly fond of the dark templar. He'd been brusque and treated her roughly when she and the other Aiur protoss had stumbled through the warp gate. She hadn't been pleased to learn that he was to accompany them. And yet now he was insisting on undertaking a mission that made the word "risky" seem like a walk in the park.

"Razturul is right," said Mohandar. "You are a strategist, Selendis. He is a dark templar warrior. Let him undertake this mission."

Still Selendis hesitated. "The human and Vartanil can repair this ship," Razturul continued. "Use it to take the crystals and flee once the ritual is complete. I will go and do my utmost to bring reinforcements." His eyes half closed and he tilted his head to the side, laughing a little. "Besides, who knows? I might elude them after all, and bring honor to my people by saving *you*, Executor."

"Who knows indeed," Selendis said, and with those words, Rosemary knew the executor had given her consent. What Razturul said was possible, sure.

But not likely.

She knelt and unpacked the small kit she'd brought with her, reaching for the tools, and looked up at Vartanil. She'd had enough of protoss farewells, and did not want to watch as Razturul made his. Vartanil nodded his understanding, and Rosemary turned her attention to the dusty relic of a vessel, preferring to focus on a centuries-old machine than a being who would be dead inside of an hour.

"We might all be dead inside of an hour," Vartanil reminded her.

"Shut up and touch the crystal again," Rosemary growled. It didn't make her feel better that everyone present saw through her façade of indifference as she started to work.

CHAPTER 20

ROSEMARY GOT THE NEWS THE MOMENT IT happened.

She had been lying beneath the ancient vessel, her hands and face and leather clothes luminescent with crystal dust instead of greasy with oil, when Razturul sent his farewell.

For a split second, she saw what he did: the sea of zerg roiling beneath him, the cloud of them descending from the air and all sides. The ground was rushing up to meet her: The ship was falling out of the sky. And then nothing.

She also knew, although she had not seen it, that Razturul had been mere minutes from making it to the portal. He had led them on a good chase, had the dark templar. And he'd almost made it.

"Rosemary?" The thought was from Vartanil, and she saw him now through blurred vision as he bent and peered underneath the ship. His concern wafted over her, comforting her, and she dragged a hand over her face quickly.

"Got some of this damn dust in my eyes," she said,

although of course she knew he knew it was a lie. "Get back in the cockpit and let's keep going."

Damn the protoss anyway, and damn herself for giving a rat's ass about them. And about Jake for that matter. What the hell was she doing here when—

The light was unexpected and elicited a sudden whoop of delight from her. The ship purred, a pleasant sound, as it awakened like a cat from a nap in a sunny window. Excitement and pride emanated from Vartanil as he gleefully sent to Selendis, "Rosemary has done it! The vessel is operational!"

"That is excellent news," came the executor's response. "And I am told that the ritual is about to finish. They are cautiously optimistic, although—"

The cool words were suddenly drowned by a rush of emotion, quickly quelled. Rosemary's heart lurched as a single word came to her: "Ulrezaj."

He was here. Somehow, damn him, the thing had found them. Information inserted itself into Rosemary's mind: He was here, he had again grown strong and powerful, and he was heading directly for the Alys'aril. Rosemary didn't need to be telepathic to know what that meant. Ethan, at least, seemed to want Zamara alive—at least as alive as someone could be when their essence had been transferred to a khaydarin crystal. And he was cruel enough to leave the alysaar and all the others, including and likely especially her, alive to dwell on their failure once his hydralisk had gotten the prize.

Ulrezaj, though, had nothing to hinder him. He

had come to destroy Zamara and likely everything and everyone else along with her.

Ethan couldn't believe what he was seeing. A frantic flicker crossed his mind: *The thing's unstoppable.* But that was nonsense. Nothing was unstoppable. He'd seen with his own augmented eyes that Ulrezaj could be wounded. Hell, his zerg had been part of it. Kerrigan had predicted that the dark archon would lead Ethan to Zamara, and of course his adored queen had been correct. What she had not predicted was that this place would also enable the nearly-destroyed Ulrezaj to recover so fully. And so quickly.

It was as if the battle on Aiur had never happened. Ulrezaj moved toward them, a roiling absence of light, as if the combined forces of protoss, terrans, and zerg had not come close to dispatching him. It was déjà vu . . . except for one thing. This time there would be no protoss psionic storms to slow his approach. Dark lightning sizzled and crackled about him as he came on.

Quickly Ethan looked through the eyes of his hydralisk. They had not permitted the zerg to enter the room, of course; but the creature was observing through an open door. Two protoss stood on either side of the door. They were unarmed; these were scholars, not fighters, but they were guards nonetheless. Briefly, he considered sending a second zerg to find out what Rosemary was up to, but then decided against it. If they tricked him, he could find her quickly enough.

Ethan could see the prone form of Jake Ramsey, lying very still on a small raised table carved from black stone. The old protoss and two assistants stood over the terran. Their hands were extended; one hand almost touching Jake's body, the other palm out toward a crystal that hovered in the air. Glowing blue lines went from their palms to the crystal. The ritual was still going on—which meant that Ethan needed to slow Ulrezaj down long enough for them to finish.

Ethan sent his zerg of course, and they obeyed like a pack of hounds on the hunt, scurrying, slithering, and flying toward the creature. The mutalisks attacked from above, spitting out their insatiable, horrific symbiotes. Ulrezaj's form pulsed, and with seeming casualness a wave of shadow spread off of him, like a pool of oil but one that moved unnaturally fast. The mutalisks were struck dead instantly, their corpses and those of the voracious symbiotes falling heavily atop their comrades, crushing several of them. Ethan caught glimpses of zergling legs wriggling frantically from beneath the mutalisk bodies. Others dropped on Ulrezaj and were turned to ash on contact.

The hydralisks hunched forward and fired wave after wave of spines at the creature. The spines, deadly when striking flesh, seemed somehow to be absorbed by the monstrous creature. Bolts of blue-white energy exploded from the dark archon, as if it was parodying the attack it had just received. The hydralisks were impaled with glowing energy, shrieked, and died, their scythe-arms—so like Ethan's own—clawing one final time in their dying paroxysms.

The zerglings descended en masse. They never even reached the foe. A single pulse and they swirled about futilely like leaves blown by a strong wind.

Ethan swallowed hard as the zerglings fell like so many dominos. Surely the attack had done something—weakened the bastard somewhat. But no. Nothing about Ulrezaj showed any kind of weakness—any kind of way an antagonist using physical means such as acid, spines, or pincers could bring him down.

Cold sweat broke out on Ethan's smooth, gray-green skin. He had failed his queen once before. He could not fail her a second time. He had hoped to save this final attack for later, but he realized he had to call out the guardians now. Crablike creatures that were even more powerful than the mutalisks they had once been, the guardians began bombarding Ulrezaj with globules of acid. Accompanying the huge creatures were dozens of tiny scourge. They dove suicidally toward Ulrezaj, their sole purpose to explode like small, living plasma bombs. This, finally, seemed to rattle the dark archon. He stopped and roared with pain, and his glowing dark aura seemed dimmer and more erratic. He turned his terrible attention to the guardians and the scourge. Some of them perished instantly, but others darted away from Ulrezaj, coming back in for another attack.

He was stopped, for the moment, and he would be slowed.

It was the best Ethan could hope for.

Which meant that he had to have another plan. A thought sent a pack of several dozen zerglings racing toward the protoss temple. The least useful of his army against Ulrezaj, they would have no trouble ripping apart a few protoss monks. Whether or not the ritual was completed, if Ulrezaj moved too close for Ethan's comfort, Professor Jacob Jefferson Ramsey and the crystal that hovered over him would belong to the zerg before the dark archon could bring the temple crashing down upon him.

The protoss were mobilizing, as best as a group of scholars could. Orders flew, whizzing past and through Rosemary's head at dizzying speed. She got a vague gist of the plan: Those who could stand against the onslaught would do so. A second time, they were in a peculiar alliance with Ethan and his zerg; neither zerg nor protoss wished to see Ulrezaj triumph.

"The protection of this place and its knowledge is vital," Selendis's thoughts, clear and hard and pure as a khaydarin crystal, rose above the jumble. "We must permit Krythkal to finish the ritual to preserve Zamara's knowledge. While it continues, as many crystals as possible will be placed in the vessel Rosemary Dahl has restored to us. We cannot possibly mount an assault with so few numbers and no weaponry. Ethan and the zerg are currently engaged in combat; we will let them weaken our enemy for us. They seem to be slowing his advance. Nonetheless, I do not believe they will be able to halt Ulrezaj, and therefore we must prepare for defense of the Alys'aril. But we will wait until the last possible moment; it will not serve us to reveal our plan too swiftly."

Rosemary remembered that someone had said something about erecting a psionic shield over the temple. It would buy them some time, but Selendis was right to save that defense, and even the knowledge that the protoss had such a defense, as the ace in the hole. Again, she approved of how Selendis's mind worked.

"But once we have begun to walk that path, we will protect the Alys'aril until our defenses are breached, and then, we will do our best to provide sufficient distraction so that the single vessel can escape to safety."

More thoughts, input from the scholars, comments from Ataldis, things that Rosemary didn't understand and wouldn't, even if she lived among them for the rest of her life. How they would defend this place, make their last stand, wasn't her concern. Getting out of it with her hide, Jake's, and whatever information they could was.

She tried to hurry through the last few checks of the vessel, wishing she could skip them entirely, too professional a mechanic to do so. When a group of several very earnest-feeling alysaar approached carrying boxes of glittering, gleaming crystals, Rosemary, glittering and gleaming herself from the crystal dust on her leather outfit, rose and examined the cargo.

"This it?" She was surprised that they had selected the most important memory crystals already.

"Oh no," one of them replied. "This is just the first sorting. There will be many more."

Her blue eyes widened slightly as she asked, "Just how many?"

"A few dozen more at least. The vessel is large enough, is it not?"

"They're all in individual boxes," she said, frowning.

"Of course," one of them said, his confusion clear. "We analyze and label every single memory crystal. How else can we catalogue the data?"

"Great for librarians, not so great for smugglers," Rosemary said. "You'll be able to take more crystals if you just pile them in. Put them in every damned nook and cranny that isn't being taken up with a living, breathing—" She paused, realizing that the protoss didn't technically breathe and amended, ". . . uh . . . existing protoss. That's how you're going to get the largest number of crystals into the smallest amount of space."

The alysaar looked as though she'd suggested cutting protoss themselves into bits in order to make them fit. "But . . . centuries of sorting, of organization—you wish to discard that labor?"

"You want to take as many crystals as possible or not?"

The protoss still looked dazed. "I—"

"Look," Rosemary said, taking pity on him, "leave

them here for now, we're still running some last-minute checks. Talk to one of your superiors and tell him what I said. These are your crystals—your people's history, not mine. I don't give a damn if we take three, three thousand, or three million." *Just as long as Jake and I get out of here safely.* "I'll take them in boxes if that's what you guys really want. But I'd think that you'd want to save as many as possible, and sort them out later on some peaceful, out-of-the-way place once we're all off this moon and we don't have zerg and a dark archon demigod on our asses."

The alysaar exchanged glances; probably they were communicating among themselves. Then they nodded, put down the boxes, and hastened off.

"How are our friends the zerg doing on the front?" she asked Vartanil wryly, scooting back underneath the vessel.

"Not well," Vartanil admitted. "He moves through them as inexorably as shadow moves at twilight, slowly, steadily, and unable to be held at bay. He has paused, for the moment, but I do not think he will be thwarted for much longer. Ethan has sent several dozen zerglings away from the attack; they sit at the base of the stairs, silent and still."

"Damn it. He's going to storm the temple and get Jake!"

"But he knows that the ritual is still going on," Vartanil replied, puzzled.

"Yeah, but he knows as well as we do that if Ulrezaj

gets here first, it won't matter if the ritual's done or not. I know how he thinks."

Rosemary felt a tremor beneath her body. More powdery crystal residue drifted, soft as snowfall, on her face. She didn't need to ask what had caused it.

Ulrezaj was approaching on the Alys'aril.

Just a little time. Time to finish this and get out of here with Jake. Jake, you had damn well better make it. That's all I've got to say.

The earth rumbled again, more strongly. This time Rosemary heard something in the ancient vessel rattle. Sweat dotted her forehead, turning the crystal powder into a paste. She couldn't take it any longer. Growling, she scooted out from under the vessel and leaped to her feet, absently dusting off the glowing crystal residue as she seized her rifle from where it was propped up against the wall and raced toward the door of this makeshift hangar.

"Rosemary!" Vartanil's mental voice rang in her mind. "Where are you going?"

"There's a hydralisk watching Jake right now that might decide to abduct him at any minute. I don't care what you all are planning, I'm going to get it before it gets him," she shot back over her shoulder.

"But—what about the ship?"

"It's spaceworthy now. You can run the final tests and put crystals into corners as easily as I can. And I can't even pilot the thing, I'm not a protoss."

"Oh . . . you are correct. I . . . had forgotten."

Even as she ran up the wide, dimly lit corridor that

led toward the surface, toward the fighting, Rosemary grinned at that. She raced down the halls, her booted feet ringing as she ran. Even now, even with an attack from a creature that shook the very foundation of this building and the sounds of battle at its doorstep, it seemed wrong to be moving loudly down these ancient halls.

She rounded a corner and kept going. She only hoped she wouldn't be too late.

Jake stared sickly at Zamara, his hands clutching hers as if he could physically keep her here, keep her from dissolving into nothingness, even though he knew that the entire encounter was taking place solely in his mind.

"Is there no other way? Couldn't—I don't know— couldn't I be put in some kind of stasis until we find another preserver?"

"Even if we did attempt such a thing, I do not know if it would make a difference. The memories are held in a human brain now, not a protoss brain. Perhaps I was fated to this the moment I bonded with you."

She reached out a long-fingered hand to touch his cheek. "And if that is so," she continued, "then it is so. Without you, I never would have had the chance to reveal my knowledge. I only hope that you survive, Jacob. You have astonished me at every turn with your ability to adapt, recover, and persevere. If your species produces individuals like you . . . then the protoss have much to learn from such an upstart race."

She was attempting to interject levity, but Jake shook his head. He couldn't believe this. Zamara had done so much. She couldn't just . . . be wiped out like this. . . .

"Zamara!" he cried brokenly. Impulsively, he reached out to hold her, to keep her here, just for a little while longer. He realized, odd as it seemed, he'd grown to love this protoss. She'd hijacked his body, brought about the death of his friends, and her presence inside him might indeed mean his own death. But he'd never before seen such integrity. She had become part of him. And now she was about to disappear. About to become lost forever.

"No," he vowed. "You won't be lost, Zamara. I'll remember you . . . the way humans do. I'll make sure that everyone knows about you—what you did for your people. How brave you were. How much you loved them. I know it's not the same thing, hell, it's not the same thing at all, but you'll still be more than just dry words locked in a crystal somewhere. I'll tell them, I swear. If you learned something about us, then I swear to you, we'll learn something about the protoss. I just wish—"

Her hand, warm, the skin slightly rough and dry, brushing his cheek.

"I know, Jacob Jefferson Ramsey. I know."

And before his eyes, she began to fade.

Even though the energy creature appeared to have a clear purpose, it seemed to dance as it flew rather than heading on a laser-straight path. Despite the urgency of the situation, Zeratul's heart lifted as he followed.

His delight turned to momentary confusion when suddenly his screen was crowded with dozens of blips with readings identical to the creature whose trail he was following. It had to be a malfunction. Perhaps there was some sort of echo that—

A few moments later, Zeratul stared in wide-eyed astonishment at what he was able to see with his own eyes.

There were indeed dozens—perhaps hundreds—of the luminous, vaguely-aquatic, wholly mysterious creatures swirling and dancing and diving together. For a long time, this glowing ritual was enacted, and Zeratul simply watched. He enjoyed the feeling of humility that rose in him as he witnessed this spectacle. He knew that if he survived what Zamara feared was coming he would enjoy the feeling again.

Abruptly, as if from an unheard signal, they all became very still. Zeratul waited, watching. And then, more swiftly than his vision could even register, they began to whirl. Faster and faster they flew until they became a blur of glowing movement, growing brighter and brighter still until the dark templar was forced to narrow his eyes and then finally shield them. A blast of light made him jerk with pain and he closed his eyes for a moment. Cautiously he opened them.

The energy creatures were gone. In their place was a hole in the very fabric of space—a tunnel, a wormhole, outlined in shining light, its center dark and mysterious and beckoning with the exception of a single world, barely glimpsed, waiting on the other side. Zeratul knew he could no more refrain from entering that mysterious doorway than he could stop his skin from absorbing nutrients from the cosmos. He was a protoss, and though he knew and understood and practiced intelligent caution, his curiosity would not let him be.

He calmed his thoughts, although in truth he was almost quivering with excitement. He would need all his wits about him if what awaited him on that world was not benevolent. For a moment, he forced himself to be still, to go within, and when he was ready, Zeratul moved slowly, steadily toward the wormhole. What was on the other side, he somehow knew, be it beautiful and wonderful or horrific and destructive, would change everything.

CHAPTER 21

THERE WAS NO THOUGHT OF BOXES, LABELS, OR categorization now. With the very foundation of their sacred place shivering beneath the figurative footfalls of the encroaching dark archon, the alysaar came at a run, their arms filled with brimming boxes or even sacks. The ship was large, but not enormous. It had been designed to carry about a dozen protoss and a fairly decent amount of cargo, presumably for shorter-term excursions. Vartanil realized, as they all did, that only a small handful of those here would make it out of the Alys'aril.

He and the others began to tear out seats. They would load the vessel with as many protoss and crystals as they could. It was the best he could do.

Ulrezaj was almost—almost—disappointed.

It had been a long time since anyone had offered even the merest possibility of defeating him in battle. He had actually worried for a time on Aiur, with the three factions attacking him simultaneously. Indeed, had he not retreated when he did, they might have won.

But it had taken all three large forces to threaten him with any real danger. Now it was the remnants of the zerg and a handful of alysaar untrained in combat who foolishly tried to stop the mighty Ulrezaj from achieving his goal.

Effortlessly, almost lazily, he continued to move forward toward the building where he had once been an eager young student. How the memories raced through him now. He thought, almost nostalgically, that he might opt to spare the building. But no—why leave anything the protoss could use against him? Better to raze it all, protoss, terrans, zerg, crystals, structure. Wipe the surface clean. Then he could return here unmolested whenever he needed to.

It was time. Ethan wondered if he wasn't already cutting it too close. At the speed of thought, his zerg acted. The pack that had been waiting like good dogs at the foot of the stairs now sprang into action. They bounded up the stairs, chittering and snapping their jaws.

They were not unseen. Selendis rushed forward, psi blades glittering, and sliced three in half almost immediately. Blood and ichor began to drip down the black stairs. Still the zerg came on, driven and utterly obedient.

Inside, the hydralisk acted. It hunched forward, firing spines from its back. The two guardian protoss immediately sprang toward it, blocking the deadly barbs with their own bodies, dying to protect their alysaar'vah and the human he tended to. They went down silently, their bodies impaled a dozen times over, blood pooling out from beneath them.

The four forms within the room remained still, as if they had not noticed anything. The hydralisk ducked its head and moved forward, sliding into the chamber.

There was no battle cry to alert it, no posturing threat or warning. Only the sudden and violent impact of spikes of quite another variety than its own, riddling it as it screamed and thrashed and twisted around to see a petite human female still firing at it.

It surged toward her, extending its scythes to separate the human's head from its body. The human didn't back down. Pale, tight-lipped, her blue eyes intense, she kept firing until, with a final faint swipe, the hydralisk toppled and hit the floor. The intense yellow of its eyes faded to dark.

Rosemary stared at it a moment, panting. It had gotten within inches of striking her. Quickly she glanced into the room. All was as it had been when she had left. Nodding to herself, she took off for the courtyard, where she could hear the sounds of ravening zerglings on the rampage.

Ethan grunted as the zerg that was his eyes on the inside died. Rosemary, of course . . . Trouble had much to answer for. Still, several zerglings had managed to get past Selendis and make it inside. The executor killed all she attacked, but the sheer volume ensured that she couldn't take down all of them. A thought sent a second group away from harrying the dark archon and rushing up the stairs.

Suddenly a soft blue-white radiance sprang up around the Alys'aril. The zerglings, running full tilt, slammed into the barrier and were knocked back. Some of them did not rise. The others kept hurling themselves at it in vain.

A psionic shield. The protoss who served in this . . . this library were not warriors, not the way the templar were on Aiur. But they had will, and they had mental power, to protect the structure.

Ethan swore. He should have seen this coming. Angrily, he summoned the guardians toward the glowing, radiant dome of energy that engulfed the temple, and had them attack.

Closer to the Alys'aril, Ulrezaj paused, mildly amused as he felt a slight brush against his thoughts and realized that the alysaar were erecting a field to protect themselves. It was . . . almost endearing, how they kept trying. Endearing, but foolish. Well, he would let them think they had succeeded for a moment or two; he found it entertaining.

The earth, already dry, turned utterly dead as he moved inexorably across it. Like a slug leaving a smear of slime, Ulrezaj left a blackened trail to mark where dark archon energy had obliterated the soil beneath him. He reached out with his mind and touched the protective shield the alysaar had erected. Grudgingly, he realized that it would actually hold against his first assault. They were stronger than he had expected; stronger mentally than he had been, before he had secretly approached the forbidden Wall of Knowledge in his youth and learned about the powers he now wielded almost effortlessly.

Yes, it would hold against his first assault. Maybe even the second.

But not the third.

It was time to end this. He had toyed with them enough. Like a careless child treading on insects beneath his feet, Ulrezaj continued to move through the zerg almost unaware of their existence beyond a mild annoyance.

The sun shone with fierce and dispassionate brightness down upon the scene of dead and dying, squirming, shrieking zerg, meditating protoss, and the great dark archon that was about to destroy them all. Its intensity did not penetrate Ulrezaj; his darkness took the light and swallowed it.

And then a shadow fell on the bright, dead ground. And another. Until dozens of small shadows danced on the earth.

And Ulrezaj shook with terrible rage as he realized that a third enemy had joined against him yet again.

Rosemary felt the shock and delight rip through her mind as the protoss saw it.

Ships—so many that the sky was becoming

crowded. Terran vessels. "I'll be damned," Rosemary said softly. "The cavalry *does* come over the hill."

Of course, this cavalry was no doubt commanded by Valerian Mengsk, and that meant trouble of another sort, but she'd deal with that later. She shot the two zerg that were bearing down on her, then raced out into the courtyard and assessed the situation as she swung the rifle into position.

She could see Ulrezaj with her own eyes now, looming toward them. His dark image was slightly obscured and softened by the blue-white shield the protoss had erected, but it was clear enough. At his feet was a vast spread of dead and dying zerg of all shapes and sizes. The hot air, so still when she had first come here as if nothing ever pierced the silence, was now swirling with dust and laden with sound. The shrieks and bellows of the zerg as they hurled themselves at the shield; the deep pulses of Ulrezaj's dark energies as they surged outward; and the more familiar sounds of Dominion vessels. Rosemary heard the reverberating spurts of plasma torpedoes, the explosions of cluster rockets, and the once-you've-heard-it-you-never-forget building, nail-biting hum of a Yamato cannon.

Some of the ships she recognized right off the bat, such as the dropships like the one she herself had piloted not that long ago. There were battlecruisers, of course. She counted four of them. She could peg them anywhere by the sound of the Yamato cannons and the unique hammerhead shape. But they looked different, somehow. And the fighters—she blinked, wondering if the waviness induced by the heat in the air was making her see things. For the first time, she understood the phenomenon of the mirage and the oasis. She was sure the thing was there a minute ago—

And then it reappeared, a zippy little planetside fighter with almost nostalgic-looking turbofans to propel it. Cloaking ability, then. It was small and swift and Rosemary felt like she was falling in love as she watched it dip and dive and unload cluster rockets.

And over there—the piece of military equipment she'd pegged as a type of siege tank had tucked its massive legs underneath it, somehow leaped into the air and sprouted wings. It had now taken flight and was diving and retreating at Ulrezaj while a mutalisk was doing the same thing.

Heh . . . talk about "air to ground," she mused. Clearly Arcturus, or at least his military people, hadn't been just sitting on their butts drinking port over the last few years.

And amazingly enough, the combination of zerg and Dominion vessels was obviously giving Ulrezaj pause.

It had been many years since Rosemary considered herself starry-eyed, and she wasn't now. Ulrezaj, from what she understood, could replenish himself easily and effectively at any point. Even as she watched, several of the fast little ships got too close to the dark archon and were vaporized instantly. Even if Valerian had brought the whole Dominion fleet with him, she wondered if they'd be able to best Ulrezaj on his home turf.

Still . . . all they needed was some time. Some time to pile into the ship, get through the warp gate, and come back with a bunch of protoss ready to . . .

She shook her dark head. No, they might get through with the vessel, a couple of alysaar, and some crystals. But even a slew of protoss who were masters at the sort of thing she'd witnessed on Aiur wouldn't be able to stop him. He'd wear them down . . . and then restore himself.

They were losing. He was almost here. Rosemary realized that at this moment, she was utterly impotent. She could do nothing. No grenades, no gauss rifles, no weapon or power she could wield as an ordinary human female was going to make a difference. It had been up to the protoss to defeat him, them and their psionic storms. The protoss here had done everything they could, she'd give them that—but it wasn't enough. It simply wasn't enough.

They were losing, and she and Jake would die.

Her brow creased in the stubborn frown that both friend and enemy alike would have recognized, had they seen it. Rosemary lifted the rifle and got the dark archon in her sights. It was a pointless and empty gesture, but if he got within range, she was going to fire on him.

At least she'd go down fighting.

Jake still held Zamara's four-fingered hands in his own. They were growing more and more transparent and felt oddly fragile, as if he were holding an empty eggshell instead of flesh and bone, as if he could crush them with a quick squeeze. Of course, both this eggshell-thin version of Zamara's hands and a more solid one were equally unreal, existing, as they did, solely in his mind.

More solid . . .

Jake stared at them. It wasn't his imagination—well, of course it was, it all was, but that was beside the point. Zamara's hands were indeed growing more solid within his own.

"What . . ." He didn't dare hope, but Zamara's eyes shone brightly.

"The crystal," she said, and he suddenly understood.

Normally, the dark templar utilized the khaydarin crystals found on Ehlna for the purpose of storing memories. But Jake had not given them an Ehlna crystal. He had given them a piece of the enormous crystal that had hovered deep beneath Aiur, by all accounts the most powerful khaydarin crystal any living protoss had ever encountered.

And this unique crystal was able to contain more than simple data.

"You . . . you won't be lost," he breathed. He felt his lips stretch in a grin that, he suspected, bordered on the idiotic.

She hunched her shoulders in a laugh. "It would appear not," she said. "Perhaps, in the future, we will find more crystals like this one. And then the dark templar will be able to preserve memories almost the way we do."

He felt almost giddy with relief and squeezed her hands, the hands that were not real. But they *were* real. They were as real as the tumble he'd taken that had kicked off the whole chaotic adventure, as real as the guilt that still racked him about the deaths of his friends, as real as Rosemary's kiss before he entered this mental state.

As real as—

"Ulrezaj!" he cried, reflexively tightening his grip.

"I know," Zamara said. Her grief was his own. "I have led him here, to this sacred place of irreplaceable knowledge, to these innocents who have had nothing to do with anything other than study. He has come for me, Jacob Jefferson Ramsey."

"He won't get you," Jake swore. "When—this is done, and you're in the crystal, we'll get you out. We'll keep your knowledge safe." *What you died for will not be lost.*

"You do not understand," she said, half closing her eyes in a smile. "My knowledge must be preserved— but so must Ulrezaj be stopped."

Jake stared at her, uncomprehending. "What do you mean? Do—do you want to get back into my head? Stop the transference?"

"No, it is too late for that. My essence is already in the crystal." Humor washed through him, shy, almost girlish. He had never thought of her as girlish, but this, too, was a part of her as much as her strength, will, and occasional acerbity. "I simply did not want to say farewell until I had to. Life is sweet, Jacob. Protoss or terran, we share that."

"I don't understand." What was she getting at. "Didn't you just tell me you were going to make it through this okay? Well—as okay as you can be?"

"I . . . had thought so. But now—Jacob, I believe I might be able to stop him once and for all."

"How?"

"The Alys'aril is constructed above one of the strongest energetic nexuses of this world. There is a nest of power here, it is why the site was chosen."

He nodded. This much he knew.

"Ulrezaj is just outside the Alys'aril. So are his adversaries—once again, zerg and terran fight together to destroy a monster who is our common enemy."

So, Ethan and Valerian had followed the dark archon. Jake's thoughts started to race—if Ulrezaj was indeed defeated, they would need to fight both Valerian's forces and the zerg. They would—

A gentle remonstrance brought his attention back to her words. "Time enough to deal with that once Ulrezaj is defeated," Zamara chided. "The three factions fight outside, but their battle will not be won there. It will be won here, inside your mind, inside the khaydarin crystal that contains what is left of me and all the memories I have stored."

"What?"

"Ulrezaj has recovered much of his strength. My guess is that this world—these energies that make the crystals what they are—are what has helped fuel him all this time. He was once a student here; here he was born, in a very real sense. And here, he must cease to be. The selfsame energies that created the monster can give me the abilities to harness him."

Jake thought he was starting to understand what she intended to do. The cold prickle of apprehension crept over him. He prayed he was wrong.

"You think . . . we can trap him in a crystal, like we're doing with you?"

"Not quite, Jacob. I intend to use a crystal to contain him, yes. But not one *like* the one that holds me."

Understanding crashed on him like an avalanche, and even deep into his link with Zamara, he felt his physical body twitch in protest.

"Oh no . . . Zamara, you can't—"

"I believe I can. If this crystal is powerful enough to contain not only my knowledge but my essence . . . I might be able to utilize its powers and those of the nexus to encase him within it. Also, it should serve as a sufficiently strong prison for Ulrezaj. At the very least, I must make the attempt."

Zamara, for the good of her people, was going to spend an eternity imprisoned with a dark archon.

He couldn't let her.

"No, Zamara, I will not permit you to do this. Hey!" He lifted his head to the utterly fictitious skies and yelled without a voice. "Hey! Don't let her!"

"Jacob—it is what must be done. I have ever served my people the best I knew how. If Ulrezaj is not contained, he will destroy me, you, Rosemary, every pro-toss here, and the Alys'aril and all the information it houses. I have done so much to keep the memories with which I have been entrusted safe."

"You think they'll be safe with—with that trapped in with them? What do you think he'll do to those memories? God, Zamara, *what do you think he'll do to you?*"

"It does not matter. I must stop him, and this is the only option I have. Jacob—please, you must release me now. You must let me do this. If you do not, you could be trapped with us."

"I don't care!" he cried recklessly, realizing he spoke the truth. He wanted to live—he wanted to be with Rosemary, to continue to explore and learn, to feel the sun on his face and taste food and run and laugh and make love. But he could not abandon Zamara. Maybe, if he were trapped with her, he could help somehow.

"No. I have damaged you sufficiently. It is time for me to go, Jacob. To leave the mind I should never have been forced to enter in the first place. I will not take you with me."

"Zamara—"

Zamara half closed her eyes and tilted her head, smiling at him a final time. A whisper in his mind, of affection, and faith in him.

He felt her extend herself, reaching out and at the same time somehow pushing him away. Once, she had descended into his mind so decisively it had been more than he could bear. Now Jake didn't want her to leave, didn't want her to sacrifice herself to—God, he couldn't even wrap his mind around an eternity with Ulrezaj as part of him. He fought her, but hers was the stronger will. When she finally pulled free, he cried her name sharply, feeling lost and abandoned and so very empty.

"Zamara!"

She was gone.

Blackness descended.

The mammoth dark being froze. Rosemary frowned and kept peering through the sights. What was going on? The mutalisks and various Dominion craft continued strafing him, but he simply . . . stood? Sat? . . . right where he was. Suddenly Ulrezaj's mass quivered and spasmed, extending an arm of darkness here, bulging out there, as if something was inside a sack and struggling, kicking, flailing to get out. Her hair and skin prickled suddenly and her gut clenched as energy crackled around her, intense enough to feel but not powerful enough to incinerate or harm. Slowly, she lowered the rifle, staring.

An eerie wail erupted and even she winced. Some of the Dominion vessels backed off, spooked by the strange motions of the dark archon and the ear-splitting cry he was emitting. The zerg kept coming, and this time, Ulrezaj did not repulse them. He simply stood, and they milled around him, doing no damage but clearly also not taking any.

"What the hell . . ." she murmured.

There was a flash of darkness from Ulrezaj so intense it was almost like a bright light. Rosemary gasped and squeezed her eyes shut for a second, then willed them to open.

Ulrezaj was gone.

She wasted perhaps half a second wondering what had happened, then a predator's grin split her face. In a single smooth movement she'd positioned herself behind a protective pillar, hoisted the gauss rifle, and began firing into the swirling morass of flesh and carapace that was the zerg.

She'd take down as many as possible, glorying in finally being able to destroy something that richly needed destroying.

And then she'd do the same to their leader.

Ethan could not believe it. He didn't know what had happened, and frankly, did not care. Grinning a very human grin, with a thought he effortlessly redirected what was left of the zerg toward the two remaining foes. He was glad that he was no longer forced to fight alongside protoss and terrans—zerg should destroy them, not cooperate with them. Zerg were the superior race, as his queen had said and as he believed. He would prove this to her, prove his worth and loyalty, by bringing her the thing she sought.

Surely whatever arcane little ritual the protoss were doing to separate Zamara from the professor's body was done by now. At the very least, he would move toward the Alys'aril so that he would be in position to snatch the prize before the terrans could claim it.

He had brought many zerg with him to Aiur, but Ulrezaj had decreased their numbers. He had further decimated them here, and Ethan felt the faintest twinge of worry as he glanced up at the skies, dark with ships. No. He was so close. He would not permit worry to distract him.

The disciplines, both mental and physical, with which he had honed his body as a mere human were every bit as strong now as they were then. He called upon them, focused his attention to laser-sharpness, and directed his subjects.

There—a single human female, hiding behind a pillar, firing at the zerg that were converging on the temple. A smile twisted his mouth. Good old Trouble. He'd have to put an end to her this time, and he was sorry in the abstract about that. But it gave him not a moment's hesitation as he trained an entire group of zerglings and hydralisks in her direction, like he'd sic a dog on an intruder.

"Bye-bye, Trouble," he said, watching as they surged up the steps to the courtyard. They were almost within range, and he saw the hydralisks lift their carapaces to expose their razor-sharp spines. They let loose a volley, but Rosemary had seen it coming and interposed the pillar between the spines falling around her like javelins and her smooth, unarmored skin. She peeked around to fire and two of them dropped.

Two, out of dozens.

No pillar would protect her from the claws, fangs, and sickles of the zerglings, who were almost on her. She had to know that, even as she fired, and he felt the respect he'd always had for her one final time before her death.

Then the little pack of zerg seemed to explode. Blood, ichor, and flesh went high into the air, raining down in pulpy fragments. It took a fraction of a second for Ethan to realize that one of the small terran vessels had hovered like a hawk just in time to fire dozens of rounds of cluster rockets into their center. Two zerglings managed to escape mostly intact, and, oozing fluid in a sluglike trail behind them, struggled to get to Rosemary. She dispatched them both swiftly, and lifted her dark head.

She seemed to stare right at Ethan.

The small fighter continued to hover protectively above her, and Ethan swore. Valerian had no doubt issued orders to guard his pet assassin. No matter. He'd get her later.

He was distracted by movement in another part of the courtyard. A protoss had suddenly emerged. He realized it was the one he had spoken with earlier, who had seemed to agree to his demands if he would only wait until the ritual was completed. Ethan growled softly. He should have known better—likely the whole story about the "delicate ritual" was a lie to buy time. He wanted to see this Executor Selendis ripped to pieces, too, and with a jerk of his hairless head another pack suddenly pulled itself from fighting the Dominion ground troops to tear off toward Selendis.

She met them halfway, leaping from the courtyard into the fray. Ethan could appreciate good fighting, and he knew what he was seeing was magnificent. Glowing blue blades erupted from Selendis's wrists and she whirled and almost danced as she fought. Her bright armor glinted in the merciless sunlight, the glare bright enough to make Ethan wince and probably harsh enough to be a weapon on its own at close range. Selendis dispatched two zerglings almost instantly, then turned on a third. The hydralisks fired a volley of spikes. Selendis cocked her head, as if listening, then leaped and flipped in midair. Her blades moved so swiftly they were a blur, and Ethan realized that she'd been fast enough to simply not be there when the spines reached her, and had sliced to pieces those she couldn't elude.

He debated sending in the "bigger guns" of his zerg army, but they were having a tough enough time holding off the Dominion attacks. Ethan realized that he was letting his emotions get the better of him. This must not become a personal battle, if he was to win it for his queen. He would leave Rosemary and Selendis to the lesser zerg; even a girl who was an expert with a rifle and a protoss executor would eventually fall.

Even as he turned his head, two battlecruisers began attacking the guardians that were spewing acid on the strange new units that were wreaking havoc on the zerg. He watched them for a moment, enough of a good sport to admire the technology. Small, sleek little vessels with sporty red trim, they came almost to ground before the wings retracted, legs extended, and the ship became a ground unit to be reckoned with. Ethan shrugged. Impressive—but once they were on the ground, the ships were easy targets for the guardians. He pulled two more in and directed them at the robot/vessels.

Valerian was not going to win this one.

Rosemary glanced up only briefly. If she had guardian angels in the forms of Dominion ships sent to protect her, then it was a fallen angel named Valerian who'd sent them. If he wanted her alive, he likely wanted something from her. Well, hell, if he was going to put his resources to saving her, then she was going to do what she burned to do.

She left the comparative safety of the pillar and raced down the steps, slipping and almost falling on zerg guts. She recovered, leaping the rest of the way to land firmly on the hard-baked earth. Rosemary had seen Ethan, flying out of harm's way on a mutalisk. She looked up at the ships overhead, waved, and pointed, then took off at full speed.

Ethan should have been harder to take down, she thought as the ships raced ahead and began bombarding him. The mutalisk screamed in agony, a horrible, screeching sound, and flailed before dropping like a stone. The ships continued to fire on the writhing zerg and its passenger.

Kerrigan saw it happen through Ethan's eyes, and sighed. She'd spent so much effort in creating him, had had such high hopes. As his body was riddled with metal, as he twitched and spasmed in agony, she experienced not a little regret. But there was nothing she could do. The task had been his to complete, and he had failed, and now he would die.

"My . . . queen . . ." he gasped in her mind.

She sent him the equivalent of a pat on the cheek, and then, unmoved by his wail of betrayal and shock, pulled out of his brain.

Still, she mused, the experiment had worked. She would simply have to create a new consort at some later date. One that would hopefully survive his first real challenge.

"Damn it!" Rosemary scowled as she ran, hoping there'd be enough left of Ethan for her to personally dispatch. The ships backed off as she entered their targeting range, unwilling to strike her.

He was still alive. She skidded to a halt and caught her breath, picking her way swiftly but carefully to avoid the pools of acid that some of the dead zerg had left as a final attack. Ethan hadn't been so lucky. His mount had fallen into one of these pools, and where he wasn't scorched, the acid was eating through him.

He did not scream, though he must have been in

terrible pain. Rosemary respected that. She regarded him for a moment as he writhed in front of her.

"Huh," she said, casually. "I'd have thought a whole bunch of zerg would be coming to you right now, to spirit you away for healing."

Ethan propped himself up on one arm and one scythe-arm. His legs were pools of liquid flesh. The tendons on his neck stood out like cables as he tried to control his pain. But the look in his eyes gave him away. Rosemary raised an eyebrow; she'd never seen such anguish. And she knew it wasn't physical, either.

"Wait, let me guess. Your connection to the zerg has been severed, hasn't it?"

His silence confirmed it.

"Wow. Nice queen you've got there, huh? Drops you the minute you need a little help from her. Looks like you're just as expendable as the next zerg, Ethan."

"No!" The word was ripped from his throat. "She will not abandon me. . . ." The protest turned into a harsh sob. "My queen . . . Kerrigan . . ."

Rosemary grinned and made a mock tsk-ing sound of sympathy. "And so you die betrayed. Hooray for appropriate ironies, you son of a bitch."

She lifted her rifle, slowly, so he could watch her, and took careful aim.

A sudden golden-blue blur interposed itself between Rosemary and her prey. Before Rosemary could react, Ethan lay lifeless before her, his head severed from his body, the flesh cauterized by a psi blade. Selendis stood before her.

"What the hell do you think you're doing!" Rosemary shrieked.

"Protecting you," the executor replied calmly.

Rosemary let loose a string of oaths. "Protecting me? You robbed me of my kill! He was all but dead! I didn't need protecting from anything!"

"I did not protect you from what Kerrigan left of Ethan Stewart," Selendis said in that oh so irritatingly quiet mental voice. "I protected you from slaughtering out of hate. We are warriors, you and I. We must sometimes take lives. But we should do so because it is necessary. Not because we enjoy it. It is my fervent hope that after this moment, you will never again have to slay with hatred in your heart."

Beneath the resentment, the anger, the shock of feeling cheated, beneath the hate that *did* still surge fiercely inside her, a part of Rosemary understood.

"I'll give you a piece of my mind later," Rosemary said, then winced at how literally that could be taken. "For now, we've got to stop the zerg—and then Valerian."

Selendis nodded, and together the executor of the templar and a terran assassin sprang into the fray.

CHAPTER 22

JAKE BLINKED AWAKE, TEARS WET ON HIS FACE. For a moment, he was disoriented. He felt as though he had forgotten something very important, lost it or misplaced it—and stared blankly up at the protoss faces peering down on him. And it was then that he realized what had happened.

Zamara was gone. She was no longer anywhere to be found in his mind or thoughts. For a second, he thought he would be sick, so overwhelming was her absence. Four-fingered hands, strong but gentle, closed on his arms, slipped under his body and eased him to a sitting position.

"She's gone," Jake gasped, reaching to clutch Krythkal's robe. "She—"

"We know," came the thought in his head. At least he could still understand them. But he felt like an amputee. God, were humans really this . . . *alone*?

Krythkal lifted his hand. Resting in his palm was the crystal that Jake had given him before the ritual had begun—the crystal that he, Rosemary, Alzadar, Ladranix, and all the others had found deep in the

labyrinthine heart of Aiur. Then, it had been luminous, clear . . . clean. Now Jake stared at the crystal fragment. Its hue was now dark, yet still glowing
somehow with a sullen purple-black hue. Something
swirled inside it, and there was the occasional spark
of brightness that surged forward only to submerge
again.

Jake took it gingerly. He had always had difficulty holding the crystal before. It had emanated
a power that gradually would hurt if he held it too
long. But that pain was somehow cleansing, scouring.
Something too strong for him to hold or wield, yes,
but not hostile.

But now, as it lay in his hand, it felt . . . wrong. He
could think of no other way to describe it.

"I . . . blacked out," Jake said, staring at the crystal.
It felt cold, and a numbness began to spread across his
palm. "What happened? Did she . . . did she do it? Did
she manage to trap Ulrezaj in there with her?"

"It is difficult to tell," Krythkal said, his mental
voice rich with sympathy. "Ulrezaj did disappear. The
Dominion and the zerg are fighting one another now.
The zerg appear to be losing that conflict. We felt—
something at the very last moment. A surge of power
from the crystal, from Zamara, reaching out . . . before
we were unable to sense her anymore."

The cold increased. Jake stubbornly refused to
release his grip on the crystal. He felt he owed it to
Zamara, somehow, to hold it as long as he possibly
could, and closed his fingers about it tightly. Just as

she had hung on to her mission as long as she possibly could. And maybe—was still holding on to it.

"Did she get all of him?" he demanded, his voice harsh with grief. "His soul, his memories, all of him?" Was it worth losing her? "And what about her? If she's in there with him—"

He couldn't speak the words, but these were telepaths, and so he did not need to. Were they trapped together in some kind of hellish, eternal battle? Was she still self-aware? And if so—was she in pain? What could he have done to stop her? Should he have done something?

Human fingers, small and warm and gentle, closed on his where they clutched the crystal and unfolded them. Jake let Rosemary open his hand and stared dully at the blood that coated the pulsing, sickly dark stone. He'd grasped it so hard he'd sliced his hand on its sharp edges. Jake looked up into Rosemary's heart-shaped face, naked pain on his own. She smiled gently and then turned to hand the stone to Selendis.

"Jacob," came Selendis's mental voice, and he dragged his eyes from Rosemary's to look at the executor. "Zamara lived, died, and found a way to live again in order to serve her people with everything she had. We must now do the same to honor her memory and sacrifice. The zerg are all but defeated, their leader slain, and that means that Valerian will soon be here. He has come for Zamara, but he must not find her."

So, Ethan was dead. Jake wondered if Rosemary

had killed him or if the Dominion or Selendis had taken him down. It didn't matter—as long as he was alive, the zerg had an intelligent leader other than Kerrigan. He had to go if they were to win. Jake dragged his arm across his eyes and nodded, pulling himself back together.

"You're right," he said. "We can't let what Zamara did be for nothing."

"Valerian does not know the transfer has been successful. If he finds you here . . ."

"Whoa, whoa," Rosemary said, frowning at Selendis. "You're just going to leave us here for him to kill? A decoy while you make off with Zamara? Sorry, that's not my idea of a good time."

Jake looked up at her. "Selendis is right. We can't let Zamara and Ulrezaj fall into the hands of the Dominion. Think what Mengsk would do with a weapon like Ulrezaj—and you know he'd try to set him loose and control him."

Rosemary's face was still contorted in a frown. Jake continued.

"Besides—I'm going to need medical care. Human medical care. The pain . . . hasn't gone away. I think the tumors are still present. The protoss are smart, but they wouldn't be able to cure me in time. Valerian's people might. And he might not be as bad as you think. There was something—genuine about him. And about that Devon Starke fellow. I can't explain it, but . . ."

He took her hand. "And . . . damn it, I'm tired of

running. So very, very tired. But . . . Rosemary, I think you should go with the protoss. Valerian won't be looking for you, just me. I can delay him long enough for you and the protoss to escape. But you've got to hurry."

In the midst of his grief for Zamara, his heart lifted as Rosemary shook her head, her fine, short black hair flying with the gesture. "Not likely," she said. That was all, but it was enough. More than enough. Whatever was going to happen, they would face it together.

Selendis cocked her head. "The tide of battle turns," she said gravely. "The zerg are all but vanquished."

Jake got unsteadily to his feet and for the first time saw the bodies just outside the door—two protoss and a zerg. "What—"

"Long story," Rosemary said.

"I will want to hear it—but not now. You need to go," he said. He looked at them in turn—Krythkal, who had possibly saved his life; Selendis, so strong and tall and proud; Vartanil, who had believed in him; Mohandar, the dark templar, who had worked side by side with Selendis and Rosemary to retrieve a preserver's knowledge. He knew they could read in his thoughts his admiration and respect.

"Jacob Jefferson Ramsey," Selendis said, "you are a hero to our people. We will not forget. You will become part of our history—a bright part of it."

"And you as well, Rosemary Dahl," said Vartanil. Rosemary's cheeks reddened.

"Hell, I'm no one's hero," she said roughly.

"You are mine." Vartanil gave them a protoss smile.

Jake hissed slightly and staggered as pain shot through him. Rosemary caught him, small and slight but strong, steadied him. Overwhelmed, he turned his face from the protoss. "Thank you. And I will not forget Zamara."

As one, the protoss bowed deeply to him. Then they turned and quickly headed down the corridor, maneuvering around large chunks of stone and debris. He watched them until they vanished from sight, going deep below the temple to the hangar and the single ship. Krythkal did not go with them.

"You're . . . staying?"

The protoss nodded. "The Alys'aril was damaged in the attack. The zerg killed many of the alysaar. Many, many crystals were destroyed. We will not leave it."

Jake and Rosemary exchanged glances. "Valerian will look at this site as a treasure trove. He's all about ancient knowledge," Rosemary warned.

Krythkal half closed his eyes and tilted his head. "He would have to be protoss to understand it."

"He'll figure that out," Jake said.

"He would doubtless plunder, as you fear, if no one were here to prevent him. But perhaps we can engage in a dialogue. I have lived here for most of my adult life. I cannot leave it, regardless. And who knows. It could be that the time has come when we will need to cooperate and share our knowledge with lower—with other species."

"Nice catch," Rosemary said dryly. "So . . . what do we do now?"

"We wait," Jake said.

They made their way out to the courtyard, where they could see the final moments of the battle unfolding. Jake's eyes were glued to the small, clunky-looking ship that Rosemary had helped to restore as it emerged from beneath the Alys'aril and sped arrow-straight in the direction of the warp gate. His heart lurched as a fighter broke formation to follow, but almost immediately it barrel-rolled gracefully and returned to its fellows. He sagged in relief. The protoss vessel had been scanned for human life-forms and dismissed as unimportant. Jake watched, a smile curving his lips, as it disappeared from view.

Krythkal stayed in touch mentally with Selendis as they raced to safety. A few moments later, he told them with quiet joy, "They reached the gate. They are safe."

You did it, Zamara. You did more than anyone could have asked of you. And now you and Ulrezaj are on Shakuras. They'll watch over him. You did it.

Jake found himself unable to stand for long and Rosemary eased him down to the stones of the courtyard. She sat down herself and gently placed his head in her lap.

He looked up at her, strangely at peace even though he suspected that torture and a particularly nasty death were but a few moments away. He saw the same odd peace reflected on her features as she ran her hands through his fair hair.

"This is nice," he said softly.

"Don't get used to it. I'm not about to feed you grapes or anything."

He laughed then, a free, pure, ringing laugh, and her full red lips, the lips he had not kissed nearly enough, curved in response.

Valerian Mengsk found them there less than an hour later. The Heir Apparent paused on the last step, accompanied by several marines with rifles and a slight, nondescript man in civilian clothing. Valerian's sharp gray eyes darted around and he lifted a hand in a quick gesture. Six of the marines hurried off, splitting up to head in two different directions.

"Professor Ramsey. Rosemary. How good to see you safe," Valerian said. The words sounded genuine. "Quite the chase you've given me. I—"

While Valerian had been speaking, the nondescript man had been staring at Jake. Now he blurted, "Sir— she's gone."

"What?"

"The protoss in Professor Ramsey's head. She's gone."

"You must be Devon Starke," Jake said. "You're right. Zamara is no longer in here." He sat up, tapping his skull. "Only thing that's in here is a very human brain and a few very painful tumors."

Valerian's golden brows drew together over gray eyes that suddenly reminded Jake of a storm at sea. "What have you done?"

"She wasn't ever supposed to be in his head in the

first place," Rosemary retorted, getting to her feet and glaring at the emperor's son. "The protoss got her out."

"Where is she?" Valerian demanded.

"Hell if I know."

Valerian swore and ran a hand through his hair. "Take them to the ship," he told the marines who remained. He turned his eyes to the protoss, as if noticing him for the first time. "You . . . are you in charge of this place?"

Krythkal inclined his head. "I am Krythkal, the alysaar'vah of the Alys'aril."

"I've been instructed to claim this site for the Dominion," Valerian said. "Your people will not be harmed if you do not resist." He glanced around briefly, and Jake didn't need to be a telepath to read his thoughts. His hunger and regret were plain on his face. Still, it was as Jake had expected. Valerian, knowledge-seeker, had claimed the site for—

Jake blinked. Had Valerian really just claimed to have been *instructed* to do something? Who could possibly . . . his eyes widened.

"I'm sorry it was damaged in the fighting. Very sorry indeed," Valerian was continuing. His gray eyes darted to Jake's. "Professor, Rosemary—you will come with me."

Jake had never thought he'd be face-to-face with the emperor of the Dominion. But then again, a lot of things had happened over the last several months that he hadn't ever dreamed would happen.

He, Rosemary, Valerian, and Starke were in Valerian's private quarters. Of necessity smaller than the room in which the Heir Apparent had entertained Jake what seemed like a lifetime ago, the rooms still painted a picture of their inhabitant. There were still ancient weapons on the walls, showcased by good lighting; a cabinet of fine carved wood that doubtless stocked rare and delicious liquor; four leather chairs instead of the sofa Jake remembered.

Arcturus Mengsk's face was oversized on the viewscreen. Jake knew that was intentional and provided Mengsk with an advantage. There would have been a time when he would be sweating bullets, but now Jake was just simply so weary that he looked the emperor right in the eye, which seemed to irritate the man.

"My son has told me a little bit about your situation, Ramsey," Arcturus said. "And I hear that you've cheated us."

Beside him, Rosemary tensed, but had the good sense to stay quiet. Jake glanced over at Valerian, but the younger man's face was a careful mask of neutrality. He would get no cues there. He—

Don't worry. Answer him honestly.

Jake recognized the mental voice as Devon Starke's, but didn't give the former ghost away by glancing in his direction. "Sir," Jake said, "Zamara's presence in my head was killing me. If she'd stayed there I'm not sure there'd be even this much left of me. As it is, I will require an operation to remove several tumors."

Arcturus laughed, his oversized face easy and inviting. "Well, I will take what I can get. I've ordered Valerian to claim the protoss temple for the Dominion, and now he's given me you."

Valerian started. "Father, what do you mean?"

"You came to me for help. I gave it to you—gave you the best vessels and pilots I had. You were to bring me the protoss intelligence you were so desperately hunting. You failed, so I'm taking the professor instead. There won't be much left of him when I'm done, I'm sorry to say. But we'll pull out everything we can."

Valerian paled, then flushed. But before he could speak Jake had blurted, "There's no need for that! I'll happily tell you everything I know! This information—it's not just for the protoss. It's for all of us!"

Mengsk's eyes narrowed and he regarded Jake speculatively. "Of course you will, son. You won't have a chance to hide a damned thing."

The old bastard . . . he lied to Valerian and to me, came Starke's voice. *Professor—the deal was to let you go. I'm sorry.*

So am I, Jake thought.

"And so we're back where we started from, when you were headed for interrogation on the *Gray Tiger*," Mengsk said with an incongruous joviality.

A muscle twitched near Valerian's eye, but Mengsk the Younger had composed himself. He sighed, straightened his shoulders, and gave a self-deprecating smile. "It's as you wish, Father. I couldn't have done it without your help. Don't suppose I could have a few of those vikings for my own use?"

Jake stared, first at Valerian, then at Starke. Starke looked disappointed, but resigned.

"I knew Jake shouldn't have stayed," Rosemary snarled. "You despicable, lying, cowardly—"

"Perhaps you'll excuse us, Father," Valerian said. "I've got a tiger by the tail here."

"Feisty little thing," Mengsk said.

"You don't know the half of it," Valerian said, smiled his easy smile, leaned forward, and switched off the viewscreen. He whirled, all humor gone from his face. "This isn't good. I thought this might happen, but I didn't know you'd need an operation beforehand, Professor."

Rosemary stared. "You mean—that was an act?"

"Of course. I had to let Father think he'd won. He's like a bulldog—won't let go unless he knows he's the victor. Now that he thinks I'm bringing the professor to him, he'll leave us alone for a while."

Jake stared, openmouthed. "I . . . I give up," he said, laughing and throwing his hands in the air. "Tell me what happens now."

Valerian sighed, running a hand through his blond hair. "Well, I'm not quite sure. I have had to stash people away before now, of course, but never anyone Father wanted as badly as he wants you."

"I meant it, you know," Jake said quietly. "I'd have told him everything. He wouldn't have had to—to rip it out of my brain."

The Heir Apparent smiled softly. "I know that, but he doesn't believe anyone would be that honest, Professor. He's so used to mistrust and double dealings he can't understand something that you and I understand very well—that sometimes knowledge is only useful when shared with all who want to learn it."

"The discovery of wonders," Jake said softly, remembering the conversation. Valerian's smile grew, and as he nodded they held each other's gaze for a moment.

"Hate to interrupt this touching moment of male bonding, but Jake has tumors in his brain and he needs a good place to escape to," Rosemary said.

"As usual, the charming Ms. Dahl has put her finger on it," Valerian said. "I always travel with the finest medical staff. They don't need to know the details of why you need to stay alive—just that you do. Come."

"Sir—" Devon Starke's voice was as pleasant and remarkable as his physical appearance was unremarkable, deep, and resonant. "Sir—you cannot do this. I can't permit you to."

Valerian smiled, but there was a glint of steel in his gray eyes. "Devon, I'm fond of you, but you do not get to tell me what I can and cannot do."

"Pardon, sir, I mean no disrespect, but—you are caught in a terrible situation." He glanced at Rosemary and Jake, seemed to make a decision, and continued. "You must either give in to your father and surrender Rosemary and Jake to them, or defy him outright. I know you do not wish to do, either."

Valerian scowled slightly. "Yes, well, I don't really have a choice."

"Yes, sir, you do. You cannot hope to stand against the emperor. And you will not let the professor and Rosemary be destroyed. There's a third way."

Jake and Rosemary exchanged glances. Once, Jake could easily have read the thoughts of anyone in the room. Now he was as he had always been—a non-telepath. Hell, he wasn't even good at reading faces or body language. He shrugged at Rosemary, who frowned and turned her blue-eyed gaze back to Starke.

"I'm listening," Valerian said quietly. "Will I like this third way?"

"I doubt you will, sir, but you'll have to take it."

Suddenly Devon Starke was in Jake's thoughts again. *I felt what you did, when you escaped the first time. When you linked us in that place where we were all a part of each other. When we felt each other's thoughts and feelings, when there was no separation.*

He continued in words that went deeper than words, and Jake felt tears sting his eyes as he remembered the connection himself. He thought of Zamara's words to him, and shared that conversation with Devon:

This changed the protoss, he had said to her. *What will it do to us?*

And her reply . . . Oh, Zamara, how he missed her, how he would always miss her.

That moment was never intended to be shared beyond our

own species. The Khala is for us, not you, and it is sacred, not a toy. . . . Truly, Jacob, I do not know what will happen. Your species is . . . young yet to grasp the true significance. Most likely, most of those who experienced it will discount it, scoff at it, and dismiss it as a momentary fancy.

But . . . not all?

No. Not all.

Devon Starke's mental voice, alive with pain and joy and hope and longing: *Not all, Professor.*

Jake stared at Devon, opened his mouth to speak, but before he could utter a word he felt the former ghost dive into his mind. There was little pain; Starke knew what he was doing, and this was a linking of human to human rather than protoss to human. But it caught Jake off guard, rather as if he had been suddenly seized, and he gasped slightly in surprise. He felt Starke rooting around in his thoughts, taking something, discarding something else—

Thank you, Professor. Thank you for everything. I'm sorry for what I must now do.

And then there *was* pain—lots and lots of it. Jake cried out sharply, stared at Starke in shock and betrayal, and slumped unconscious to the floor.

CHAPTER 23

"STARKE! WHAT ARE YOU DOING?"

Valerian's normally modulated, smooth voice was deep and rough with anger as he rushed to the fallen bodies, checking for pulses and then lifting his gray eyes, storm clouds now, to the former ghost.

"They're unharmed," Starke assured him. "And you'd best get the professor into surgery as soon as possible."

Having assured himself that both Ramsey and Dahl were all right, the sharp edge of Valerian's fury was tempered, but only slightly. "I assume you've got a reason for doing this."

"Indeed I do, sir. I do what you cannot."

Valerian rose. "Explain."

"Your father wants a pound of flesh. Let it be me."

Valerian's eyes narrowed. "What are you talking about?"

"Sir, there's no way that you can defy your father and come out of this well. I made a vow to serve you to the utmost of my abilities, and that is what I intend to do." He hesitated, a self-deprecating, almost shy smile curving his lips. "You saved my life, Your Excellency. I've been on borrowed time ever since. I believe in you, sir. In you and in Professor Ramsey. Let me trade my life for the three of you—for your continued safety and freedom. Give me to your father and his ghosts."

Valerian had been trained from childhood to play the fine game of politics. He had carefully schooled himself to not reveal his emotions. But for the second time in almost as many minutes, his veneer of poise was shattered.

"What?"

"I dived deep into Professor Ramsey's mind. I extracted quite a lot of information. Arcturus will send ghosts to get that information, and there's enough there that they'll think they've learned all there is to know. I'll put up enough mental barriers so they'll have to really dig for it—that way it will seem believable, and also buy you, Ramsey, and Dahl some time. You'll have the chance to hide them somewhere far away, where your father won't find them. I fear I caused the professor quite a bit of pain—do apologize for me, won't you?"

"Devon . . . if they are forced to extract the information with you fighting them . . . that's going to kill you, isn't it?"

The former ghost shrugged his thin shoulders. "Possibly. At the very least, it will shatter my mind. I'll be quite useless to anyone afterward." He said this with only the faintest tremor. Anyone who didn't know him well would have thought he was discussing the weather.

"As for you, sir, I'm a trained ghost. Any memories I have of this conversation will be so scrambled and disjointed by the time they reach them that they won't be sure what's a lie and what's the truth. You'll be completely off the hook and able to claim that I acted totally independently."

"There has to be . . . we could find another way." Even as he said the words, Valerian realized that they were nothing more than wishful thinking.

"Sir, with all due respect, I don't think so. You needed to call on the emperor to recover Professor Ramsey. We're here at the crossroads, and this is the only viable path."

Slowly, Valerian nodded. "Is . . . well, there's no one I should notify, is there?" Devon Starke had been separated from his family since he had been conscripted for the ghost program. No one would miss him—except for Valerian.

"No, sir. But if you'd do something for me, I'd be most grateful."

"Name it."

"That bonding that Ramsey did—it's part of why I'm doing this. That, and my loyalty to you. Don't forget about that. We can become better than we are, sir. I know this. I've tasted it."

Valerian extended a hand and clasped Starke's. "I won't forget, Devon. Not that, nor you, nor what you've done. I promise."

• • •

Jake blinked awake. He was lying on a small bed in an alcove cut into a wall. The sheets were comfortable and he was tempted to close his eyes again when a soft voice said, "Well good morning, Sleeping Beauty."

He turned to see Rosemary sitting curled up in a chair, smiling at him. Her chin was propped up on her hand and her bangs fell into her face. His heart turned over.

"What happened? Devon—what did he do to us?"

"Turns out Devon Starke had a bit of a knight-in-shining-armor complex."

"Had?"

Rosemary's grin faded a bit. "Well, he's still alive. For now. He took information from your brain and volunteered to distract Arcturus long enough for Valerian to get us safely away."

Jake stared. "He's . . . they'll kill him."

"He knew that. It was his idea."

"But why?"

"Loyalty to Valerian . . . and something about that mind-link thing you did to us all really got to him."

Jake nodded slowly. "I understand."

"On a happier note, the tumors were removed. You're well on your way to a full recovery. Although you're bald now and you'll have quite the wicked-looking scar."

Jake's hand flew to his skull. Rosemary was right—his head was smooth as a baby's bottom, and there were bandages on it.

"Guess now I'm an egghead in all meanings of the word," he deadpanned.

The quip caught her off guard and she laughed, as much in surprise as in humor. His smile, tinged with sorrow at the loss of Devon Starke, grew a little.

"Come on, Eggy," she said. "Mr. V is waiting for us."

Soft music was playing and their erstwhile captor, now host, had his back to them as they entered. Valerian turned, smiling, and Jake saw he had a glass of a golden liquor in his hand.

"Professor. I'm told the surgery was an unqualified success. They've assured me that you'll be able to travel within a day or two. It's even safe for you to have a drink with me, if you like."

Jake inclined his head. "Thank you, sir. I will."

"I'm having pear brandy, but you may have whatever you like."

"That will be fine, thank you."

Valerian himself poured the drinks. At Jake's curious look, he said, "Remember, you're technically prisoners. Whittier shouldn't see us sharing a celebratory glass together." He grinned as he handed the small glasses to Rosemary and Jake. Jake took a whiff of the fragrant liquor; it was almost achingly sweet and made his mouth water. He sighed softly as he remembered another moment, seemingly so long ago now, when he had been about to taste something new.

"Sammuro fruit," Rosemary said quietly.

"What, now you're the mind reader?" Jake said jokingly.

"No. I was thinking of it too."

Jake wondered if the protoss would ever return to Aiur. There were some protoss left, he was certain of it, even in the wake of zerg and Ulrezaj and the horrific grip of Sundrop. They were survivors.

Valerian lifted his glass. "The day I'd hoped for has finally come," he said, smiling at each of them in turn. "We are about to sit down together—not as employer and employees, not as perceived enemies—but as friends. I've looked forward to this day."

"It's been bought at a cost," Jake said. Rosemary lifted an eyebrow and nodded slight approval at his boldness. "I understand Devon Starke is being a decoy for us . . . and that he is likely not to survive the undertaking."

Sorrow flitted across Valerian's patrician face. "This is true. I wasn't expecting that from him. It was a brave gesture."

"And you've taken control of a protoss sacred site," Jake continued. "Forgive my boldness, sir, but after being as close to them as I have been—that doesn't sit well with me."

"Nor with me. Unfortunately it was necessary at the time, if I was to find you. However, you'll be pleased to hear that a few hours after you went into surgery, your protoss friends returned. With lots of company."

"They came back for us," Rosemary said. She

directed her gaze toward her glass of pear brandy, but the corners of her lips were turned up. "Huh."

Jake's heart soared. They hadn't abandoned him, or the dark protoss. Somehow, he wasn't surprised—although he was very happy.

"They did indeed. I was forced to return Ehlna to their control or have my father's lovely and very expensive ships blown out of the skies."

"But . . . all that knowledge . . . that's exactly what you've been looking for," Jake said. "Hell, it's what *I've* been looking for."

"My father would exploit it, and if he could not, he would destroy it. I'd rather the information be preserved, protected—even if it means I never learn it myself. And I confess, there's a small box of crystals tucked away in my quarters for perusal at a later date."

Jake smiled a little and sipped the brandy. It was almost unbearably sweet, the ripe kiss of the pear warm in the sunshine ready to fall from the tree, thick and syrupy and golden. For a moment, he thought about the last time he and Valerian had shared a drink.

I know some have notions that this is a very romantic, exciting profession. But really, it's a lot of hard work and practical puzzle solving. It's a wonderful intellectual challenge, certainly, but there's little romance in it when all is said and done.

"What are you grinning about?" Rosemary said. He smiled down at her.

"I was remembering what I said to Valerian the first

time we met. That there was very little romance in archaeology. I was wrong and you were right. This has been . . ."

He could find no words, nor could he link minds anymore to express in thought what words could not. "I . . . I'm not just a detached observer anymore. I'm not a preserver, not the way the protoss are, but I'm a storyteller now. A keeper of the lore. I've always been the skeptic, the scientist. But you were right, Valerian. It *is* about the discovery of wonders."

He looked at Valerian's face, with its barely concealed curiosity and excitement and eagerness to listen. He looked at Rosemary, even more beautiful now than she was when he'd first seen her, as she looked back at him with a soft smile. Thoughts and images tumbled in his head: Darius, Kendra, Rosemary, Devon Starke; Alzadar and Ladranix and Vartanil; Selendis and Mohandar and Zeratul; and at the beginning and end of it all, a protoss spirit with a wry sense of humor and a great heart named Zamara, trading a peaceful passing for eternal battle. Impulsively, he lifted his glass.

"A toast. To courage, and curiosity, and sacrifice, and . . . and the stories." The little glasses clinked and Jake, surprising himself and the other two, downed his in a single gulp. He held out the glass and, grinning, Valerian refilled it.

"Let me tell you about what happened," Jake said in a voice that shook with deep joy and pride. "Let me tell you . . . *everything*."

Award-winning author Christie Golden has written over thirty novels and several short stories in the fields of science fiction, fantasy, and horror.

Golden launched the TSR *Ravenloft* line in 1991 with her first novel, the highly successful *Vampire of the Mists,* which introduced elven vampire Jander Sunstar. To the best of her knowledge, she is the creator of the elven vampire archetype in fantasy fiction.

She is the author of several original fantasy novels, including *On Fire's Wings, In Stone's Clasp*, and *Under Sea's Shadow* (currently available only as an ebook), the first three in her multibook fantasy series The Final Dance from LUNA Books. *In Stone's Clasp* won the Colorado Author's League Award for Best Genre Novel of 2005, the second of Golden's novels to win the award.

Among Golden's other projects are over a dozen *Star Trek* novels and the first two books in this StarCraft Dark Templar trilogy, *Firstborn* and *Shadow Hunters*. An avid player of Blizzard's MMORPG, *World of Warcraft*, Golden has written several novels in that world—*Lord of the Clans, Rise of the Horde*, and most recently, *Arthas: Rise of the Lich King*—with two more in the works. She has also written two Warcraft manga stories for Tokyopop, "I Got What Yule Need" and "A Warrior Made."

Golden is currently hard at work on three books in the major nine-book *Star Wars* series Fate of the Jedi, in collaboration with Aaron Allston and Troy Denning. Her first book in the series, *Omen*, is due out in July 2009.

Golden lives in Colorado with her husband and two cats. She welcomes visitors to her website, www.christiegolden.com.